Praise for Stephen Grace's Under Cottonwoods:

"I read *Under Cottonwoods* with my thirteen-year-old son and we both loved it—he for the fishing action, I for the novel's flawed, searching, and wholly sympathetic characters. Stephen Grace has crafted a humane and hopeful story that will engage both nature lovers and champions of the human spirit."
—Wally Lamb, author of *She's Come Undone* and
I Know This Much Is True

"*Under Cottonwoods* is the reason people still read."
—Tim Sandlin, author of *Honey, Don't*

"With strong big-hearted prose, Stephen Grace charts the mysterious waters of an unlikely friendship between two damaged and yet optimistic men who lean on, carry, and challenge each other to heal and forgive. *Under Cottonwoods* is that rare novel that manages to be both generous and wise without condescension or syrupy sermons."
—Elwood Reid, author of *If I Don't Six* and *Midnight Sun*

"*Under Cottonwoods* is as shimmering and hearty as trees on a riverbank. Stephen Grace's compassion for his characters and his intuition about the outdoors recall the best of Thomas McGuane and Jim Harrison."
—Alyson Hagy, author of *Keeneland, Graveyard of the Atlantic, Madonna on Her Back,* and *Hardware River*

UNDER COTTONWOODS

A Novel

STEPHEN GRACE

THE LYONS PRESS
GUILFORD, CONNECTICUT
AN IMPRINT OF THE GLOBE PEQUOT PRESS

The Lyons Press is an imprint of The Globe Pequot Press

10 9 8 7 6 5 4 3 2

Printed in the United States of America

ISBN 1-59228-165-6

Library of Congress Cataloging-in-Publication Data is available on file.

For My Parents

Acknowledgments

I am grateful to the clients of CES, who gave much and asked for little in return.

I appreciate the support and encouragement I received at the Jackson Hole Writers' Conference—especially from Carolyn Lampman and Tim Sandlin.

Cheers to all the men and women working to protect Wyoming's wild places.

Thanks to the following:

The WKC, for teaching me when to fight and when to turn away. Mike, for showing me that getting off the mountain alive is more important than getting to the summit. Tim Cully and Dave Wickline, for teaching me how to catch trout and how to let them go. Anna Loomis, for the helping hand with the coconut. Shirley and Warren Brewer, for my stay at their storied garret in Cambridge. The Splore staff, for guiding me down the river. William Meredith and Richard Harteis, for their demonstration of courage. Wally Lamb, for helping me understand I'd stumbled onto a story worth telling. Harvard's Stratis Haviaras, for his love of language: *il miglior fabbro*. My agent, Esmond Harmsworth, for his patience.

Thanks to all my family—especially my grandparents. Thanks to Tom Bissell, Sheree Bykofsky, Gelert and Radley, Kathy Helmers, Deborah Kisling, Katherine Saul.

Thanks to my editor, George Donahue, for believing in my story.

And thanks to Amy, for believing in me.

PART ONE

≈ 1 ≈

Slashback

In the early summer, when the swollen rivers of spring had lowered and cleared, I invited Walter to go fishing with me.

"Can't leave my job," he said when I mentioned the trip to him over the phone. "They need me. If I go, the boxes won't get emptied, and stuff won't get labels on it, and then people won't know how much to pay for it, and—"

"I already talked to your boss at Kmart. He said it's all right for you to take a day off. We can head over to Jackson and fish the Snake."

"Who's gonna empty boxes and put labels on stuff?" Walter asked.

"They'll find someone to fill in. It's no big deal."

"No big deal my ass! It's a huge big deal, Mike. If I don't put labels on stuff nobody knows what to pay for it."

"Your caseworker told me you haven't had a vacation in over a year. That's a hell of a long time. You're due for one."

"If you promise someone will put labels on and stock the shelves while I'm gone," said Walter, "then it's a deal. You think we'll catch fish?"

"I'm sure we will, Walt."

"We don't have to kill 'em though, right? I don't like to kill fish."

"We don't have to kill them."

⌒

I walked to a side channel of the Snake River and watched Walter looping out line as he moved his flyrod back and forth. Past him, the Tetons rose from the valley floor of Jackson Hole, Wyoming. There was the vast sagebrush flatness of the valley and the steep granite rise of the mountains. There was nothing in between—no foothills, no gradual heightening of the landscape, no transition.

In the shade of a cottonwood tree I sat down, leaning against its trunk, smooth where the bark was bare—either weathered off or peeled away by an animal. Up above, its branches brushed the blue sky.

After tightening the chinstrap on the helmet he always wore in case he had a seizure, Walter arced his line out far behind him, then looped it forward and dropped it in a pool behind a log. He jigged the tip of his rod, giving life to the fly he'd managed to tie to the delicate end of his leader after several fumbling attempts. Walter had trouble moving the left side of his body. There was no easy fix—no surgery, no magic pill. The only treatment was for Walter to exercise his left side.

Walter had taught himself how to flyfish after his accident, forcing his damaged body and brain to cooperate. He was fascinated with casting: he spent so much time watching his neongreen line loop through the air as he worked his rod back and forth, his flies were rarely in the water.

For me, flyfishing was a link to my father, a gruff and quiet man who was all motion, few words. In a damp corner of our basement he had taught me a style of fighting he'd picked up in Okinawa when stationed there in the Marine Corps. At the end of each lesson, after we'd hit a canvas bag stained with the blood from our scuffed knuckles, he told me that the better I could fight, the more chances I'd have to lead a peaceful life. One day I asked him what that meant. He told me it was something he'd learned in Asia, something I might understand when I was a man; and he said that little boys shouldn't ask questions like that, they should shut up and hit the bag. But with unwavering patience my father taught me how to fish and ski, and every weekend we left my mother and the rest of the world to go into the mountains. That time was ours; after he died it was

still ours. At his funeral, when I was thirteen, I remembered his sandpa-
pery fingers guiding my hand across a flyrod he'd built for me in his basement workshop, and at the moment of that memory I understood that
he'd shown his love for me in subtle ways—a lesson patiently taught, a
gentle touch.

A seedpod dangling from a branch brushed my face. I gripped the
soft fiber of the pod between my fingers, rubbed it back and forth, then
dropped it on a bed of pebbles. I picked up my rod and walked downstream from Walter, stopping to cast my fly into a riffle. The choppy water
glinted in the sun.

After a few casts I felt a fish strike; I lifted my rod to set the hook.
The fly shot out of the water and sailed over my head, wrapping my leader
around a branch.

Walter's laughter rose above the sound of rushing water. "I didn't
know trout lived in trees, Mike. Or do you got your bird license? Are you
trying to catch birds?" He laughed until he doubled over and dropped
his rod.

I walked upstream and sat next to him on a big rock smoothed by
the river.

"Catch any birds?" he asked.

"Haven't seen you catch any fish, smartass."

"I had some strikes," Walter said, picking up his rod. "I put a dry fly
on 'cause I saw fish rising. Some big ones, too. My fly's gonna catch one.
I'll show you how it's done."

Our relationship had begun with flyfishing. The day I first met Walter, I had overheard him ask a flyshop employee where he could go to
catch trout. The guy gave him directions to a riverbank trampled
smooth—one of the places employees sent tourists. I pulled Walter aside,
and staring at his eyes, one which seemed normal, the other drifting in its
socket, I told him about a stretch of river my father had shown me, a
channel pinched off from the main current and hidden by cottonwoods.
As Walter nodded and turned to leave, I said I could take him. He turned

back and stared for a long and uncomfortable moment. Finally he told me that if first I drove him into the mountains to a meadow where wolves were rumored to hunt, he'd go fishing with me. He said he wanted to see a wolf but it was too far to ride on his bike; then he made me shake his hand, made me promise we had a deal. No masquerade for him, I thought as he stumbled from the shop, his dragging foot catching on the doorsill: no costume could cover his damage. He was an honest mess; I was just a better actor.

Walter worked his rod back and forth, feeding out line in a long neat loop. He brought the rod forward and let the line fall to the river on a sluggish bend. His fly dented the water and spread widening circles across the calm surface. A fish splashed a few feet away from the fly.

"What's the matter, Walt? That fish didn't like your fly."

"I didn't want to catch that stupid little fish anyway. The big trout just suck the flies down. They don't hardly make a splash." Walter raised his rod and worked his line back and forth, then set it down farther upstream, near the bank, where the dirt had been cut under by the current. "I'll bet a big one lives under there. A monster of a trout."

A few fish splashed near the bank, tufted with green grass, but nothing attacked the fly. Walter wiped his cheek, pinched something between his fingers, and held it out for me to see. "That's what they're eating," he said.

I stood up and walked over to see what he had. A fat yellow stonefly, winged and tenacled, wriggled between his fingers.

"I got one that looks just like that," he said. He flicked the bug onto the river; as it touched the surface, a fish dimpled the water and sucked it under. "That was a big trout! It didn't splash, just gulped that stonefly down."

He pulled a metal box, shiny in the sun, from his vest. He clicked it open and found a fly that looked like the insect the fish had devoured. "Tie it on," he said to me.

"Do it yourself. I'm not going to do it for you."

"But I don't want to waste time. Fish are feeding right now. Tie it on for me!"

"Nope," I said. "Show me how it's done."

"Fine!" He pinched the fly with his strong right hand and tried to thread the line through the hook with his trembling left.

"Other way," I said. "Hold it with your left. Tie with your right."

"Always yelling. Always telling me what to do."

After Walter switched hands, he tied a good knot, moistened it with spit, and pulled it tight. He grabbed a pair of clippers from his vest and trimmed the tag end of the leader. I sat back down to watch. A breeze that had been stirring cottonwoods along the riverbank stopped. The white clumps of seedpods halted their drift from the branches. The air suddenly felt warmer, and everything was perfectly still.

Walter worked his line out and dropped it a few inches from the bank. His fly floated onto the water, sending rings across the glassy surface of a deep pool. The rings spread, then melted back into the river. I saw Walter holding his breath and realized I was holding mine.

With a subtle slurp, the fly disappeared. No loud splash, no big disturbance. Just a little dimple and a sucking noise, like the sound of the last bit of water spilling down a drain.

Walter pulled his rod back, setting the hook; line hissed off his reel as the fish sped upstream. Walter was still holding his breath. Neither of us made a noise.

The breeze picked up, shaking the cottonwood branches, scattering their fluffy pods, which danced and darted through the restless air. Walter held his rod high and fought the fish. He pulled against the steady pressure, reeling in line, letting line pull out, reeling it back in. His face was red and tense, his arms tight, his feet motionless in the black dirt. He finessed the fish away from a tangle of logs near the bank, taking in line each time it paused in its struggle. Finally it tired and rose to the surface, swimming in muscular circles. Walter reeled in the last few yards of line; the circles slowed and weakened, then stopped. Walter scooped his net under the limp body, then lifted the spent fish from the water. I walked over and looked at it, golden and finespotted, its body quiet, its mouth pumping open and shut, its small sharp teeth showing brightly in the sun. There were crimson stripes under its jaw.

Walter took a deep breath and whistled. "Cutthroat, Mike. Big one."

"It's damn big. Probably twenty inches."

Walter dipped his hand into the water, moistening his skin; then he ran a fingertip along the side of the fish. "It's so smooth," he said. He turned the fish over. A long gash ran from its belly up to the top of its back. An old wound, knotted with scar tissue.

"What is that?" Walter asked.

"Might be from a bird. Maybe an eagle or an osprey caught it in its claws, but it slipped away before it got eaten."

"Maybe a bear grabbed it."

"Could be."

"Or maybe somebody shot it with an arrow."

"You don't want to keep it, do you?"

"No way am I gonna kill it. I'm gonna let it go back."

The breeze stiffened, wrinkling the river and swirling seedpods through the air, across the ground, onto the water. One tuft stuck to Walter's vest.

"Slashback," Walter said. "That's what I'm naming him." He ran his finger along the raised rib of the scar. "Slashback's got himself a wound, but he's still a strong fish."

"Want me to get my camera? I could run back to the truck and grab it."

"I'm gonna let it go now."

Walter pulled a pair of forceps from his vest, scooped his shaking left hand under the fat belly of the fish, and gripped the fly. He carefully pried the hook out, then turned the trout upstream. Walter pulled his trembling hand away. The fish rested a moment, holding in the current, then drifted away from the shore and sank into the deep green water. For as long as I could I watched it, turning from a bright and slippery trout into a dark fish shape, then a shadow, then nothing.

I looked over at Walter, who was still staring into the river. Without turning to look at me, he said, "I showed you, didn't I."

I reached over and pulled the cottony seedpod from his vest. Dropped it, let it drift onto the water. The current swept it away.

"I liked Slashback's scar," Walter said.

"It made him interesting."

"I like him 'cause he had stories."

Walter looked up, over the river, into the cottonwoods. "Hey, Mike, looks like the wind's blowing snow out of the trees!" He dropped his rod and plucked a fuzzy seedpod from the air. "I just caught a monster of a fish named Slashback, and now it's snowing from the trees in summertime."

⌒

That afternoon, before leaving Jackson Hole and driving back home to Kingfisher, we went to a brewpub to celebrate Walter's fish. I ordered a beer. No alcohol for Walter because of his seizure meds; he had a Pepsi. We sat outside on a deck and stared at the mountains, watching clouds build. They puffed up, then scrapped apart over the peaks.

Walter seemed down; the excitement of catching the fish had already worn off.

"What's the matter?" I asked.

"I want a girlfriend." He was silent a moment, then said, "I don't want a girlfriend like me. That'd be two stupid heads and that's even worse than one. But maybe that's the only girlfriend I'll get."

"You'll find someone who's right for you." I took a drink of my beer. "Have some faith. It'll happen."

Tears glistened in Walter's eyes. "Fuck faith. And fuck my stupid broken head."

I reached over and squeezed Walter's shoulder, let go, leaned back in my chair. "You're right. I shouldn't make it sound so easy."

Two tears spilled from Walter's eyes, one down each cheek. "You got a wife," he said. "You're lucky."

"Look, it's not that simple. My marriage is a damn mess. I haven't told Nora everything. Maybe if—"

"What?" Walter yelled. A young couple with sunburned faces turned from the table next to us to stare. I stared back until they looked away.

Walter lowered his voice. "You got a wife and you should be happy. You don't have a broken head."

Clouds raced toward mountains, joining and shredding above the stony peaks. Between pulls on my beer, I said, "I am lucky. Don't let me forget that."

"If you help me find a girlfriend, then I'll make you remember."

"You've got a deal."

Walter raised a trembling hand and brushed away the bright bead of a tear. A smile spread across his face. He laughed, and again the people next to us stared, but neither of us paid attention to them.

"It was snowing from the trees today, huh, Mike?"

"It was."

"And my fish, Slashback—he was big?"

"He was huge."

"I can still see Slashback," Walter said, wiping his damp cheeks, smiling. "He was gold and there was bright red on his jaws—bright like a sunset. And there were little black dots all over his skin that you could hardly see. And he was smooth when I touched him. And his scar was thick and bumpy. . . . And I think I felt him shake—not 'cause he was cold, but 'cause he was scared."

"He was a beautiful fish," I said.

"Whatever caught him first and left that mark dropped him into the river by accident. But I did it on purpose. I just let him go."

❦ 2 ❧

Wildfire

A few weeks later I reached for my wallet. It wasn't in my pocket. I thought I might have left it at Walter's; I drove to his apartment. As I knocked on his door I heard beeping—the sound of a smoke detector. I knocked again. No answer. I turned the knob, opened the unlocked door. A blue haze clung to the ceiling in the living room. As I stepped into the apartment, smoke coated my throat, stung my eyes.

"Walter?"

No answer.

I ran through the living room, coughing, following the confusion of smoke. In the middle of the kitchen, Walter stood below a detector with a blinking red light, swatting at it with a broom. He held the handle, cornflower blue, in his strong right hand, wielding the broom like a sword.

"Where's the fire?" I yelled. "What the hell are you doing?"

"There's no fire. I burned dinner. This stupid thing won't shut up. Just keeps on beeping."

"Have you tried taking the battery out?"

Walter gritted his teeth, pulled back the broom, and gave the smoke detector a vicious swipe. "Can't reach. Can't get to the battery." He whacked it again; the cover popped off, exposing the insides: tangled wires of red, black, and blue. The light continued to flash, and still it beeped.

"He's down but not out," Walter said. "One more ought to do it." He wound up for the final blow.

I grabbed the broom with one hand; with the other I reached up and pulled the battery out. Dropped it into Walter's shirtpocket.

"I would've had it. One more thump and I would've shut that damn thing up for good."

I coughed and spat into the kitchen sink. Phlegm flecked with soot oozed over the stainless steel. I opened a window and gulped fresh air. When I stopped coughing I laughed—laughed so hard I started coughing again.

"So what happened?" I finally asked.

Walter was still holding his broom. He looked poised and ready, as if the smoke detector might come back to life and need to be dealt with.

"In there," said Walter, pointing at the oven. "Take a look."

Tendrils of smoke curled from the edges of the oven. I stretched my sweatshirt over my nose and mouth, unlatched the door. Scraps of blackened cardboard, the remains of a box, lay in a smoldering pile on the top rack. I grabbed a pair of tongs from the counter, peeled the charred layers apart. Inside the box was a pizza—a charcoal disk.

"What the hell, Walt?"

"I forgot to take it out of the oven. I was making my puzzle and I didn't remember."

"But the pizza's still in the box."

He shrugged his shoulders. "Guess I forgot to take it out of the box, too."

I shut the oven and started to lecture him about kitchen safety, something I'd promised his caseworker I'd do. It wasn't the first time he'd almost burned the apartment down. But as I explained how to use a timer—along with the importance of removing a pizza from the box before putting it in the oven—I looked at Walter, his head tilted to the side, listening attentively, still gripping the broom, and I had to swallow a laugh. "Walter, you've got to—"

"I thought you'd be proud of me. Mitch and I left the battery in the smoke detector. We didn't take it out to put in our radio."

"But you've got to be careful with the oven. You could—"

"We left the battery in just like you said."

"You want to try again?" I asked. "Want to make another pizza?"

"That was my last one."

"Got anything else to eat?"

"Peanut butter."

"What else?"

"Cheese."

"Any bread?"

"Mitch ate it all. He likes toast."

"Want to go out to eat?"

Walter dropped the broom and hurried toward his room. "I'll bring my photo album," he said.

"The one with pictures of Kmart in it?"

"You haven't seen this one before."

⁓

After we slid into a booth at Kingfisher Inn, Walter dropped his photo album on the table, then reached into his pocket, handed me my wallet. "I counted your money," he said. "You got lots in there. You got a nice truck, too." Walter took a sip of his ice water and blinked hard. "You rich, Mike?"

I stared a moment at Walter, at his left arm curled against his chest, not unlike the foreleg of a praying mantis. Then I looked through a window at the street outside, where light from a neon sign bled into a puddle, and flinching from the pain of memory, I told Walter that I had some money from my parents' life insurance policies. My dad had been killed in a car wreck when I was thirteen, my mom died from cancer when I was fifteen.

"You didn't have no parents after that?" Walter said.

"I lived in a foster home until I was eighteen."

He tilted his head. "Why don't you ever talk 'bout your parents?"

I kicked him under the table. "How come you never told me how much you wanted a girlfriend?"

Our waitress came over and said, "Hey, Mr. Walter. Missed you yesterday."

"I didn't have no money, Martha. Mitch borrowed it all."

"You tellin' the truth?" She put her hands on her hips. "You didn't go and eat at Denny's, now did you?"

"I didn't have no money—I swear! You know I only eat at Kingfisher Inn. It's dirty and small but it's got the best French fries."

Martha winked. "All right, Mr. Walter. I guess we'll let you get away with it this time. But I best not catch you at Denny's."

When Martha left, I took a sip of ice water and my teeth went numb. "Why'd you only order fries?" I asked. "What about a burger?"

"I won't have enough money for a tip. Martha has a hard job. It makes her feet hurt. I tell her I'll rub her feet for her and she laughs and pats me on my helmet." Walter thumped the top of his helmet and grinned.

"I'll buy you one," I said. "Think of it as a reward for finding my wallet." I waved Martha back and ordered Walter a burger. Didn't order one for myself because I was supposed to have dinner with Nora later that night, I told Walter.

"I wish I could go out to dinner with Nora," he said. "I wish she was my wife."

"You'd rather eat with her than with me?" I laughed, but Walter's face stayed serious. Finally he smiled, and then he started to laugh, a gurgling sound like water bubbling through pipes. He reached over the table and used his left hand to punch me in the arm. "You keep telling me I can't fight good if I only use my right," he said. "So I started practicing with my left. I hit the back of my couch every day. I asked Mitch if I could practice on him but he said no."

"Do I have to separate you two?" Martha said as she set down a plate that held a tall burger and a thatched pile of glistening fries.

"This guy's got a mean left jab," I said.

Martha put her hands on her hips. "You doin' some boxin', Mr. Walter?"

"I gotta keep him in line," Walter said, pointing his shaking left hand at me.

After Walter finished his food, he opened his photo album, its cover ringed with stains from coffee mugs, its pictures yellowed with age, their corners curling away from the adhesive that held them to the page. Walter pointed to a snapshot of a little boy with bowlcut hair and a gap-toothed grin. "That was me before I was broken," he said.

Next was a Polaroid of Walter from when he was a few years older. His head was dwarfed by a baseball cap with the Denver Broncos' logo on it.

From across the table Walter looked at me, his blind eye drifting, his good one staring, and he told me his dad was a Broncos fan. A couple years after his accident, right after his mom died, his dad had stopped calling and writing. His dad sent him checks for his birthday and for Christmas but never talked to him, Walter said.

I looked out the window, down a road damp from afternoon rain. The wet asphalt beneath a streetlight was as smooth and shiny as porcelain.

"Cancer in her breast—that's what killed my mom." Walter tilted his head and looked at me. "What kind of cancer did your mom have?"

I told him it started with a tumor in her colon, then spread through her body.

"Did doctors make her radioactive?" Walter asked. "They gave my mom chemicals and radioaction."

I smiled. "Chemo and radiation?"

"It made my mom barf and all her hair fell out. I bought her a wig 'cause she was embarrassed 'bout her bald head. The wig was too small but she told me it was a good present."

We sipped our water and looked outside. In the last light of day, grassy hills turned limegreen, then dulled to gray. Stars winked above mountains, and bats with crooked wings flew drunkenly, chasing bugs into the night.

I pulled the album toward me and looked at the next picture.

"That's a bike my dad built for me," Walter said.

"He made it?"

"He built it out of pipes. He's smart like that. He can build anything." Walter pointed to another photo and said, "Here's the house we lived in." Rows of singlewide trailers stretched down a potholed street.

I swallowed. My throat felt small, constricted. When my dad was alive we lived in a brick house with a finished basement and a sprawling yard, I told Walter. But when my dad died, before the insurance company paid up, my mom and I moved into a trailer on a gravel plot. I rubbed my finger against the plastic covering the page. A bubble that had risen above the photo crinkled and collapsed.

I turned the page, saw a picture of Walter climbing a ladder into a treehouse. It didn't look like the jumble of scrap lumber a little boy would piece together; it was made of choice wood and precise angles. Clean lines and sanded edges. Something a father would build with his own tools, and maybe buy a few new ones just for that project. Something a father would craft with love.

It was a blur: a mad dash through Walter's life, a glimpse of what he'd been. I took a deep breath and looked out the window, across the street. Under a blazing light a guy with a red tangle of hair was working on a VW van. He pounded a wrench against a part he'd pulled from the engine, the wrench soundlessly meeting metal. A hippie blacksmith in a silent forge.

"You paying attention?" Walter frowned, seaming his forehead with wrinkles.

Martha cleared Walter's plate away and joked with him, but it all seemed so distant, as if I'd entered someone else's dream. I stared at Walter, wondering what fractured thoughts he had, what jumbled scenes his damaged brain perceived.

Football pictures covered the next few pages: Walter in full pads and a crisp uniform, kneeling next to his dad. A shot of a huddle, Walter surrounded by teammates. A picture of him running, the ball tucked under his arm as he sidestepped a tackle.

After the football photos was a picture of Walter with one tennis shoe lifted off the floor, scratching at a pantleg of his jeans. Next to Walter, her arm around his waist, stood a girl with eyes like black opals and chocolate hair spilling over her shoulders.

"She was my girlfriend before my accident," Walter said. "We were gonna go to college and then get married. When I was in the hospital in a coma she came to visit me every day. I could hear her talking but I couldn't wake up. She sat next to my bed and prayed and told me jokes and said how scared she was. One day she didn't come see me no more."

Again I stared out the window, across the street at the guy working on the van. He was half in the engine compartment, half out. He tossed a screwdriver over his shoulder. It hit the asphalt and bounced without sound.

"It would've been easier for everyone if I'd died," Walter said. "Then they could've gone to my funeral. They wouldn't have to know the new Walter."

"Don't say that." I looked past the van, where mountains rose in humps and spires, shapes darker than the starlit night.

"Don't tell me not to say it. 'Cause it's true."

Pictures of river trips covered the next few pages: Boys with their arms around Walter's shoulders, rapids and waves, rafts rigged with gear, ready to float into the wilderness.

Walter pointed at a photo of a cliff. In the surface of the rock was some kind of etching, a stick figure. "That's a picture Indians made," he said. "We found it next to one of our campsites."

According to Walter's caseworker, the accident had happened while he was on a rafting trip the summer he turned fourteen. Most of the boys on the trip were a few years older than Walter and more experienced with rafting and rock climbing. One evening he left camp and scrambled up a cliff. He didn't fall far—ten feet or so—but he landed on his head and his brain swelled and bled. It was the next day before his friends could get him to a hospital, where doctors searched his brain for blood clots to remove, and scans revealed deep wounds for which there was no repair— smashed cells that would never recover, severed fibers that would never rejoin. When Walter woke from the coma, he was born anew with diminished IQ. And with this new life most everything was lost to him but his memories—the imprints of the past more durable than the damaged flesh that stored them.

He turned the page and pointed at a photo of him with a walker, moving down a hospital hall empty and bright, polished floors reflecting the light.

Next came pictures of cars and boats made of plastic, lined up in neat rows on bookshelves. Walter said that at first he couldn't make his left hand hold the models, but he practiced all day long because he had nothing else to do. And flyfishing—he'd worked at that when he got out of the hospital, he said. His doctor had given him a flyrod and told him it was good therapy because he had to use both hands to cast, his right clasping the rod handle, his left working the line.

Outside, the man was gone, but next to his van the light still shined, draping shadows across the street.

Walter pushed the album closer to me. There was one photo in the center of the last page: Walter's dad in cutoff jeans, one arm around his wife, one around his son. Walter's hair was a black dome parted on the side. Mountains were hazy in the background; the sky looked as smoggy as Los Angeles. Walter's mom was holding up something that sparkled in the sunlight.

Walter grinned. "My mom lost her earring, and a mom who's lost an earring isn't a happy mom. But my dad and I found it for her."

They had taken the ski lift up Snow King Mountain in Jackson Hole to a deck on the summit, Walter said. It was his mom's birthday; his dad gave her some earrings on top of the mountain. When she put them on she dropped one. It fell through a crack in the deck and rolled into a pile of gravel, where it shined in the light leaking between the boards. Walter lay down and looked at the earring; his dad crawled under the deck. If his dad went toward it Walter yelled "hot," and if he went away from it Walter yelled "cold." His dad finally found the earring and came back up on the deck to give it to Walter's mom. He told Walter he had good eyes, and he hugged Walter and his mom at the same time and had a tourist take their picture. That was Walter's favorite photo in the whole album, he said. That's why he'd put it at the end by itself.

I stared at the mountains in the background of the picture. Haze had blued them: nearby mountains dark blue, distant ranges pale blue, remote peaks blending with the haze on the horizon—a blurry seam where summits merged with sky.

"Were there forest fires that summer?" I asked.

Walter looked at me, tilted his head. "There was hardly no rain at all. And then there was a storm but water didn't come out of the clouds. Just lightning and thunder. There was a bunch of forest fires 'cause of that storm."

I remembered the summer Walter was talking about—the summer the West had burned. It had been a dry year; the valleys were crisp and brown. To find animals and green plants, to find life, you had to go up into the mountains or down into the riverbottoms. Wind rarely stirred the sky; the air was a hot and stagnant mass. When a breeze did blow, it spun funnels of dust across the parched earth like a sandstorm in the Sahara. I carried a waterbottle with me so I could rinse off the grit that coated my teeth and clogged my throat—wash away the taste of the drought.

After waterless storms and lightning strikes, wind finally came; it fanned the flames, spread the wildfires. When the fires stopped, when they were either put out by people or they burned themselves down to nothing, the sun was an orange disk in a hazestained sky, and the earth was coated with ash. Autumn snows fell, dusting the mountains white; winter blizzards buried them. The snow melted off in spring, and from the charred and ashy ground sprang wildflowers, carpeting the earth with violent color.

We'd reached the end of the album. Walter closed it. "It's hard to remember who I was," he said, staring at me. "But sometimes I need to. Sometimes I think that's all I got."

I nodded and pushed the album toward him, understanding that his memories were reminders of what he had been, reminders of what he now was not. The pictures of Walter from before his accident made immortal a boy healthy and whole. But those images were the measure of his loss, for they contained the likeness of the man he would have become if he hadn't fallen. Walter's father had loved the boy in the pictures, but he'd stopped talking to the man who sat before me. A labeler of boxes, a stocker of shelves. A fisherman.

Pieces

The next night, after arguing with Nora, I drove to Walter's apartment.

"Come in," he finally yelled after my third round of knocking. He was sitting at the kitchen table, working on a puzzle, his helmeted head bent low. He shuffled through a mound of pieces, then pushed one next to an empty spot in the border of the puzzle. He flicked the piece away. It slid across the polished tabletop and dropped to the floor.

"Want to go out, Walt?"

"Too busy with the puzzle. It's a hard one. It's got dogs on it."

I leaned against a wall, listening to the hum of the refrigerator and staring at a puddle of light that glared on the linoleum floor. "I'll take you out so you can dance."

"This puzzle's got a billion, zillion pieces."

"You told me that besides flyfishing, dancing's your favorite thing to do."

He tried to force the wrong piece into an empty spot, then flicked it away, across the table, onto the floor.

"There's a good band at Spirits."

Walter swiveled around to look at me. Studied me without saying anything. Then he turned back to the puzzle and picked up a piece. "You want to go out, don't you," he said.

I tapped my fingertips against the table.

Walter, still staring at the puzzle, said, "I'll go if you help me with my buggy. My tire's flat like pancakes." He stood up, steadying himself with his right hand, then headed out the kitchen door, his gait wobbly at first, steadying after a couple steps. I went to my truck and grabbed a toolbox, then followed Walter into an alley that seemed to run all the way to a range of folded mountains, disappearing into their shadowed pleats. In a garage facing the alley was Walter's bike with four wheels, a canopy, and a recumbent seat—his buggy as he called it.

Walter shuffled over to the bike and tilted his head to the side as I explained how to work the tire bead off the rim, slip the punctured tube out, and search the tire's inner surface for hidden sharps—thorns and glass that could flat the new tube.

"You do good work," Walter said. "You're hired."

"Why don't you give it a try?"

"Nope, can't do it. My left hand don't work so good."

"You should learn how to do this yourself."

Walter kicked a tire pump. "I told you," he yelled. "I can't do it!"

"That's bullshit. Your hand works fine when you make yourself use it. It works when you make puzzles. You use it when you cast a flyrod."

"Always yelling at me. Always telling me what to do."

I handed Walter a tire lever and said, "My dad used to tell me that if I just watched him and didn't do it myself, I'd never learn."

He grabbed the lever and threw it at me; it glanced off my shoulder, then skittered across the cement floor. "I said I can't do it!"

"No, you *won't* do it. And I'm not going to do it for you." I pushed past him and walked out of the garage. "I'm trying to be your friend, not your damn babysitter." I stomped through gravel, grinding sharp stones into the ground and kicking at rocks, bulleting them into wooden fences. After a few laps up and down the alley, when my frustration had drained away, I walked back and watched Walter throwing rocks with his left hand, chucking them against the cinderblock garage. As each one hit, it made a dry clack, loud in the windless silence, and it left a tiny cloud of rockdust. The buzzing of mosquitoes bothered the air. Walter pulled a tire lever from his pocket and walked inside; I followed him into the garage.

I uncapped the valve stem of the sagging tire, and with the corner of my thumbnail I pressed the pin, letting the last few pounds of pressure hiss and sputter out like the life of a wounded animal expiring. After I'd bled out all the air I showed Walter how to slip a lever between the rim of the wheel and the tire bead.

With a lever clenched in his right hand, Walter gave the flat tire a violent jab.

"Easy," I said, molding his fingers around the handle and helping him wedge the tongue of the lever under the tire and then hook it to the wheel.

Sweat varnishing his face, Walter raised his trembling left hand and gripped the wheelspokes to steady the rim; then he pried the blunt end of another lever under the tire's edge and popped free the bead, loosing the rubber, exposing the damaged tube within. I punched him in his shoulder. "See that? You're on your way to becoming a bike mechanic."

The muscles in Walter's jaw squirmed to stop a smile from spreading across his face.

After we'd nested a fresh tube in the tire and worked the bead back onto the rim, then pumped the tire full and capped the valve stem, I wiped my hands on a rag, handed it to Walter, and asked him how long it had been since he'd gone on a date.

"I haven't gone on a date in . . . years, or even months . . . I don't know, but it's been a long time. Probably years or something." He wiped his hands, folded the rag, put it in the basket on his bike.

We walked from the garage, back into the alley, our shadows striding next to us. Birds flew overhead, wheeling and swooping as they chased insects. All around us was the steady hum of mosquitoes, their buzz as annoying as their bloodthirst. I crushed a plump one on my forearm, wiped away the crimson splotch.

Walter said, "How come you don't got a date with Nora tonight?"

"Tomorrow we're going to a concert. One of her friends plays the cello. I can't stand classical music, but I promised Nora I'd go. She's mad enough at me already."

"Why do you two always fight?" Walter asked as he picked up a rock and threw it at the garage.

Through a puncture in the clouds I saw windblown snow smoking off the tops of distant mountains. Then the cloudgap closed, and it seemed the hole had been a brief opening to another world. A land of white volcanoes coughing ash into a clear and sparkling sky. I looked at Walter. "What happened on your last date?"

He dropped a rock and folded his arms across his chest. "Tell me why you fight with Nora so much and then I'll tell you 'bout my date."

I looked away from Walter. "Nora says I need to grow up. She wants to have a baby but I told her I'm not ready. She wants me to get a job. And she thinks I drink too much."

"How come you don't work?" Walter asked. "You could put labels on boxes with me. I could talk to my boss at Kmart."

I laughed. "Maybe when my parents' life insurance runs out I'll take you up on that."

"So that's it?" Walter asked. "Nora wants you to make a baby and get a job?"

I looked down the alley. "Mostly it's stupid stuff. This morning we argued about whose turn it was to do laundry."

"Do you love her?" Walter asked.

I nodded that I did.

"Then you better not fight with her no more."

I shoved him. "All right, marriage counselor. Tell me about your last date."

Walter said that his caseworker, Nancy, had set him up on a blind date with a woman named April. April came to the date in a wheelchair, and she needed help eating—one of her staff came along to feed her. April drooled. And she must have put her lipstick on herself because it was smeared all over her face, Walter said. April's staff, a big hairy guy who looked like a gorilla, picked Walter up in a van at his apartment and took them to Dairy Queen. Walter didn't have any appetite because April kept drooling.

Walter stopped talking as a delivery truck drove down the alley. When the roar of the engine faded, he told me that after dinner they'd gone to a park. It was April's idea—she went there every week to feed the ducks. As they tossed breadcrumbs into a pond, April told Walter the story about the ugly duckling, a story her mom had told her every day when she was a little girl. April had wobbled around on crutches and choked when she ate and drooled when she tried to talk, but her mom had promised her that someday she'd be beautiful like the ugly duckling that turned into a pretty swan. April was mad at her mom for telling her that story. She was no swan, she told Walter.

Another truck rumbled through the alley, and again Walter fell silent. Overhead, clouds fanned out, ruffled by wind. I heard the soft thump of a bird's wings as it passed.

Walter said that April had started crying. She made a sound like choking. Walter told her he thought she was pretty, and she said bullshit, he was lying. He tried to give her a hug; she hit him with one of her crutches. Her staff, who'd been sitting in the grass with his shoes off, came running over and grabbed Walter. His feet were hairy and wide like Bigfoot's. April told the Bigfoot staff that Walter was trying to squeeze her breasts; he took Walter back to the van and drove him home while April waited in the park.

Walter and I got into my truck to escape the mosquitoes. I pushed a pile of empty beer cans off the passenger's seat, onto the floor. "Did Nancy try to set you up with anyone after that?" I asked.

Walter climbed onto the seat, shut his door. "Nancy was mad. She kept asking me if I'd squeezed April's boobs. I told her no, but I don't think she believed me."

Where the alley ended, watery light washed over rumpled hills. Mountain peaks flashed in the distance when clouds parted, disappeared when they joined. As we left the alley and drove down a paved road, yellow lines rushing toward us and scrolling out behind, Walter told me that after his date with April he'd tried a dating service—it had been Nancy's idea. He went to an office and filled out forms. He had to write down how tall he was and his favorite food and his hobbies. Then they made him take his helmet off and comb his hair, and they took a picture of him. A couple weeks later a woman called Walter and they made a date. She asked him on the phone if he was drunk; he told her he couldn't drink because of his meds. He had written down on a form that fishing was his favorite thing to do; that was her hobby too. They met in a parking lot next to a river. Nancy dropped him off.

Walter laughed. "I thought my date was gonna have a heart attack when she saw me."

She just stood there and stared at him, he said. She told Walter she hadn't wanted to use a dating service, but ever since her husband had left, her friends had tried to talk her into it. She asked Walter if he was a joke, and she asked him how much her friends had paid him to do it. Walter told her he wasn't a joke. He told her he'd had an accident and broke his head. She told him she was going to break her friends' heads for talking her into using a dating service.

She had a spinning rod and a jar full of nightcrawlers with her, Walter said. He told her he was a flyfisherman and he could teach her how to do it so she wouldn't have to use worms. She shook her head and said she'd sue the dating service for setting her up with a retard. Walter told her she was fat and he didn't want her for a girlfriend anyway.

Walter looked at me and grinned. "She told me who cares what a retard thinks. Then she drove away."

Walter said that Nancy had planned to pick him up in three hours, so he went fishing by himself. When Nancy came and got him and asked him how the date had gone, he said he'd caught three trout. Then he told Nancy he didn't want to go on any more dates for a while.

A car appeared behind us. It sped past, then dissolved in the distance ahead; its taillights traced red lines across the dimming sky. I downshifted as the road climbed a hill. Through a thinning in the clouds I watched a banner of snow flag off the summit of a faraway mountain.

I said, "After our fishing trip on the Snake the other day—that's the first time you've told me you wanted a girlfriend."

"I always wanted one. But not many women'll go on a date with me." Walter grinned and thumped his helmet with his strong right hand. "And the ones who go are usually crazier than I am."

⁓

Walter scooted onto the dancefloor when we got to Spirits. I sat down at a table and ordered a beer. The band was hammering out "Hotel California" by the Eagles.

At first Walter moved wildly, twitching his hands, kicking his feet. But after a few minutes his movements smoothed, as if his body were soothed by the music. He got a few looks at first, and I noticed some people straining not to stare at him.

Walter's caseworker had discouraged me from taking him out to dance. She was afraid he'd get laughed at. And sometimes he did.

After a couple songs, a guy with a baseball cap perched crookedly on his head ran onto the dancefloor and followed Walter. He flailed his arms; drips of beer flew from his bottle and sprayed across the floor. "Check it out! I'm doing the seizure shuffle," he yelled to his friends, who raised their drinks and yelled.

I grabbed Walter and walked him out of there. "We don't have to go to bars anymore," I said when we got outside. An engine turned over in the distance, then quieted. Past the street rose a black bulk of hills, and mountains jutted against the sky, pinwheeled with galaxies and dotted with stars.

Walter stopped walking and turned to stare at me. "I just think 'bout the music and then I forget 'bout my accident, and I forget 'bout that guy making fun of me. Fuck that guy. I don't care 'bout him."

I let Walter choose; we went back into the bar.

I gulped down beers as fast as the waitress could bring them. My pits dripped, my forehead pebbled with sweat. I reached under the table, scraping my nails into the wood and pressing bumps of old gum between my fingertips. I tapped my other hand on the tabletop. Beating the shit out of the frat boy who mocked Walter would have felt damn good, but I knew that Walter wouldn't approve.

I fidgeted and drank as I watched Walter, spinning and looping across the dancefloor with his eyes closed, oblivious to the heartless shadow that mimicked him. The guy flailed around as if he were being electrocuted. But Walter ignored him, and eventually the guy lost interest. Laughing and swigging beer, he walked back to his group of friends, on the lookout, I imagined, for an easier target.

Walter kept his eyes closed as he danced, but he never bumped into anyone, like a dolphin navigating by sonar. As the music slowed, couples pressed their bodies together. Walter's jerking hands and feet quieted, then smoothed to a gentle tic. He turned, moving in circles, spiraling toward the center of the floor. Couples drifted away, not seeming to notice Walter but clearing a path for him. When he reached the middle, he stopped turning and stood with his feet rooted, his arms at his sides, his body swaying to the music. I left my table, and pressing through a sea of bodies, I made my way to the edge of the dancefloor to watch. Walter's eyes were clenched shut and he was smiling. Sweat dribbled down his face, the wet beads sparkling gemlike in the pulse of the strobe lights.

～4～

Pimples

"She wants to go dancing with me," Walter yelled into the phone.

I rolled over in bed and checked the clock: 1:30 A.M.

"She watched me at Spirits last night and today when I saw her she asked me if I wanted to go dancing with her!"

"What are you talking about?"

"She's got pimples . . . not pimples really—those scars people get when they're all grown up but they had pimples when they were a kid."

"You know what time it is, Walt?"

"She has old pimples but she doesn't have a broken head or anything like that."

"*It's one-thirty in the morning!*" I drew back a curtain and looked outside. Aspen branches shook in a night wind. A car drove by, its headlights moving shadows across my bedroom wall.

"Did I wake Nora up?" Walter asked.

"She's not here."

"Did she finally get smart and leave you?"

"She said she'd be back in a couple weeks. She went to her sister's house. Said she was sick of us arguing."

After a pause: "Mike, I think she really likes me."

"Look, Walt, if you don't start at the beginning and explain what the hell you're talking about, I'm going to come over to your apartment and kick your ass."

"You think you could take me? My left's getting strong. I got a mean left jab—you told Martha that."

"Walter!"

"Okay, okay. Always yelling. No wonder Nora left you."

I swallowed a yawn. "Did you call to give me marital advice?"

"I called to tell you 'bout Louise. She works at the fishing store where I always go. Come over here and pick me up. Then we won't have to talk on the phone."

⌒

As we slid into a booth at Kingfisher Inn, Martha winked at Walter. "How's my favorite customer?" she asked.

"I got a date, Martha."

Martha looked at me and frowned. "She ain't too pretty, Mr. Walter. I reckon you could do better." She wheezed a raspy smoker's laugh, and with a finger dyed yellow from nicotine, she poked me in my chest.

"Not him," said Walter. "I got a real date with a girl. She used to have pimples but she don't have a broken head like me."

Martha winked at him. "She's a lucky woman."

After Martha left, Walter told me about Louise, an employee at a fly-fishing shop who'd watched him dancing at Spirits the night before. She said maybe they could go dancing together sometime; Walter told her he was free every night that week and every night for the next week, too. Louise told him she could go on Friday.

Walter leaned back and grinned. "I told her she wouldn't fit on my bike. She said I was funny. But guess what, Mike? Louise's got a car and she said she could drive us." With an open hand he whomped the top of the table, wobbling ketchup and mustard bottles. "You still mad at me for calling so late?"

"That's great news, Walt."

"Hey, Mike?"

His lips squirmed. I could tell he was trying not to smile.

"If things don't work out with Louise, and if Nora don't come back to your house, maybe I could call Nora and go out with her."

I scooted toward Walter in the horseshoe booth, put him in a head-lock.

"Well maybe it really is a date with you two," Martha said. "It's starting to look like the last one I went on." She set down mugs of hot chocolate with leaning white hats of whipcream.

"Mike's jealous of me," Walter said as he jabbed me with his left hand. "I got a date and he don't."

⌒

"Want to tell me about it?" I asked Walter a week later as we drove away from town, toward a range of mountains gray and squatty. Walter had said he went on the date with Louise, but he hadn't told me how it had gone.

"Don't want to think 'bout it right now," he said without looking at me.

In the distance clouds clumped together and settled on top of barren hills like powdered wigs on bald heads. "Tell me about the date when you feel like it," I said. "Let's just worry about catching some fish today."

"That's a deal," Walter said as we pulled onto the highway.

After parking at the trailhead, we hiked toward a river. Ravens, their wings spread and steady, soared on updrafts. All around us stood hills furrowed and red, as if the eroded earth were leaking blood that stained the thinly grassed soils.

"This place don't look so good," said Walter. "Hardly nothing's growing here. Are you sure the river's got fish in it?"

"My dad brought me here. This is where I caught my first trout." I looked at Walter. He tilted his head; sunlight sparkled on his helmet. I cupped a hand over my eyes, asked him if he'd polished his helmet.

Walter told me he had. He'd wanted to wear a tie for his date with Louise but didn't have one, he said. He looked in Mitch's room and all he could find was a wide one with red and orange stripes that looked like a clown's tie. He rode his bike to Salvation Army and found a gray tie with blue dots on it for twenty cents. He gave the woman at the counter a quarter and told her to keep the change.

Walter stopped talking. At the side of the trail, in the shade beneath a haven of pine trees, butterflies tumbled, blown by wind. "I thought you and me made a deal," Walter said. "We were only gonna worry 'bout catching fish, and I didn't have to tell you 'bout the date till I was ready." He started walking down a bouldery path, wobbling as he sidestepped rocks that blocked his way.

After a few minutes of hiking we turned a corner and stepped onto a broad shelf of stone with a commanding view, like a balcony in a theater. A wasteland of bare and crumpled hills sprawled into the distance. Past the hills was a mountain, its base hidden behind haze, its peak hovering above the mist like a palace in the sky. Over the dry earth in the foreground floated dustclouds, thick and golden in the bright noon light. And below us flowed the river, splitting and joining in quicksilver channels where the water spread over a gravelly bed.

"It's like a bunch of little rivers," said Walter, pointing his curled left hand at the braided waters.

I rolled the tip of my tongue over suncracked lips, tasting blood laced with salt, and I looked at a landscape that seemed more likely of a dream than of the daylight world.

"Does it look different from when you were a little boy and you came here with your dad?" Walter asked as we dropped down the path, heading toward the water. He tripped over a pile of shattered sandstone. A broken man in a broken land.

"I remember where I caught my first fish," I said as I grabbed the back of Walter's shirt to steady him. I stopped walking, thought a moment. "There was a big boulder with green lichen all over it. There wasn't much grass, hardly any bushes or trees. Like that lichen was the only living thing."

A bird flew by, passing so close I felt its wingtip brush my cheek. Its body a flash of blue, its head helmeted with a crest of feathers, its whirring wings invisible, the kingfisher disappeared into a ravine.

I followed Walter as he shambled through stony rubble, then slipped down the last few feet of path and waded into a ginclear trickle. Dirt banks lay dry and fractured, cracking in the sun like shattered crockery. The waterline along the shore, marking where the river had risen when spring snowmelt bloated it, was littered with tiny bits of wood and the castoff husks of streamborn insects.

I heard a splash. "Trout?" Walter asked, tapping me with his flyrod.

"Probably just a frog," I said as I headed toward the next channel, walking over rocks that made a hollow clatter when they rubbed together, crunching a sunbleached fish skeleton beneath my boot.

"I'm going there," Walter said, pointing his rodtip past a shallow riffle, at a cliff face where water pooled. "Where the water's green—that's where the trout'll be."

Walter was right: no trout swam in the transparent water of the riffles; and none in the shallow pools, where the water turned the pale green of a lima bean. Only in the deep holes, only in the places where the riverbed was buried beneath the darkest seagreen—only in those places did we find fish. In the deepest pools we caught trout that rose to the surface to take our flies. And then we let them go, watching the fish slip from our hands, back into the river, back into the bottomless green.

I walked the shore until I found a slab polished by wind and rain and time. I sat down on the smooth rock and watched Walter cast, his rod waving back and forth, his line looping. My eyelids sagged, and my face in the sun, I fell asleep. I dreamed of my father. I saw his hands, knotted with callus, saw his thick fingers twine with mine as he showed me how to hold the handgrip of a rod he'd made me. And I heard his voice, his deep and gentle voice, the rhythm of it real but the words unclear.

"Think we better go back 'fore it gets dark?" Walter asked, pulling me from the dream, waking me as watery shadows dribbled across the ground. I rubbed my eyes, watched birds darting against a dim sky. I glanced at my bare wrist; I'd left my watch in the truck.

"Did you find that boulder?" Walter asked as I gathered my gear. "The one where you caught your first fish?"

I told him I'd found a few rocks that looked like it, but I hadn't seen the bright green lichen I remembered from when I was a boy. I stopped breaking down my rod and looked at Walter.

"You miss your dad?" he asked. "And your mom—you miss her too?"

"Yeah, Walt. I miss them both." I picked up a rock tumbled smooth by the river, stuffed it in my pocket to give to Nora.

"Do you miss Nora?"

I pretended I hadn't heard him. A breeze rolled along the river, shivering the bushes that clutched its banks. I finished taking my rod apart, then put it in its case and tied it to my backpack, glancing skyward as I slipped my arms into the packstraps. Squiggly clouds covered the sky like children's cursive written on a blue slate, like a scribbled message I couldn't read.

Walter started to laugh.

I pushed him. "What's so funny?"

"I'm not pretty like Nora but I won't leave you. You need a dog, too, Mike. They never get mad and go away." He fell silent a moment, then said, "What were you two fighting 'bout anyway?"

"Nora says I'm not a good communicator. Imagine that." I looked at him and smiled. "She wants me to see a shrink so I can learn to talk about things."

"A shrink can make you talk more?"

"Nora doesn't know any better—she's from New York."

Walter nodded. "So are you gonna see one?"

"I told her I don't need to pay some stranger to give me advice.

You're pretty good at that. And you don't charge by the hour. All I have to do is take you fishing."

Walter tilted his head. "Does Nora ever get mad 'cause you go fishing with me all the time?"

"Actually, she told me it's about the only thing I've done right in the past year."

"Then maybe you should pay me," Walter said as he used his left hand to punch me in the solar plexus.

I fought to get my breath, then offered to continue his boxing lessons if he kept going fishing with me. He told me we had a deal.

After finding a path that led away from the river, we passed through a scrubland of dead plants, their dry pods clacking in the wind. We traveled a stony waste, then went by trees with blackened bark. Blades of grass, newly green and thin as hair, grew from the cracks of logs split by fire.

Back at the truck Walter finally told me about his date. He said he hadn't been able to figure out how to make a knot in his tie. He looked at himself in the mirror and tried to tie it, but the knot didn't seem right. He asked Mitch to help him. Mitch got the tie all tangled up and Walter yelled at him. Mitch told Walter that since he couldn't get the tie on, at least he could have a shiny helmet for his date. They tried furniture polish but that didn't work, so they used Crisco.

A windgust that carried a spatter of rain shook bushes. When the wind died, except for a few raindrops pinging against the truck, all was silent and still. I finished putting our gear in the bed, shut the creaky tailgate. "So did you go to Spirits?" I asked.

"Louise picked me up right on time. I didn't dance as good as I usually do 'cause I was nervous. And that guy was there—the one who made fun of me last time. He followed me around."

"Did you ignore him again?"

Raindrops dimpled the dirt at my feet. Walter looked away from me, toward the lifeless hills that hid the river. He told me that Louise had gotten mad and yelled at the guy, and then she'd started to dance. It was smoky and she was moving her arms above her head. Walter could see her hair and her eyes but he couldn't see her pimple scars. He tried to kiss her cheek. Louise pushed him away and went outside. He followed her out and told her that when they were dancing he couldn't see her pimples and she'd looked so pretty he wanted to kiss her. Louise drove him home and didn't say anything to him when she dropped him off. When he got out of the car, Walter tried to apologize for kissing her and for saying something stupid. He told her he didn't care about her pimples, but she slammed the door and drove away.

I nodded, waited for him to continue. He said nothing. The sky darkened from gray to deepening black, and all but the faintest stars appeared. "Have you talked to her since then?" I finally asked.

"I walked by the store where she works and looked through the window. I saw her but I couldn't go in and talk to her. I did that for three days—looked through the window. Yesterday I went inside and I tried to tell Louise sorry again. I tried to tell her 'bout my stupid head—how it does things and says things that it shouldn't."

A breeze stirred, rustling dry and crackly grass, flinging drips of rain against us.

"What did she say, Walt?"

"She wouldn't listen. She wouldn't look at me."

≈5≈

Searching for Gold

"Whose dog?" Walter asked as he climbed into my truck one morning in mid-September.

"Meet Cap'n," I said as I scratched the dog's ears and tried to find its eyes, buried beneath brows that looked like twin dust mops hanging from its shaggy head. "That's Cap'n—as in Captain Hook. I'm going to get him a peg leg with a hook."

Cap'n settled into the backseat, his face disappearing as he curled into a ball. Rumpled and dusty, he looked more like an unmade bed than like a dog.

"Does he bite?" Walter asked.

"Only if you bite him first."

"I bet he don't run so good with three legs."

"He still gives squirrels a hell of a time," I said. "It's like the Serengeti in my front yard."

Cap'n stretched himself into the front of the truck and rubbed his furry head against Walter.

I told Walter that Cap'n had spent about an hour trying to hop after squirrels with his three legs. That didn't work, so he switched tactics—became a stalker instead of a chaser, turned himself into a cat. He learned to wiggle through the grass, creeping up on squirrels like a lion stalking a gazelle.

My buddy Todd and I had been driving around, having a few beers, I explained. Buck—that was Cap'n's name when he had four legs—was standing in the bed of the pickup, barking at deer and dogs. I asked Todd if Buck was going to be okay riding around in the back like that. Todd said it wasn't a problem, said he did it all the time, said Buck was a surfing dog. Buck had good balance. Just stood there and barked, never fell down— even when we got shitfaced on Jim Beam and Todd was sliding through gravel, riding on two wheels around turns. Buck was fine until he saw a squirrel. He dove out of the truck to chase after it. Didn't have a graceful landing, broke his leg in four places.

Walter reached over, scratched the dog's head. Cap'n raised a fluffy eyebrow, exposed a dark eye. Dropped the brow, went back to sleep. "Doesn't your friend Todd want him?" Walter asked.

"I'm going to keep Cap'n for a while until I find a home for him." Yellow highway lines zipped toward the truck; in the rearview mirror I watched them unroll behind us.

Walter and I were searching for ponds that were rumored to have golden trout and grayling. Stories circulated around Kingfisher about fishing guides at the turn of the century who'd left the valley and headed into the mountains on horses packed with canvas bags full of water and fish fingerlings: exotic species for their wealthy clients to catch, something other than the native fish—cutthroat trout. Oldtimers spoke of dozens of ponds dotting a meadow, high and hidden in the mountains, the waters so tiny they hadn't been named by Forest Service mapmakers. But the springfed ponds were rich with insects, and with plenty of food and little fishing pressure, the grayling and golden trout had thrived, it was said. The few people who found the hidden waters guarded the secret. Directions couldn't be coaxed out of them—unless they were drunk. On a summer climbing trip in the Wind River Mountains when Nora and I were in college, an old man with a face like a walnut, wrinkled and brown, and a white Santa beard that gave the illusion of wisdom, spoke of the ponds as we sat next to him in a bar. He explained the directions more to his beer mug than to us, and that summer our search began.

After a few years of looking, Nora and I had figured that either the ponds didn't exist or the drunk in the bar had given us bogus directions. But still we searched. Looking for the hidden ponds was like traveling into one of the blank spaces beyond the edges of the known world on an ancient map, a place rumored to hold treasures and monsters both.

About five years back Nora and I had stopped bringing a GPS unit; we seemed to get lost more when we had it with us than when we left it behind. Two years back we stopped bringing the pistol: a .357 Magnum we thought would protect us from bears. The place where the ponds were supposed to be was smack in the middle of prime grizzly habitat. The hunters who invaded the area every fall told us that if we had a pistol and got charged by a grizzly we had better make damn sure we hit the bear in its heart or in one of its lungs on the first shot. Otherwise we'd do nothing but piss it off—really give it a reason to maul us. They said that unless we could hit the bear in one of its eyes, we shouldn't aim for the head: bullets would just ricochet off its thick skull. I couldn't shoot a billboard from ten feet away. We finally decided to leave the gun at home when a crusty, grayhaired hunter laughed so hard he doubled over with a cackling cough; when he came up for air he told us that shooting a charging grizzly with a pistol was like plinking a pissed off Mike Tyson with a pellet gun. Forest rangers encouraged us to carry cans of pepper spray, but it was hard to imagine pepper spray stopping a quarter ton or more of angry bear.

In bars around Kingfisher we had heard stories of grizzlies attracted to the places where hunters gutted the elk and deer they killed. The bears caught the scent from miles away and made beelines for the leftovers— rich and easy meals. The bears would charge anything that got in their way. When they burst from the woods into clearings, they ran faster than horses gallop. And a grizzly could knock a man's head from his neck with one pass of its paw.

We had heard of a grizzly sow with cubs chasing a hiker to the top of a tree. After she'd tried to climb up, and five hundred pounds of bear bulk had sheared all the low limbs from the flimsy pine, the grizzly sat at the base of the trunk for three days, waiting. Dehydrated but unscathed, the treed hiker needed more counseling than medical treatment when the bear finally ended her siege.

We had heard of wolves that either had escaped the machine guns and poison of extermination programs or had been restored to Yellowstone and then strayed from the sanctuary of the park into the wilderness of northwestern Wyoming. Deep in the backcountry, people had seen canine pawprints big as human hands. Hikers had heard howling that didn't sound like coyotes. Hunters, when glassing distant ridges with their binoculars, had glimpsed fourlegged animals as bulky as professional wrestlers; but they disappeared before the hunters could get their rifle sights lined up and take a shot. Some people thought the "wolves" were just well-fed coyotes. Others said they were dogs that had strayed from ranches—dogs that had gone wild and formed a pack.

I pointed out the windshield at the Tetons rising in the distance. "Know what 'Teton' means?" I asked Walter as we crested a hill. "It's a French word—means 'tit.' French fur trappers named them."

"Must've been some lonely trappers," said Walter. "They don't look like tits at all." He squinted and stared out the window, then said, "Well, maybe really pointy ones."

As we climbed into the mountains, gravel shot out from under the truck tires and ricocheted between trees. Dust poured into the cab. I rolled up the windows, but still it worked its way in—crept through seals, sneaked through cracks. I coughed and sneezed, and my jawbone chattered as the truck jounced along the rutted road. A valley dry and brown stretched out below, and haze from a wildfire rimmed the world, spreading gauzy white against the spotless blue of the sky.

Walter said, "How come Nora's not going with us?"

"I don't want to talk about it."

He punched me in my shoulder. "We'll just worry 'bout finding fancy fish today."

I glanced at him and grinned. "That's a deal."

When we got to the parking area, the truck was furred with dust. As Walter wrote "wash me" on a window with his fingertip, and Cap'n peed on bushes and sniffed the ground, I kicked around in the sagebrush and found a half dozen roses wrapped in cellophane. The bar code was still attached; the price had been peeled off. Couldn't tell the color of the flowers: the petals were as dark and dry as old autumn leaves. Next to the roses lay a pair of tube socks with orange stripes. I carried the socks and flowers to the truck, dropped them on the hood. "Reminds me of a game I learned in college," I said.

"What kind of game?" Walter asked. "Like Monopoly?"

I told Walter I'd had an English professor who wore a bowtie every day and began each class by explaining how worthless our generation was. The professor told me I was lazy because I wrote in fragments; I told him we lived in a fragmented world where everything around us and inside us was broken. He said that's exactly the kind of rationalization he'd expect from someone without any discipline or ambition, someone who'd never been to war. I told him his explanation was what I'd expect from a dickhead in a bowtie; he kicked me out of his class. But the bowtied professor did have one good idea: he'd make us walk around campus and look for unusual things, and then we'd have to tell a story about what had happened. For example, if we saw a woman sitting on a park bench crying, we'd have to explain what she was crying about, how she ended up there, where she'd go after she got up from the bench and left the park.

Walter pointed at me. "You start," he said. "Make up a story 'bout why roses and socks are in the middle of nowhere."

I paced around for a few seconds, then began: "A man declared his love for his girlfriend here. He thought it would be romantic to bring her into the wilderness, give her some roses, tell her he'd love her forever. But she wasn't having any of it—just wanted to keep things simple. Wasn't interested in love. She handed the roses back to him and ran off. She hitched a ride back to town with a hippie in a VW van before her boyfriend could catch up with her."

"What was a hippie in a VW van doing out here?" Walter asked.

"That's a different story. Let me finish."

Walter drew his index finger and thumb across his mouth—zipped his lips.

"So the boyfriend drove home alone. At first he was sad, but by the time he got back to town he was pissed off that he'd gone to so much trouble and gotten screwed over. So he bought some black roses, drove back to this spot, left the roses here—a memorial to his dying love. Then he tore off his socks. They'd been a birthday present from his girlfriend— his *ex*-girlfriend—and he threw those on the ground and left them."

I said, "How about you? Got a story?"

Walter grinned and tilted his head. "A man and a woman loved each other so much they caught on fire."

"Spontaneously combusted?" I asked.

"No," said Walter, "they just burst into flames."

I smiled and nodded.

"The woman dropped the roses when she caught on fire," Walter said. "The man had on fireproof socks. He was a firefighter. He was late to pick up the woman for their date. He couldn't find no normal socks that were clean, so he put on his firefighting socks. All that was left after they burned up was some ash, the socks the man wore, and the roses the woman dropped. And the message of my story . . . Is that what you call it? The message?"

"The moral."

"The moral of my story is that love can be a dangerous thing."

While I clapped, Cap'n tilted back his head and barked at birds that dipped and veered above.

We hiked past the parking area toward a ghost town—a dude ranch that had been abandoned just before World War Two. Some cabins sagged and leaned, some were piles of lumber and shingles, crumbling back to the ground from which they had been raised. Yet all the chimneys stood, their rocks and mortar intact. Pillars rising from the ruins.

We passed a barn that was tilted so far to the side it seemed a gentle breath of wind could knock it over. Walter stepped off the path and gave the barn a push. I joined him. We dug our feet in and grunted and shoved; the leaning barn creaked. It swayed but wouldn't fall.

We got back on the trail, following it around piles of boards, avoiding rusty nails as long as railroad spikes. At the top of a bushy knoll the trail split into three faint paths that snaked through sagebrush. Without hesitating, Walter followed a path toward a timbered ridge below. Cap'n hopped along beside him. I walked behind Walter, catching him when he stumbled. We headed into the wilderness, searching for waters that we probably wouldn't find, that maybe didn't exist. The ghost town disappeared as we dropped downhill, without protection, without guidance, the promise belched out by a drunk old man in a bar almost a decade ago still echoing in my head. The promise of fish rare and beautiful.

The trail split, and again Walter chose with neither comment nor hesitation. We left the open sagebrush plain and entered a dark and woodsy place. Trees were tightly clustered; their branches twined together, roofing the forest and blocking the light. We tripped over logs, caught our boots in bushes, slipped on moss. Cap'n hopped toward squirrels and made them scamper up trees. From boughs far above, the chattering squirrels knocked down tiny pinecones that pelted us like hail. Squawky jays flapped their wings.

Finally the dim and noisy forest ended; we walked into a meadow, treeless and green. In its sunken center was grass so bright it glowed like fluorescent paint. Around the edge of the acidgreen grass were rocks velveted with dark moss—round stones marking where the shore had been. We were in an old lakebed, I said to Walter. Nora had told me that as soon as a lake fills, it starts to dry out. It turns to spongy earth, then solid ground. Walter walked toward the shriveled stems and wrinkled caps of mushrooms arranged in a ring. "It's so round," he said. "Like somebody planted it."

They grow in a circle like that because the mushrooms have a central root system, or something like roots, that links them together, I told Walter. Nora called them fairy rings. She said that in Ireland they have legends about fairies that dance all night, and when they disappear in the morning, the ring of mushrooms pops up, marking where the fairies danced in a circle.

In a rubble of boulders something scurried and squeaked. Like a plump gray mouse with round ears and a twitching nose, a pika climbed atop a rock. "What is that funny thing?" Walter said. "A fairy?" Peeping and chirping, it stared at us. Walter answered the pika: squeaked back at it. It turned, then vanished into a crevice between boulders in the center of the clearing, the place like some strange feverland of hallucinated plants and animals.

"Maybe this is where the fish lived," said Walter as he kicked at the loamy dirt, the glowing grass. "The fancy fish we came to find. Maybe they're fertilizer now."

I looked at my watch, glanced at the sky. "We've only got a few hours of daylight. Think we should head back?"

From a bush Walter plucked a feather as long as his forearm. A feather from an eagle or a hawk—a bird brown and big. He stuck it in a vent on his helmet and said, "I want to keep going. If those fish still live here, I'll find 'em."

As Walter and Cap'n walked across where the lake used to be, Walter stopped and pointed to a rock outcropping. "See the cave up there?" he said.

I stared at the cliffside where he was pointing, saw a black cleft big enough to park a tow truck in. "I'll bet that's the home of a wolf pack," I said. "The cave is like a maze inside, and a boy lives in the middle of it. When he was a baby his family came out here for a picnic. He wandered away and got lost. The wolves found him and took him back to their cave and raised him. If someone goes in looking for the boy, the wolves split up and scatter through the maze. The person has to leave some kind of trail—something to help her find her way out, or else she gets lost and dies in there."

Walter tilted his head, stared at the cave. "An old man with a big beard lives up there. He don't like people but he likes animals. He feeds the animals and fixes 'em when they get broken. The ones that don't heal up good—he lets 'em live in the cave with him. And he can talk to the animals. He knows all their languages. He forgot how to talk like a man, but he can chirp like a bird and growl like a bear."

We left the sun and the green grass, headed back into the forest. Back into the clustered trees, the piney dark. Scurrying squirrels and cackling jays greeted us. Trees groaned and swayed when wind raced through the forest, bouncing limbs whiskered with pine needles. We hiked singlefile, Walter in front so I could catch him if he stumbled. Cap'n circled around us, moving us closer together as we walked. It was the sheepdog in him: he liked to keep his flock together. I wandered off the path, started to walk through the woods by myself to see what would happen. Cap'n yelped and chased after me, nudged me back toward Walter.

The dim forest lightened as we neared a clearing, and we stepped out of the trees, into sunlight, streaming through a sky hazed with smoke from wildfires. Before us was a vast meadow, and through its center coursed a stream with water so clear it was invisible. The instant before my pupils narrowed to the light I saw bubbles and ripples floating like clouds above the gravelly bed. Trout scattered as Cap'n hopped toward the bank; the fish seemed to fly through the air. As my eyes adjusted, I followed Cap'n to the edge of the stream, studying the panicky trout as they darted between a riffle and a pool.

"Look," Walter shouted. "Dolphins!"

Four animals, glossy and slim, swam toward us. Their backs arched above the water and then they dove. Then reappeared. And arched and dove. . . . And for a moment, before my mind made sense of what I was seeing, they were dolphins. A pod of dolphins swimming through a mountain stream. One of them surfaced near me, stuck its head out of the water like a periscope. Its whiskered face looked old and wise—out of place on its sleek and playful body. A river otter.

Walter laughed so hard he had to sit down.

The otters swam around, studying us, some upright with swiveling heads, others floating on their backs, paddling the water with flippery hands and feet.

Cap'n hobbled toward the shore, a low growl rumbling in his throat, his ears flattening and his backhair bristling. He gave a few barks, and the otters scattered and dove, then reemerged downstream. And again they dove, disappearing beneath an undercut bank.

I heard the slow beat of broad wings, then saw a shadow, and finally noticed a bird flying overhead: an osprey, colored like a pinto horse—white, blotched with brown. Beneath the bird dangled a limp fish, iridescent in the sun.

"Looks like that bird's carrying a rainbow in its feet," Walter said.

"It's a grayling." I pointed at the fish, at the rectangular fin on its back, as the bird passed by.

We followed the stream, hiking along the bank, watching fish scatter: all cutthroat—no grayling, no golden trout. We shoved through a tangled net of alder bushes and climbed onto a beaver dam. Above the dam was a pond, a perfect mirror, a miniature of the sky. With fins poking out of the water, fish cruised through the shallows like tiny sharks, gulping insects from the glassy surface.

"What are they?" Walter whispered.

The pond exploded. I saw a waterspout erupt; then a bird with its wings folded back, a streamlined missile, shot out of the water, into the air. A trout of shiny gold struggled to escape its claws. The bird, another osprey, flew away, its wings beating slow and steady, the fish bright in the sunlight—a miracle of color in the smoky sky.

We didn't speak, didn't move. Even Cap'n was silent and still. I finally turned toward Walter. He was staring at the spot where the bird had disappeared, an inky place in the huddled trees beyond the meadow. He said, "I thought somebody was throwing rocks into the water to scare us."

"I thought we triggered a landmine," I said. "I've heard that the people who find the ponds do everything they can to guard the secret. Thought maybe somebody booby-trapped this place. Did you see the fish that osprey had? Looked like gold jewelry sparkling in the sun."

"It looked fake," Walter said. "Maybe the old man who lives in the cave painted the fish."

I shook my head and laughed. "That's a hell of a theory."

"If dolphins can live in the mountains in Wyoming, then crazy old men can paint fish."

I climbed to a high point on the beaver dam and looked across the meadow, crisscrossed with dams, studded with dozens of ponds, like glistening eyes gazing up from the earth, staring into the sky above.

I glanced down at my legs, zebraed with dirt: grit clung in black stripes to my white skin. I pulled off my damp shirt, kicked my boots off, then jumped into the pond. A couple degrees colder and it would've been ice. I tried to scream but my body and mind were paralyzed. I just stood there in the chestdeep water, silently begging my heart to not stop beating. I convulsed with shivers; my teeth hammered together so hard I thought my fillings would pop out.

"How is it?" Walter asked.

"Not bad," I stammered through clattering teeth.

Walter took off his shirt and boots, peeled off his socks, climbed in. "Not too bad," he muttered, his purple lips stretched tight.

We started swimming like maniacs, flailing around, trying to generate warmth, battling the shriveling cold. We roiled dirt at the bottom of the pond; murky clouds spread through the clear water. Fish flashed as they appeared and disappeared, darting between billows of silt, swimming around the edges of the pond, then back toward the center. Every few seconds I felt one touch my leg. Felt the slippery fishflesh against my goosebumped skin.

Cap'n jumped in and swam around. His soggy eyebrows rose up, revealing dark and uncomprehending eyes. He kept paddling in circles, tilting to the side. It was the first time he'd been swimming since losing his leg.

"He leans to the side like a broken boat," Walter said.

I couldn't stop laughing. Laughed so hard I warmed myself up.

When we finally crawled from the pond, back onto the beaver dam, a seam unraveled in the blanket of haze above. The sun burned through, drying our shivering bodies. We spread our clothes across the beaver dam, making soft beds over sticks with ends gnawed sharp by beavers' teeth. And we lay in the afternoon sun.

As we hiked out of the forest, past the fluorescent grass and mushrooms in the dead lake, Walter said, "I'm gonna come back here with my flyrod. I've never caught a golden trout or a grayling before."

I stopped hiking. "Nora and I've been searching for those ponds, for those fish, for almost a decade. And if it wasn't for you, we'd probably still be looking for them. Doesn't seem right to catch them somehow."

After a few minutes Walter said, "I'm not gonna catch 'em either."

I turned to look at him.

"If the old man in the cave paints 'em, then they're his fish. I'm not gonna catch 'em and make the old man angry. I got enough problems without having a crazy caveman mad at me."

Gusts of wind surged through the woods, screeching between branches. A few yards ahead of us, a dead pine groaned as it bent toward the ground. In a sudden blast of wind the tree popped apart—sounded like fireworks exploding. The branchy crown fell to the ground and the trunk snapped upright: a splintery stub poking the sky. As we walked down the path, dry branches crunching beneath our boots, the wind shifted and the smell of rot burned our noses. We pulled our shirts up, covering our faces like bandits as we passed a bloated deer carcass.

When we left the woods we saw the ghost town—sagging buildings and straight chimneys on the hill above us. I stopped hiking and turned toward Walter. "I don't know what Nora and I are going to do now that you found the fish. We'll have to meet some other drunk in a bar, scruffy and pissed off at the world, blabbing into his beer about secret ponds."

As we topped the hill and passed the chimneys, straight and tall, dark columns against the glowing sky, Walter asked me what the ponds were called.

"The old geezer got right in my face and whispered. I can still smell his breath—like garlicky hamburger and stale beer. Smelled as bad as that dead deer. Told me if he said the names of the ponds out loud they'd dry up."

The failing sun threw bars of orange light across the ground, the buildings, the chimneys. We passed a ring of stones holding the gray ash and blackened sticks of a long-ago fire; then we saw the barn we'd tried to tip over. Walter stopped and stared, told me he wanted to try again.

Braced and breathing deeply, we counted to three, and together we pushed while Cap'n barked and hopped around us, as if encouraging our efforts. The leaning barn creaked and swayed, then fell to the ground with a final groan and puff of dust as the walls thudded into the dirt. Walter wiped his hands on his shirt, smiled at a job well done, then headed through the maze of crumbling buildings with Cap'n hopping next to him, glancing up at Walter through dark eyes beneath shaggy brows, looking at him as though he'd known him all his life.

Across the valley a thunderhead towered over a mountain. Bolts of blue lightning flashed and forked without sound, showing the peak in a light unreal. As if the summit were a dreamshape, a sorcerer's castle with turrets spiraling into skies ablaze with electricity, sparks arcing from castle to cloud and back like a fantastic nexus between heaven and earth.

At the edge of the parking lot Walter and I stopped to study tree graffiti: carvings in the tender bark of aspen, where people had left their marks in black welts against the white—initials, hearts, vows of love.

"Maybe someday I'll have a girlfriend to put on the tree," Walter said, looking at the ground and kicking a pile of stony rubbish. As I circled the aspen, my boots crunched crackly plants withered and brown. And I noticed bushes that were reddening and yellowing—turning to their fall colors weeks before plants in the valley would begin to change. In the mountains autumn was near; on the valley floors it was distant—the days were summerhot, the nights still warm.

As we drove toward town, dropping from the mountains back to the valley, clouds of dust boiled up beneath the truck and lingered in the air, stretching out behind us like a banner announcing our return.

Walter, his fingers pressed to the glass, was staring out the back window. "We must be important people 'cause we found the secret ponds," he said. "And red sunbeams are crossing the road like those lasers that set off an alarm when somebody walks through 'em. And dustclouds are shooting out behind the truck like smokescreens." Walter raked the fingers of his withered left hand through Cap'n's fur. "I feel like I'm James Bond and we're in a secret spy truck with lots of weapons." Then he shook his head and spoke so quietly I might have imagined it: "Spies in the mountains, cavemen painting fancy fish, dolphins in Wyoming. I'm gonna write my dad a letter and tell him 'bout all that."

≈6≈

Horse Tamer and Lightning Legs

A few weeks later, when the aspen leaves in the valley were gilded at their edges, and the days were still warm but the nights crisp, Nancy called me. She said that Walter and Mitch had ridden so far from town they hadn't been able to make it back. They'd left their bikes on the roadside and hitchhiked home. Nancy had to leave town for a conference; she asked me to help them get their bikes back to their apartment and to talk to them about bike safety.

They were in the living room watching TV when I got to their apartment. A black-and-white western was playing with the volume turned off. The curtains were shut; it took a few minutes for my eyes to adjust to the dimness. The apartment had a peaty stink, like rotten compost. Walter nodded as I walked in but said nothing. Mitch leaned toward the TV, glowing in the murky living room.

I pulled a curtain back; sunlight streamed into the room. I pushed at the window but it wouldn't budge. The paint at the seam where the window nestled the sill looked intact. "You guys are like vampires," I said.

Mitch laughed. "Yeah, yeah. Like Dracula."

I pushed until the seal of paint broke and the window popped free. Air rushed in, freshening the musty apartment.

Mitch hopped up, jingling, and shut the window. Mitch always jingled when he moved: a metal ring full of keys dangled from a beltloop on his pants. A few of the keys probably served a purpose—his apartment door, a locker at work. But there were dozens of keys on the ring. Keys to locks he'd lost long ago, keys to locks that were broken, keys he'd found, keys people had given him as gifts, keys to nothing.

Mitch pulled the curtain across the window; then he sat back down, looked at the TV, and said, "Got a joke."

I flopped down on the couch. "Let's hear it."

Without looking away from the TV, Mitch said, "An old guy backs up his car. Puts it in reverse, runs a chicken over."

"He runs over a chicken?"

Mitch clapped his hands. "Yeah, yeah. Chicken's dead. The old man gets out of the car, picks up the chicken. He gives it to the old lady. The old lady says, 'That's not my chicken. It's too skinny!' "

Mitch looked at me for the first time since I'd come in and said, "Funny, huh?"

I clapped my hands. "That was a good one."

"That's not my chicken," Mitch repeated, still staring at me. "It's too skinny!" His thick glasses made his eyes look enormous; they changed shape, stretching and bulging through the smudged lenses as his body shook with laughter.

Walter was eating pickle relish, scooping it from a jar with his fingers. Mitch turned back toward the TV, smeared mayonnaise on a slice of American cheese, stuffed it into his mouth, and washed it down with a swig of Pepsi from a two-liter bottle.

"Good lunch, guys?"

"We were supposed to have pizza," Walter said. "But we just ordered Pepsi."

"What about pizza?"

"Forgot."

"So you had Pepsi delivered and nothing else?"

"I asked the delivery guy if he could go back and bring us a pizza, but he just stared at me like I was crazy."

"Heard you guys had a little adventure yesterday," I said as I got up and walked toward the door. "Want to go get your bikes?"

Mitch fumbled with the remote. The sound kicked on. He shuffled over to the TV and turned it off, then unplugged it. "Safety first," he said.

As Mitch pushed past me and went outside, I noticed a bulge in his shirtpocket. The first time I met Mitch, I had thought the bulge was some kind of growth: it looked like a tumor protruding from his chest. When I asked him about it, he reached under his sweater and pulled out a lumpy package wrapped in plastic grocery bags and masking tape. He held it out for me to see, then stuffed it back under his sweater. "Just stuff," he said when I asked him what was in the package.

Once, as a favor to Nancy when she was pissed because Nora and I had taken Walter camping without asking her, I helped Mitch clean his room. I found all sorts of treasures in his dresser drawers and under his bed: single shoes, unmated socks, surgical gloves, a garden hose, deflated basketballs, a baby carriage, a rack of barbecued ribs, and packages of all shapes and sizes wrapped in plastic and tape. He wouldn't let me throw anything away, except the ribs—and even for that I had to bribe him with a can of Pepsi. I finally gave up cleaning and organizing his room when I tried to hang up one of the framed pictures he had stacked in his closet. He pulled it from my hands, stuffed it under his bed, then chased me from his room, slammed the door, and told me that you can't just go around hanging things up, because that's how they get stolen, and maybe I should go bother Walter and leave him and his stuff alone, and who the hell did I think I was, anyway?

When I reported back to Nancy, she told me that Mitch had spent most of his life in a state school, a gray building with rows of tiny windows and a flat roof. She showed me a picture: far from any town, it was perched on a hill like a ridgetop battleship. The residents there lived not in rooms but in cubicles, Nancy explained. Tiled cubicles were easy to clean: attendants soaped them and sprayed them with fire hoses. The residents were allowed few possessions; what they could keep was usually stolen by the biggest, toughest residents, or by the staff.

Walter told Mitch I was okay, promised him I wouldn't steal anything. But still Mitch chased me away every time I walked by his room; and he fidgeted, pawing at his clothes, adjusting his glasses, and picking at his ears whenever I got near him. There was, however, one thing that always drew him from his shell: masks.

An art teacher at a local high school had put on a ceramics class for people with disabilities. Nancy talked Mitch into taking the class; he loved it. That is, he loved the mask part of it. Bowls bored him; the salt and pepper shakers the teacher encouraged him to make were uninspired lumps; he got through the M and I of a name plaque but fizzled before finishing the T. But then came the first night of mask making. Mitch couldn't get enough. The teacher set up a private class—just for Mitch, just for masks. And masks he made: surreal blends of man and beast, grotesque and beautiful. The teacher's sister owned Kingfisher Inn, which sometimes doubled as an art gallery. For a few weeks Mitch's masks were featured there. A local paper did an article with a picture of the grinning artist next to one of his favorite creations. A framed copy of that photo hung in Mitch's bedroom—the only picture he allowed out of the closet and on his wall.

"I've got something for you, Mitch," I said as I climbed into my truck. Mitch and Walter had already piled in, Mitch in front, Walter in back. I pulled a book from under my seat. Handed it to Mitch. "They're Native American masks." I reached over and flipped through the pages until I found what I was looking for: a mask that looked like a man's face, but with a long, twisted bird beak and a circle of feathers haloing the head. "Looks like the ones you make."

"What's it say 'bout that?" Walter asked as he leaned over Mitch and looked at the book.

I read the text beneath the picture. "Says it's a ceremonial mask for a shaman."

Walter shrugged his shoulders. "A what?"

"It says here that shamans are sick or crazy in the ordinary world, but they have power in the spirit world. Some Native American cultures believe shamans use the spirit of a bird to soar in and out of people's dreams. Says that shamans are healers, and the medicine they use is magic."

Mitch pointed at the mask. "Looks like Walter. Has a long nose like him."

"Shut up, Mitch," Walter said. "Your feet smell." He thumped Mitch's head. "See that, Mike—I used my left hand! Just like you taught me."

"No hitting," Mitch squeaked. "Safety first." Mitch's eyes bulged when he said the safety slogan—something he'd picked up at the institution where he'd grown up, according to Nancy.

Walter kicked Mitch's seat.

"No kicking," Mitch said. "Safety first." He looked up from the picture and peered at me through his thick glasses. "Maybe I'll make a birdman mask like that," he said, pointing at the picture in the book. The smile that spread across his face grew so big it shrank his bulging eyes to slits.

I backed out the driveway and drove through town as Walter and Mitch flipped through the book and bickered.

"Want to tell me why you rode your bikes out into the middle of nowhere?" I pointed out the windshield at the highway ahead. It snaked through a canyon, then climbed red hills, capped with crumbled rocks, dotted with scraggly trees. The outlines of mountains were sketched in the hazy distance.

Walter told me that he'd gone to his weekly appointment at a clinic where they helped him do exercises to strengthen his weak arm and leg. A physical therapist named Susan was there.

"She's always real nice to me," Walter said. "She helps me with my stupid arm and leg and she's patient. . . . And her eyes—I like her eyes. They're smiling eyes."

"Eyes can't smile," said Mitch.

Walter kicked Mitch's seat.

"Safety first! No kicking, Walter."

"I'm not kicking Walter."

"Real funny," said Mitch. "You should be on TV you're so funny."

"Eyes can too smile, Mitch. You're wrong 'bout that. Her eyes smiled at me." Walter fell silent and stared out the window. After a few minutes: "I asked Susan if she wanted to go to Kingfisher Inn with me after my appointment."

A hawk dropped from the sky, landed on a coyote carcass next to the road. It closed its wings, then spread them like a shawl as we passed. Sunlight burned through the red tips of its feathers.

"Susan said I was nice but she didn't think it was a good idea. . . . Her mouth kept smiling while she stretched my arm, but her face looked funny. Her eyes—they weren't smiling anymore. I went home, got Mitch, and he knew I was mad and we started riding."

I glanced back at the hawk, receding behind us. It folded its wings and turned its head to the side, revealing a curve of beak long and slender. I pointed at the side of the road. Past the pavement, sagebrush raced by in a whizzing blur. "There's not much of a shoulder here. What about safety first?"

"People honked and yelled," Walter said. "I couldn't hear what they said but I don't think it was 'Have a nice day.' One guy gave us the finger. Mitch gave him the finger back."

I stared at Mitch, saw my reflection in his glasses. My face looked ridiculously long—distorted like an image in a funhouse mirror. Mitch was blind in one eye; the sight in his other eye was poor. Walter was blind in one eye too, but his good eye was better than Mitch's. Walter was responsible for finding things in the apartment—especially small things that Mitch misplaced, like his toothbrush. Because he was afraid that someone would sneak into the apartment and steal his toothbrush, Mitch kept it in his bedroom, and sometimes he forgot where he'd stashed it. Walter, with his keen eye, could spot the handle poking out from under Mitch's mattress or from the pocket of a coat hanging in the closet.

Walter had lost his sense of smell when he had his accident; Mitch had a good nose. If it wasn't for Mitch, Walter probably would have burned the apartment down: when Mitch smelled food burning he'd tell Walter, who'd pull from the oven the blackened lump of what was supposed to be dinner. And Mitch's sense of smell saved Walter from food poisoning. Walter would get confused and keep gallons of milk months past their expiration dates; Mitch would sniff the milk and pour it down the drain if it smelled sour.

Walter asked me why I was laughing.

"You guys are funny."

"Funny like *ha ha* funny?" Walter said. "Or funny like the way Mitch's feet smell?"

"How do you know his feet smell? Thought your nose didn't work."

"Nancy said they stink. She told Mitch he has to wash his feet."

Mitch pressed his hands against his ears. "I'm not listening to you no more, Walter."

I glanced in the rearview mirror. "What if you hadn't been able to hitch a ride home? What would you have done?"

Walter lifted his shoulders, let them fall. "We could've camped out."

"Did you have a tent with you, or food—or anything for camping?"

"Next time we'll bring a tent," Walter said.

"Nancy might take your bikes away if you guys keep doing dangerous stuff."

"You think you're so smart, Mike. Before I fell and broke my head I was smart. I used to ride my mountain bike real fast 'cause it felt good, and sometimes I fell off and got hurt but no one could take it from me. . . . Now, just 'cause I got a broken head people want to take my bike away. It's my bike and it's my choice if I want to ride it."

"Look, you've got to stay on the shoulders, off the roads. And you've got to stop going on these adventures. You can't ride off into the middle of nowhere with no plan for getting back."

"If we're more careful you won't let Nancy take our bikes away?" Walter asked.

"I can't promise anything."

"But you'll try to talk Nancy into letting us keep 'em if we're careful? My life would be shit without the bike."

I watched Walter in the rearview mirror. He turned to look out the window at the world flashing by. "I'll try," I said.

"Fine," he said. "That's a deal."

The road rose up, then leveled as it passed over the flatness of a vast plateau. The wind was constant, and the few trees that lifted above the sagebrush were bent and twisted from the steady pressure. Next to the road clouds of dust swirled like miniature tornadoes.

"Right up there," Walter said. "There's our bikes."

I saw a glint of metal in the green sage. I slowed down, started drifting toward the gravel at the edge of the road. A big, boxy RV sped by; my truck shook in its wake.

"Look out!" Walter yelled.

Two animal shapes—one small and black, the other large and white—leapt from the sagebrush onto the pavement. I rammed the brake pedal; my truck turned to the side, across the road, as it skidded to a stop. Next to the passenger side stood two horses. The larger one, white as bone, shook its head and whinnied. Its twitching eyes and the dark caves of its flared nostrils were a few feet from the window. Mitch scooted away from the glass; Walter leaned toward it, staring. The small black horse, with head tossing, eyes rolling, and mane frothing, turned and ran off the road, back into the maze of bushes that it had burst from. The big white horse stomped and snorted, standing its ground.

"That's one mean horse," said Walter in a voice that barely lifted above a whisper.

Mitch covered his face with his hands and peered at the horse through fingergaps.

"He don't have a saddle," Walter said. "Maybe he's wild."

The horse lowered its head and stepped toward the truck, then shuffled back and snorted. It seemed to look through the window, right at Walter, who pressed his face to the glass.

"Angry horse," Mitch said. He leaned farther away from the window, still peeking through his hands.

Walter pushed the front seat forward, then reached for the door handle and started to open it. "I want to see that horse up close," he said as he shoved the seat, pushing Mitch onto the floor. Mitch balled himself up, then covered his face with his hands and said in a muffled voice, "Bad idea, Walter. That's not safety first."

Walter flung open the door and began to wiggle out of the backseat.

"He's just a horse," said Walter. "He's not so mean." He pressed the seat all the way forward, squashing Mitch, who moaned and said, "Bad idea. Very angry horse."

Walter swung his feet onto the pavement.

"Get back in the truck," I said. "Right now."

He stood up, holding the edge of the seat to steady himself.

"Walter, get back here!"

Mitch uncovered his face and grabbed Walter's shirt. He tugged with both hands, trying to pull him in. "Be careful, Walter," he squeaked. "Safety first."

The horse lowered its head and snorted. The white bulbs of its eyes darted back and forth. I climbed over Mitch, reached for Walter.

Mitch squealed and said, "You're squishing me."

I grabbed Walter's shirt, then crawled closer and tightened my grip. My knee sank into Mitch's back. "Ouch," he yelled. "I'm squishing!"

I yanked Walter into the truck. Mitch was on the floor, wedged between the dashboard and the seat, clenching the console with his hands. His glasses were beaded with fog.

"You all right?" I asked.

"Can't see so good. But I'm not squishing no more."

Walter stared at the horse through the open door. I reached down to wipe Mitch's glasses with my shirtsleeve; as I let go of Walter he scooted out of the truck and shut the door behind him. I crawled over the seat, trying to avoid Mitch, who curled into a ball and said, "Oh no, more squishing."

I opened the door, slid over the seat, and when I dropped onto the road a grasshopper leapt from the pavement at my feet, fanning open its paperthin wings of yellow and black. Walter took a few steps toward the horse; it backed away from the helmeted human that limped toward it.

"What the hell are you doing, Walt?"

"Safety first!" Mitch yelled.

I'd forgotten that my truck was turned sideways, across the road, blocking it. Cars coming from the opposite direction had stopped on the other side of the horse. I couldn't see the drivers through the glare on the windshields; the sun was high and hot in a cloudless sky.

Walter took a step forward. The horse turned to the side and puffed out its flanks, showing Walter the full white bulk of its flesh. Walter took another step. The horse swung around, its meaty sides rippling over its ribcage, lids stretched back over eyes that looked as round and white as cue balls.

"The hell you doin'?" someone yelled from one of the cars. "You some kinda maniac or somethin'?"

"Knock it off, Walt," I yelled. "Get back in the truck!"

Walter took another step, stumbled, steadied himself. The horse whinnied and rose up on its back legs; with its front hooves it pawed the air. It teetered forward and fell back to earth, its hooves sounding off like gunshots as they smacked the pavement. The black hollows of the horse's nostrils were inches from Walter's face. It rolled its eyes drunkenly and peeled back its lips, showing teeth yellow and frothy. Walter straightened his back and stood up tall. His helmet glowed in the fiercebeating sun; his face was a dark smudge below the brightness. Walter pressed his head forward until, from a distance, it seemed his face touched the mouth of the horse and his sunbright helmet merged with the horse's white flesh.

"The hell is he doin'?" drifted from a car.

"Safety first!" Mitch yelled.

I ran toward Walter and the horse, stopped a few yards away from them. Walter had his eyes closed. When I was near enough to reach out and grab him, he opened his eyes, stretching his lids so far back his eyeballs looked like eggs. The horse, with its eyes rolling in their sockets and its yellow teeth still showing, stood perfectly still. With eyes wide open, Walter pulled his lips back, baring teeth that shined as brightly as his sundrenched helmet. Sweatbeads spilled from his forehead, wandered his cheeks, dripped onto his shirt.

As I reached out to grab Walter and yank him away, the horse reared up again, swiveling on its hind legs, kicking the air with its front hooves. Its white bulk passed before the sun, casting a shadow over Walter and me. I stared up at unshod hooves, scraping the sky as if trying to grip an icy slope. The horse turned to the side and crashed down a few feet away. The impact of its landing quaked through the pavement, shot up my legs, climbed my spine. I shuffled toward the truck, dragging Walter with me. He was limp and sweaty and smiling.

"What the hell did you think you were doing?" I asked when we were back in the truck. Walter gazed out the window, said nothing.

Mitch climbed off the floor, into his seat. He wiped his glasses, then turned around, reached into the back of the truck, and patted Walter's knee. "You forgot safety first?"

The horse was off the road, galloping across the plateau, its white body parting the sea of green sage. I backed the truck up, straightened it, then drove past the line of cars, the people inside them staring. As we went by a man with his jaw hanging slack, his mouth agape, I rolled down the window and said, "Don't worry, we do this all the time. We're horse tamers."

"It's okay," Mitch added, waving at the man.

I glanced at Walter in the rearview mirror as I drove. He stared out the window and smiled, watching the horse, a white streak in the green of the sagewrapped plateau.

"Was that some kind of seizure or something?" I asked.

"I knew what I was doing," he said quietly, firmly.

"Were you trying to kill yourself?"

Walter said nothing. He was still staring out the window. He forced open his left hand and pressed his moist palm to the glass.

"Bikes," Mitch yelled. "There!" He pointed behind us. I pulled off the road and backed up to the edge of a clearing, where the bikes were chained to a lone spruce standing straight and tall. Scrawny pine trees twisted by wind surrounded it, as if the tortured pines had gathered around the spruce to seek counsel on avoiding the wind's abuse. I climbed onto the hood of the truck and watched Mitch. He pulled a bundle from his shirtpocket and unwrapped newspaper and tape, revealing another package. And inside that package was another—like Chinese boxes or Russian nesting dolls. Finally the last package was opened and a silver key fell to the dirt at Mitch's feet. He picked it up, held it to the sky and smiled, then wiped it on his pantleg and unlocked the bikes.

"Remember what we talked about," I said as Walter plopped down on the seat of his fourwheeled rig and Mitch got onto his mountain bike. Next to my face, gnats clustered in a hovering ball, a black cloud writhing with life.

"Go slow," I said. "And make sure you ride singlefile on the shoulder."

A hawk soared overhead, its shadow skimming Walter's bike, then breaking apart in the sagebrush. A few dry leaves scuttled through the dirt.

"Safety first," Mitch said as he passed by me, following Walter across the road and onto the shoulder.

I watched them ride off: Walter in front, Mitch close behind, focusing on Walter's bike—the only thing he could see with his one good eye peering through glasses with lenses smudged and scratched. I hopped into my truck and drove behind them. Mitch rode in a low gear on a level stretch of road; he pedaled like crazy to keep his bike moving. For months I had tried to teach him about shifting and matching his gears to terrain, but he had nodded and smiled, then jumped on his bike and left it in the lowest gear, no matter where he was riding, uphill or down. His legs rotated so fast they were circular blurs.

"Be careful, Horse Tamer, be careful, Lightning Legs," I yelled out the window as I pulled onto the black ribbon of pavement and drove next to Mitch and Walter. Safety flags, triangular and orange, trailed from their bikes. Mitch pedaled furiously; Walter pushed his legs slowly, steadily. I glanced in the rearview mirror at Walter as I passed him. His bike was shiny against sagebrush and crumbled rock. Mountains, shimmering and purple, rose from the tabletop flatness. I stared into the mirror at the peaks fading in the distance behind me; then I focused on the road ahead. Beyond the plateau more mountains loomed, crusted with snow, horribly bright in the hotbeating sun.

I stopped the truck, then backed up until I was next to Walter. "What the hell were you doing with the horse? Were you trying to get yourself killed?"

Walter stopped pedaling, turned to stare at me. "I got a body that don't work too good, a broken head, no girlfriend, and a dad who won't talk to me. And now Nancy wants to take my bike away." He started pedaling again, and as he rolled away, down the gravelly shoulder, he said, "I wasn't trying to kill myself. I was just trying to live."

PART TWO

~7~

Duct Tape

In early November, when the aspen were no longer spangled with autumn leaves and their limbs hung bare in a wintry wind, Walter told me we'd known each other for almost a year—he'd tracked the time on a calendar. On the day of the one-year anniversary we had dinner at Kingfisher Inn and I gave him a bamboo flyrod my father had made.

A few days later I loaded Cap'n into my truck and went to Walter's apartment, driving under a sulfurous sun in a blushing sky, heading toward a road that rose above the valley on ledges blasted into a mountainside. The sky turned to pewter, then blanched, and heavy wafers of snow drifted on the wind.

Walter grinned when I walked into his apartment. After scratching Cap'n's ears, he scurried into his bedroom. A closet door opened, closed. I pressed my forehead against a window, feathery crystals of frost growing at its edges.

"Shut your eyes," Walter shouted.

I listened to him pad across the carpet toward me.

"Okay. Now you can open 'em."

I turned around. He was standing in front of me, arms extended, holding two packages wrapped in newspaper, crumpled and torn and gobbed with tape. "Presents for you," he said.

"I told you not to get me anything."

"Don't worry—I didn't have to buy 'em. And I wrapped 'em myself."

"No kidding? These weren't done professionally?"

"I'll keep 'em if you're gonna make fun of me." He handed the packages to me—one a large circle, the other a tiny cylinder. "Open 'em," he said. "Hurry!"

I sat down on the couch and tore into one of the packages. A ballpoint pen fell out. Medium blue. Slightly used.

Walter clapped his hands. "I wrote my grocery list with it once. It didn't smear or nothing. Open the other one. Open it!"

I tore apart the circle of paper. Inside was a roll of duct tape, silver and shiny.

"Duct tape?" I asked.

Walter sat down next to me on the couch. Stared at me. Told me that the first time I'd taken him fishing he'd caught his fly on my shirt. It ripped a pocket when he tried to pull it out. I got a roll of duct tape out of my truck and taped the shirt together. Walter said he'd wanted to buy me a new fishing shirt but it was too expensive, so he found a roll of duct tape in his apartment to give to me instead.

I laughed and looked outside, staring at spindly aspen branches twitching in the wind. Hailstones big as grapes pelted the apartment windows.

Walter said, "When you picked me up to go fishing that day you told me Nora gave you that shirt. A fancy fishing shirt. You said you liked it."

Outside, the hail turned back to snow. In the blizzarding sky, flakes darted and dodged in the wind, as if debating which way to go. Walter's helmet shifted to the side. He pushed it back to the top of his head. "I'm glad you took me fishing again after I ruined your shirt." He balled his left hand, cuffed me on my shoulder. "Are you still gonna go fishing with me when you come back from Utah?"

I shoved him. "You can't get rid of me. And guess what: you're coming to Alta. Nora bought you a plane ticket for a Christmas present. She thought you could use a real vacation."

"What 'bout Kmart? If they don't have labels—"

I told him I'd worked it out with Nancy and his boss. If he flew to Utah instead of driving with me, then he wouldn't miss as much work. I'd pick him up at the airport in Salt Lake and take him to Alta.

Walter tilted his head. "Is Nora gonna be there?"

"We haven't decided yet. She's still staying at her sister's. We're spending some time apart."

"She left you for good?"

"We're still trying to work things out."

"Then I guess I shouldn't call her and ask her out on a date yet."

Donna

At Alta a few weeks later, after skiing with some friends from college, I went back to the lodge where I was staying. When I got to my room I turned on the light, an electric light fashioned like an oil lamp, and I sat down on the bed and parted the curtains. Outside a swirly wind frenzied the snowflakes—like in a paperweight you shake to make the snow scatter crazily through a miniature world. I grabbed the phone, gave Walter a call to see how his packing was coming along.

"I got a question," he said. "I like Donna."

Donna was a chubby woman who lived in an apartment in Walter's building. They had gone through the same brain injury rehabilitation program. Walter's caseworker, Nancy, was also Donna's.

Silence.

"Thought you had a question."

He said nothing.

"Are you all right, Walt? Have you started packing? You ready for the trip?" I stared outside, through the snowy sky, at a distant lodge covered in twinkling lights. Snowfall thickened; the lights vanished like diamonds dropped into a bucket of milk, sinking to the bottom, disappearing in the whiteness.

"How do I ask Donna to go to dinner with me on a date?"

"Just ask her."

"I like Kingfisher Inn. They got good steaks there. . . . Maybe she likes steaks?"

"Walter! Just ask her."

"Fine. Always yelling. Can I kiss Donna when the date's done? I want to kiss her lips. They're red. Her hair's good too. It looks different when the light changes. Sometimes it's brown like dead grass. Sometimes it's the color of a penny. . . . Can I kiss her?"

"That's up to you. And her. You have to make sure it's all right with her."

"Do I ask if I can kiss her?"

"No, you can just tell."

"How?"

"It's hard to explain. . . . Her eyes, I guess. And if she leans toward you. And—"

"If she leans her eyes towards me I can kiss her?"

"Okay, maybe you should ask her."

"What if Donna says I can't kiss her?"

"We'll cross that bridge when we get to it."

"What bridge?" said Walter. He started shouting: "We're kissing lips, not crossing bridges. What if I can't remember where Kingfisher Inn is at? Donna'll think I don't know anything. She'll think I have a stupid fucking head and she'll hate me."

I opened the curtain, stared into the sky. Past the storm a sliver of moon hung in the night. "You go to Kingfisher Inn almost every day— you won't get lost. And Donna will like you. Just—"

"But I can't read the menu too good. My head gets confused. Burger King don't have a real menu—they just got numbers. But Kingfisher Inn's got a menu. If I get confused I point at the pictures and Martha brings the pictures to me and I eat it. That's our system."

"You can do that if you go there with Donna."

"What if Martha's sick? The new waitress won't know my system. She won't know how to do it if I get confused."

Outside the window, on a corner of the lodge, a bulb burned in the murky night. Snowflakes drifted like moths from the darkness toward the light.

"Walt, you'll be fine."

"How am I supposed to be fine? Remember my date with Louise? I don't want to mess up again."

"Everyone's afraid on a first date."

"Is Donna scared like shit?"

"She probably is."

A long silence opened.

"I shouldn't go," Walter said after a few minutes. "I should stay inside and make my new puzzle."

"You said you like her lips, right. What else do you like about her?"

"Every time I see her she smiles."

"There you go—just think about the good things."

After a pause: "What if you like someone but she don't like you back? What if you think she wants to be your girlfriend but you're wrong 'bout it?"

"That can happen."

Silence. Snowflakes stung the sky.

After a few minutes: "But it's worth taking a chance—don't you think?"

"Maybe she does like you, but then she has to leave or something and you can't be with her no more."

"Isn't it worth trying?"

"You don't try very hard with Nora. All you do is fight with her."

Through a hole in the clouds a dark dome of sky appeared, as though it were a separate world beyond the pale and swirling storm, and the stars it held seemed tiny openings to another world, one of cold and lonely light beyond the black night.

"Maybe Donna'll like me, but her parents'll take her away and I won't be able to see her no more. Maybe they don't want her to go on dates with me and my stupid head. I met her parents once. They looked at me funny. 'Cause I was in that program with Donna—they know all 'bout my broken head."

"Ask Donna out, Walt. You can't hide in your apartment making puzzles for the rest of your life."

After a moment: "Mitch got a job at the fish hatchery. He made me promise to tell you he feeds the fish."

"Bet he likes that better than pushing carts around Kmart."

Static crackled in the phone. "The sky looks angry," Walter said. "I think a storm's coming. I gotta go close my windows. I opened them to let the smoke out when I burned dinner."

As I thrashed in bed later that night, trying to fall asleep, my gut and brain burning from the Jim Beam I'd downed (my college buddies had talked me into touring all the bars at Alta and Snowbird, a shot at each one), I thought about Mitch, about his job at Kmart. He'd been responsible for bringing in carts from the parking lot. There were problems. Once he pushed a cart all the way home to his apartment. Sometimes he forgot what he was doing and scraped a cart against a car. And almost every day he tried to take carts from customers before they finished with them.

When Mitch saw a cart in the parking lot, he wanted to take it back inside—whether it was empty or not. Never being done frustrated the hell out of him: as soon as he put a cart inside the store, somebody would take another one out into the parking lot. Same thing over and over, never any closure.

I had seen Mitch in action once. Nancy had been getting complaints from his manager. She didn't have time to check on him; she asked me to. With a pair of binoculars and a sixpack, I sat in my truck in the Kmart parking lot like an FBI agent at a stakeout. Sure enough, a few minutes into his shift, before I'd finished my first beer, Mitch snuck up behind a lady unloading gardening supplies into the bed of her pickup. When she turned to drop a bag of fertilizer into the truck, Mitch grabbed her cart and shuffled away, head down, his feet blurring like a cartoon character's they moved so fast. The woman ran after him, tried to take the cart back. Mitch wouldn't give it to her; the tug-of-war lasted a minute or so. The woman let go first, stormed off, came back with a manager—a bigbellied guy with a shiny baldspot on his head. He pried Mitch's fingers off the cart, returned it to the woman, apologized for all he was worth—did everything but bow down and kiss her feet. The manager's baldspot turned red as he yelled at Mitch. The woman listened and nodded. Walked away with her cart.

I gave a full report to Nancy. She said she'd start looking for another job right away. Nancy tried to find Mitch work, but he was tough to employ. When Walter started getting in trouble at Kmart she tried harder— went to every business in town, tried to talk them into giving Mitch a chance. Walter was one of the best stock clerks Kmart had: he'd been employee of the month more than anyone else. But Walter worried about his roommate, his friend. He'd wander away from his stocking duties, leaving boxes and labels sitting in the aisles so he could check up on Mitch; and when he saw him wrestling with a customer over a cart, Walter would try to pull him away. For most people, the combination of Walter and Mitch was too much. Customers would abandon their carts, leave their merchandise behind, get the hell out of there. Walter would grab the stuff from their carts and chase after them, limping and yelling, trying to return groceries or lawn furniture or clothes, dropping things all over the parking lot, leaving a trail for the manager to follow. Some people just drove away and counted themselves lucky to escape. Others tracked down the manager and demanded justice.

The job at the fish hatchery sounded perfect for Mitch: he loved trout. I had tried to teach him to flyfish. I'd found him a rod and reel setup at a garage sale, showed him how to cast. Mitch nodded and said, "Yeah, yeah." When I handed him the rod he dangled it over the water like a canepole and asked me if I had any worms. I put Walter to work, encouraged him to teach Mitch, to show him what he knew. Walter didn't get any further than I had.

Walter and I finally accepted that Mitch would be a worm fisherman, and we tried not to think any less of him for it. Walter got angry with Mitch for hooking the fish too deeply: they'd gulp down the worms, get the barbed hooks buried in their stomachs. When Walter pulled the hooks out and released the fish, some of them floated belly-up in the water, spilling their blood into the stream. Walter would lecture Mitch about not killing fish and he'd explain how flies were better than worms. Mitch would nod, smile, tell Walter, "Yeah, yeah," then point at the fish, floating on top of the water. "Resting fish," he'd say. "Tired fish."

"No," Walter would tell him. "That fish is dead, Mitch. Your stupid worms killed him."

They'd go back and forth: Mitch insisting the fish was resting, Walter telling Mitch it was dead.

I had started taking them fishing separately: Mitch to stocked ponds for dullcolored and dimwitted hatchery trout that Game and Fish employees replenished every month; Walter to mountain streams for wild cutthroat, brightcolored and savvy. The flycaster and the wormfisher: best friends and roommates, but incompatible on the water.

At the hatchery Mitch could feed the fish, fatten them up so they'd be big and strong when he caught them. I just hoped he didn't try to wrestle the fish away from the hatchery biologists; I hoped like hell he didn't decide the fish were his and take them home to hide in his room. I made a mental note to do random fish inspections of the apartment.

Before I slipped into a drunken sleep I saw with perfect clarity a scene in the Kmart parking lot: an old lady, bluehaired and pissed, chasing Mitch, trying to reclaim her cart, swinging her purse above her head like a medieval ball and chain. Walter in hot pursuit, shuffling after both of them, trying to restore order. Trying to help Mitch avoid the wrath of the Kmart manager—peering through a window, watching the chase, his baldspot turning red as ketchup.

A couple days later, with snow still dumping at Alta, I gave Walter a call, made sure he'd started packing, and then asked him about Donna.

"You did go out with her, right? Don't tell me you made a puzzle instead." I walked to a window and watched the storm swallowing trees, rivers, mountains. There was the snowbleached sky and nothing else.

"What's wrong with puzzles?" Walter yelled. "My new one's got dogs on it."

"I thought you decided to ask her out."

"You decided that—not me. I wanted to work on my puzzle."

The storm slacked for a moment and mountains appeared. Shafts of sun brightened a peak, impossibly bright in the distance. Then the storm revved back up, and behind the pale sky, thick with falling snow, the mountain faded.

"Yesterday I saw Donna. She said hi. And she smiled at me. She always smiles at me. . . . And she said she liked my helmet. She told me that again—that's two times! She said I have a handsome helmet."

"That would've been the perfect time to ask her out to dinner."

"But she was carrying groceries," Walter said. "She was gonna cook her dinner, I think."

"You could've asked her if she wanted to go out to dinner with you on a different night." I pressed my face against the window, watched my breath fog the cold glass. Pellets of snow pulsed in the wind, swarming like insects—an invasion of white bees. Walter was quiet a moment, then said, "Can I cook Donna dinner? In my apartment? I make spaghetti good."

"That's a great idea."

"Does she like spaghetti?"

"You have to ask her."

"What if she don't like it?"

"Ask her what she does like."

"What if I can't cook it? I can't cook fish. It burns too easy. I hope she don't like beans. Beans give you gas and if I fart at dinner she'll—"

"Walter!"

"What if I fart? Broccoli makes you fart too. It's got more gas than beans. Most people don't know—"

"Just relax. You'll be fine."

"You relax!" Walter yelled. "I'll bet Donna won't smile if I fart. She'll think I'm a stupid fucking farter! She'll think—"

"Remember the good things—her lips, her hair, her smile. The compliments she gives you." The falling snow had turned from pellets to fluffy flakes, like snippets of cotton batting.

"She likes my helmet. It's handsome on me—that's what she said."

"There you go. Just think about that."

After a few minutes Walter said, "Maybe I'll finish my puzzle before I ask her to have dinner at my apartment. The puzzle's on the kitchen table and we won't have nowhere to eat. I'll finish it first, then I'll ask her. That's how I'll do it."

Snow Sports

"Lean into the turn!" I yelled to Walter. He'd flown into Salt Lake City that morning; it was the first day of his weeklong stay at Alta. I was following him downhill, holding straps attached to a sit-ski: a plastic chair with skis under it that Walter could ride down the slopes. I held the straps, tethering him, making sure he didn't tip the chair over when he tilted into a turn.

"Having fun?" I asked as we came to a stop at the bottom of the hill. Powder sprayed into the air as Walter skidded the sit-ski to a stop. Faint birdtracks and the tiny pawprints of mink and squirrel were stitched across the snow's surface. Over a foot had fallen in the night, and early that morning clouds had thinned, giving way to blue sky. Fresh snow covered everything, burying bushes and boulders in its glittering folds, muffling sounds, smothering the earth. As if the world were brand new, and from an ocean of snow all else would come.

"I want to try four-tracking," Walter said. "I want to stand up on skis like I used to."

With four-tracking Walter would have to do all the work; I couldn't tether him like I was doing with the sit-ski. I slapped a pole against his shoulder. "Think you're ready for that? You'll have to steer and keep yourself in control. I won't be there to stop you."

"My left side's getting stronger." He flexed his arm, pointed to the muscle that lumped up beneath his parka. "I've been punching my couch every day."

As we walked toward the ski school office, Cap'n jumped out from a cluster of pines and hopped next to Walter, licking him and barking.

Scratching the dog's dust mop of a head, I said, "Walter can stop taking showers if you lick him like that. All he needs is a bar of soap and a bottle of shampoo when you're around."

"How come Cap'n's here?" asked Walter. "They let dogs stay at the lodge?"

"I sneak him in. Most of the employees don't care."

Cap'n hopped toward a fir tree, chased a squirrel up the trunk. The squirrel chattered from the safety of a high branch as Cap'n circled the tree, jingling.

"Why's Cap'n got bells on him?" Walter asked. "He sounds like Mitch with all his keys."

I had watched him catch a little finch in my front yard, I told Walter. Cap'n snuck up on the bird, pounced, pinned it to ground. He sat there and held it for a few minutes; then the bird got out from under his paw and flew away. I wasn't sure if it escaped or if he let it go. I put the bells on him after that.

Cap'n hopped next to me, nuzzled my hand. "Damn thing's turned into a cat," I said, giving him a push. "Right, boy? You're the world's biggest, ugliest cat."

"Are you still trying to find a home for him?" Walter asked.

"Put an ad in the paper, only got one phone call. Not too much interest in a threelegged dog."

Seth, the guy who'd answered the ad, asked me to bring Cap'n to his house, I told Walter. He showed me where he'd keep Cap'n: chained to his back porch. Seth said he wasn't home much, but he figured Cap'n would be all right. Said he'd leave food and water for him, maybe buy him a doghouse.

I didn't understand why Seth was interested in Cap'n; I thought there was something he wasn't telling me. I decided to give it some time, decided to get to know Seth. I went out with him one night. We had a few beers, and finally he told me why he wanted Cap'n. He'd been sitting in a bar one day, looking out a window, watching the street, when a guy walked by with a golden retriever that was missing a leg. Seth saw four women stop and pet the dog and talk to the guy before he got to the end of the block. Seth figured he could get a lot of ass for a minimal investment: buying a bag of generic dogfood every month would cost less than putting an ad in the newspaper personals, and it would probably work better, too. Seth figured he'd have a leg up—pun intended, he told me with a wink—on all the desperate guys looking for love. I told Seth I had to take a leak. Went past the bathroom, snuck out of the bar, left Seth with the bill for the beers. Took the ad out of the paper the next day.

Walter and I walked across a meadow, where tumbling water echoed in hollows beneath the snow. We stopped and listened, and through windows of ice we saw a stream. Bubbles formed and rose. Trapped between water and ice, the pockets of air stretched and bulged like cells dividing.

We brushed the snow from boulders and sat down to rest. In the vaulted blue above, a plane passed without sound—just a glint of silver and a white vapor trail. "How's your bike?" I asked. "Had any more flats?"

"Mitch and I went for a ride and it started to snow so much we got stuck. We hitchhiked home."

"You left your bikes?"

Walter threw up his arms. "It's not our fault it snowed."

"A bike's a big responsibility."

"That's what the cop said."

"What cop?"

"He had a badge and a gun and everything. Nancy had him come to our apartment to talk to us. Mitch ran in his room. He thought the cop was going to take him back to that place where he used to live. He hid under his bed. I told Mitch he didn't have to go back but he didn't believe me. He stayed under the bed all night. I had to put his dinner under there."

We walked the rest of the way to the ski school office and got the four-track setup: two regular skis and two outriggers—arm braces attached to mini skis for support and steering. Four skis, four tracks in the snow. An instructor showed Walter how to use the equipment, gave him a lesson; then Walter, Cap'n, and I headed to the chairlift.

The lift operator glared at us. "No dogs. That's the rule, fellas."

"Cap'n here is part of the adaptive ski program," I said, mussing the dog's matted fur.

The guy scrunched his face. "Like a Seeing Eye dog?"

"Exactly."

He shrugged his shoulders, then helped Cap'n hop onto a chair, told us to hang on to him.

After we got off the lift, Walter glided down a slope, cutting turns slow and wide as Cap'n hopped next to him and barked. Halfway down the run, Walter crossed the tips of his skis and plunged facefirst into the snow; I helped him up and gave him a few pointers about how to keep his skis in a wedge. He made a couple turns, caught an edge of a ski in the snow, spun around and fell onto his back. And as he got up, he tripped and stumbled, screaming about his head and the equipment and the snow and a list of other things I couldn't quite make out. He grabbed one of the outriggers and beat it into the snow, then threw it across the slope. I sat down behind him; Cap'n ran to him and licked his neck. After a few minutes Walter got up, gathered his gear, cleaned the snow from his goggles, and headed downhill. He made some shaky turns, then grinned and yelled that he was getting the hang of it as he swooped into a big arcing turn, his skis raising snowflakes bright as mica, soft as talc.

A few runs later, after Walter had found his rhythm and was linking turns without falling, we got off the lift and pushed through a hiphigh bank of whorled snow, then skied to the edge of an open slope scoured by wind. I warned Walter about the tricky snow, let him go ahead of me. He cut a giant turn, shoving his skis into the windpacked crust; it split apart with an even ripping sound, like the unfastening of a giant zipper.

At the bottom of the run, as we glided across the flats toward a lift-line, I tapped Walter with my pole. "I thought you might have some trouble in that crusty snow, but you looked good."

"I used to ski all the time. My dad and me would go to Colorado. We wouldn't take my mom. It was a boys-only trip—that's what my dad told her."

For the next run we headed off trail, plunging into windbuffed powder, smashing through the pillowing fluff. Each turn coughed up clouds of flakes, sent them spewing into the air. Cap'n swam down the slope, disappearing into the snow, rising above it, diving back in like a dolphin. Walter and I yelled as powder rolled over us in waves and plumed behind us. As I pushed through a deep drift, snow covered me. Swallowed me. I couldn't see, couldn't hear, couldn't breathe—there was the whiteness of snow and nothing else. A white chamber. As if I'd entered a place in which to immerse and cleanse myself, like some rite of purification. I burst through, coughing snow from my lungs, listening to Walter laugh and Cap'n bark, squinting my eyes against stabs of light that poked through my frosted goggles.

We kept skiing until the lifts closed that afternoon, each run fresh, windblown snow healing the skicuts in the slopes. When we got back to the lodge, the sun had dipped behind a mountain; the sky yellowed to the color of sunlight filtering through an amber beer bottle.

"We have two options," I said. "We can march right through the front door with Cap'n and hope the guys working the front desk don't care, or we can try to sneak him in."

"Maybe we should disguise him," said Walter. "We could pretend like we're janitors and he's our mop. Or a bedspread—we could act like we're housekeepers."

We both looked at Cap'n; then we looked at the lodge. Lights blinked on in windows, squares of light against the dimming sky.

Walter picked up a chunk of snow, tossed it toward Cap'n. He snatched it from the air, munched it as though it were a treat.

"My dad sent me a Christmas check," Walter said.

I tossed a snowball at Cap'n, watched him pluck it from the air, heard it crunch between his teeth.

"He wrote 'Merry Christmas' on the check," Walter said. "Maybe he'll write me a letter if I send him another one." Walter flipped a snowball in the air. It rose, stalled, spiraled down. Cap'n tilted his head back and caught it. Hopped away and hid it under a log as though it were a bone.

"Wait here," I said. "I'm going to find out about Cap'n." I raised my parka collar against the cold and pulled my hat down, then headed toward the lodge.

"We're in," I said a few minutes later as I jogged toward Walter. "But we have to wait an hour. The lodge manager leaves a little after five. I talked to the guy who covers the front desk at night. He's fine with Cap'n staying. And get this: he gave his buddy in the kitchen a call. Hooked us up with some steak for Cap'n."

"What're we gonna do for an hour?" Walter asked. He shivered, zipped his parka up to his chin. Mountains silvered under the rising moon. Overhead, stars burned bright and steady. Pine trees nodded in a rush of wind. Their smell spiced the air.

"I know what we can do," I said. "Sledding."

We went around the lodge to some Dumpsters behind the kitchen. Found the cardboard recycling bin, pulled out a stack of flattened boxes. "Choose your weapon," I said.

"We're going sledding on boxes?" Walter asked.

"A good sledding box is made of thick cardboard with a waxy finish. Slick and durable. Like this one." I dropped all the boxes but one.

Held it up to the light streaming through a kitchen window. "See the sheen? This, my friend, is a good sledding box."

Walter pulled one out of the Dumpster, held it to the light, smiled. "I got a good one too."

"Grab another," I said. "We'll need one for Cap'n."

We found a hill behind the lodge and hiked to the top. Walter sat on his box, and I plopped Cap'n down on his; then I gave them both a push. Cap'n barked and Walter yelled as they slid down the slope, dry powder hissing beneath the cardboard. At the bottom of the hill they fell off the boxes and rolled through the snow. I jumped on my box, followed them down. Wiped out at the bottom, crashed into the snowplastered pile of person and dog. Cap'n barked and jumped on top of me, mashing me into the snow. I chucked a snowball at Walter; he threw one back. We hurled them as fast as we could; Cap'n hopped in circles and tried to snatch them from the air. We crawled across the ground, searching for shelter from the pelting missiles, maneuvering across the firing zone and targeting each other like kids playing a game of war. When we tired, we lay on the ground and watched Cap'n, wandering in circles, his nose furrowing the snow. When he stopped and lifted his head to look at us, his face was frosted. With white whiskers and drooping brows, he looked like a man ancient and wise.

Later that night, by a fire in the lobby, with Cap'n curled up at our feet and snoring, his belly filled with steak, I helped Walter write a letter:

Dear Dad,

I'm at Alta with my friend Mike. Today I rode a sit-ski. Then I learned how to stand up on skis and use outriggers. That's called four-tracking. That was more fun because I did it by my-self. Then we went sledding on cardboard boxes.

Cap'n is here too. He's Mike's dog. He has three legs.

Thank you for my Christmas check. I'll use the money to

buy new gloves so my hands don't get cold this winter.
    Please write me.

                            Your son,
                            Walter

*P.S. Remember that bike you built for me out of pipes? That was
a good bike.*

≈10≈

Where Mountains Go

A couple days later, when all the fresh snow on the slopes at Alta had been packed down, Walter and I decided to take a break from skiing and go horseback riding. In the early morning, before the sun had climbed above the mountains, we loaded Cap'n into my truck and headed away from the lodge, squatting against the dawn. The road was enameled with ice; the truck's rear wheels fishtailed over the slick pavement. We drove by Mt. Superior, its jagged bulk plunging upward. Past it, rows of mountains faded into the distance, disappearing in the haze of the horizon like ripples on a pond spreading away from a disturbance, melting back into the water.

"I never rode a horse before," Walter said as we cornered a roadbend and saw smokestacks rising from the brown fog above Salt Lake City. "But once I walked right up to a wild horse. I wasn't afraid."

"I remember, Horse Tamer."

"Is it hard to ride them?" Walter asked.

"You'll be a natural."

Cottonwoods leaned from both sides of the road, their arched branches touching overhead. We drove out of the canyon and onto an open bench, slabs of granite tilting like the stonework of ancient masons. The rock, polished smooth by glaciers, gleamed in the early light. We headed south. I had some friends who owned a ranch outside of Provo.

They were out of town; they'd told me that Walter and I could use their horses for the day.

Walter needed help mounting and dismounting his horse, but once he was on top he rode like a cowboy. I walked beside him awhile, showing him how to hold the reins, how to steer. And a few minutes later he was on his own. Back straight, body relaxed, legs gripping the sides of the horse, he looked comfortable and confident.

Between the horses' bouts of whinnying there was a perfect stillness, a roaring silence. Drifting on their backs across the muffled earth, their hooves sinking soundlessly into snow, we passed a moose. From a stream choked with pondweed the moose raised its head, plants hanging from its face like a drooping mustache, the palms and points of its antlers bright in the midday sun. It glanced at the horses, then dropped its head to slurp plants from the boggy ground.

"Good thing we left Cap'n at the barn," said Walter when the moose was a black shape in the distance behind us.

No wind blew; the still air was cold and bright with winter sun. Steam drifted from the horses' skin and puffed from their nostrils. We rode along a ridge, then dropped into a ravine and headed toward a river. We passed through a grove of aspen, then through stands of cottonwood, their branches feathered with thin twigs. Beneath a leaning tree the snow had been scraped away down to autumn leaf litter: an animal hollow. A warm and sheltered place for an elk or a deer. We stopped and had lunch, rested under the tree. Walter and I left the horses and walked down to the river. We tossed rocks, watching them pierce the water. Snowdrifted riverbanks deadened all sounds: the crashing rapids, the splashing rocks, our voices.

"What's going on with Donna?" I asked. "Did you go out with her?"

Walter paused, then said, "Don't want to talk 'bout it." He picked up a rock, chucked it into the river. It tumbled through a foamy wave, then sank to the bottom of a pool, deep and green.

"How about your latest bike adventure," I said. "Want to tell me about that?"

"We didn't know it was gonna start snowing."

"Did you check the weather forecast?"

"We had clothes and food for camping. We had a tent, too. An army tent that Mitch bought."

I picked up a smooth oval stone, like the fossilized egg of an extinct bird. I tossed it into the river. "Where were you planning to go?"

"We wanted to see the wild horses. Mitch didn't get to see 'em before—his eyes were closed 'cause he was scared."

"Did you guys make it out that far? All the way to the plateau?"

They got to the top and it started to snow, Walter said. Not light snow, either—a blizzard. They put on their hats and gloves and kept riding, but the snow got so deep they started skidding all over the place and getting stuck. Walter tried to set up the tent but couldn't figure it out. Mitch told him sleeping in a tent in a blizzard wasn't safety first, anyway. He went back to the road and put out his thumb.

A lady with blue hair gave them a ride back to town, Walter said. Mitch kept giggling and saying, "Yeah, yeah, blue hair," but the lady couldn't understand him. She took them to Kingfisher Inn and bought them hot chocolates. Walter told her about the wild horses and how they were going back to see them, and she told him about her husband who'd been in World War Two and how he'd died from a heart attack. He'd been watching the Broncos on TV. She went to get her hair done, and when she came back her husband was still sitting in front of the TV and the Broncos were still playing and he was dead, Walter said.

I picked up a rock, white with hoarfrost. I hurled it, watched it thud into the water. Watched the splash it made disappear in the churning current. "What did Nancy have to say about the bikes?"

"She just twisted up her mouth like she was chewing a squid. Then the cop came to talk to us."

In a meadow past the river, grass tufted up from the snow like a scruffy coat of fur. A deer moved from the meadow's edge into the shadows of trees.

I turned and looked at Walter. "How many times do we have to go over this? Nancy's given you so many chances. You don't listen, you keep doing crazy stuff on your bike. Do you want her to take it away?"

Walter dropped a rock he was holding, turned to face me. "It's my bike and I want to keep it. You crashed on your mountain bike before. You showed me the bruises and cuts. Nobody took your bike away."

For a few minutes neither of us said anything. I picked up rocks and chucked them into the river, listening to the current, the sound of spilling water.

"Mitch—he's never gone on adventures," Walter finally said. "He lived in that stupid . . . intuition."

"Institution?"

"They never let him do nothing there. People took care of Mitch his whole life. All they taught him 'bout was safety first."

"I could've driven you guys to see the horses."

"We need to do some things by ourselves. Mitch and me—we need our own adventures."

Under a tree at the river's edge, where water rushed through the winter stillness, the white silence, I reached over and hit Walter's shoulder. "Promise me one thing," I said. "Promise me you'll tell me what happened with Donna before you leave Alta."

He nodded that he would, and we walked away from the river, stepping on mudpuddles covered with skims of ice. Walter jumped up and down, watching cracks spiderweb when his boots punched through and sank into the water below, as thick and brown as chocolate milk. He stopped in front of a tree. "In the trunk," he said. "There's a face with a crazy mouth."

I crunched and sloshed through the puddles until I stood next to him. I followed his pointing finger, stared at the trunk, saw the face. The stub of a branch as a nose. Two little knotholes as squinting eyes, one large knothole as a puckered O of a mouth. A face with a surprised and gasping stare, the look of someone who's just been goosed or punched in the belly.

A breeze rushed through the canyon, rattling dead plants that poked above the snow. On a log at our feet, where strips of bark had unwrapped, the stringy wood was bare—like skin peeled away from a cadaver, exposing the muscle beneath. I ran my hand along the rough wood.

"Look," Walter whispered. "Up in the tree."

Perched on a limb above us was a bird with tufts atop its head—an owl. It swiveled its face and stared at us. Walter hooted. The owl blinked, then opened yellow eyes, glowing in its shadowy face like flashlights shining in a dark forest. Walter hooted louder. A gust of wind fizzed through the trees, shivering their branches.

We left the owl and walked across the clearing to the leaning cottonwood where the horses stood, their bodies still, their eyes closed. The rise of their chests was so faint it seemed their breathing had slowed so they could sleep through the winter. The ancient tree above, the horses silent and still—it seemed a spell had been cast, a spell that could be broken by the slightest sound. Walter and I stood and stared and said nothing.

Before we left the ranch and drove back to Alta that night, Walter and I took a walk. Cap'n hopped from the barn, following us into the forest under the starsprinkled blackness of the sky. A plump moon lit up Walter's face and silvered his helmet. His eyes seemed to sponge up the moonlight: they gave back only a hint of brightness, a reflection drained of silver.

"What's the matter?" I asked.

Walter shook his head. "Nora. It's not fair."

We sat down in the snow. Above us, through a gap in the trees, stars sparkled like flecks of quartz trapped in tar. As a breeze picked up, trees twisted and groaned. The shadows of their branches moved across the ground.

When Walter spoke, his teeth were pearly in the light of the moon. "Do you ever get jealous?"

I watched Cap'n circling the top of the hill, his mouth against the ground. He was eating sticks, chewing on rocks—putting everything in his mouth, like a mythical beast devouring the earth.

"You're angry at me?" Walter asked.

"Why would I be mad at you?"

" 'Cause I think Nora's pretty. And 'cause I think you're stupid for fighting with her."

Cap'n lifted his head and stared at me. His face was bearded with snow. I looked at Walter. His lips curved up into what was almost a smile. "I'm cold," he said.

I broke a limb off a dead tree, scraped a hole in the snow, made a fire on the bare earth beneath. Twigs quickly flamed, then turned to molten wires. Sap bubbled and steamed as the branches caught. I stretched out, listening to the crackling wood and staring into the core of the fire, where coals crumbled and glowed. In a blast of wind, flames lashed the snow like a thing alive. Walter's face burned orange in the flowering light; he looked like a demon born from the moonwashed night.

A branch snapped, releasing a bundle of sparks. Bright flecks lifted into the sky, blended with the stars above. Walter stood up. His shadow, thrown by the firelight, was tall as a tree. A tower of smoke rose from the flames in the windless air, collapsed when a breeze blew.

I pointed at Cap'n, still rooting through the snow, chewing everything he found. "Maybe that's where mountains go," I said. "Maybe animals eat them. Someday there won't be any more mountains. The world will be flat and everybody will live in cities and the rivers will dry up and there won't be any more fish to catch."

I watched Walter walk away, Cap'n hopping next to him, their bodies blackening, then merging with the night. I kicked snow over the fire, covered the pulsing coals. They hissed and died.

I heard boots scuffing snow. I turned my head and stared behind me, and when my eyes adjusted to the shadows I saw Walter, his arm pointing at the sky, at a gap between clouds. "I know what those stars are," he said. "They're snowflakes that're up there till people get married." Walter grinned. "Not when people get married and divorced. Not like that. When two people know they'll be together till they die—then the snowflakes aren't stuck no more and they fall down. Sometimes when people love each other so much it's a blizzard."

"What about in summer?" I asked.

"The snowflakes turn into rain."

"Who puts them up there?"

Walter tilted back his head. "There's an old lady who lives up there. She wants people to get married. She makes the snowflakes and puts 'em in the sky. When they fall down she's glad and she makes more."

≈11≈

Space

The next night Walter and I rented snowshoes at Alta and walked away from the lodge under a moon full and yellow. A moon like a lidless eye, bulging and jaundiced, staring madly out of the black night.

We brought headlamps with us, but after a few minutes realized we didn't need them. We clicked them off. I told Walter I'd read in a newspaper that the moon was at its nearest point in its orbit to the earth, and the earth was at its closest point to the sun. And it was a clear night and the moon was full. All those things hadn't happened together in over a hundred years.

Walter tangled one of his snowshoes in a bush. He yanked it free, then said, "I wanted to study space in college. My dad and I used to build rockets and shoot them off from the roof of our trailer and from my treehouse."

A thin cloud drifted in front of the moon, ringing it with an iridescent glow, like the skin of a soap bubble, or the sheen of oil that scums parking lots.

"See that?" Walter said. "Looks like a rainbow around the moon. A moonbow." He pulled a dead branch from a bush and threw it. It sliced through the air like a boomerang, then disappeared between trees. Cap'n hopped after it.

"Wish I had a dog like Cap'n to chase sticks," Walter said. "I think

I'm gonna be ready to get one pretty soon. I've been taking good care of myself. I haven't left any more pizzas in the oven. Can I keep Cap'n?"

"Have you left any more pizzas in the boxes when you put them in the oven?"

After a moment: "Only one."

We started to walk again, lifting our snowshoes as we passed over the tops of buried trees, stepping like giants. We headed up a rise. Reached the top with a few long steps, the snow crunching under us. I felt like a monster in a fairytale striding over mountains, smashing the earth.

"How come you don't want a baby?" Walter asked.

I stopped with one snowshoe raised in the air like a freezeframe sports replay. I stared at Walter. He stood darkly against the snow. Stars swarmed in the endless black above. I set my snowshoe down.

He shrugged his shoulders. " 'Cause you got a wife and you're old enough. And Nora wants you to. Why don't you make a baby with Nora? I would."

I had the urge to tell him it was none of his business. "I guess I'm just not ready," I mumbled.

We started walking again. From the branches of halfburied pine trees hung clumps of moss. Like dwarves with drooping beards.

"So what about Donna?" I asked as we reached the top of a hill.

"What about her?" Walter said, his voice edged with anger.

The temperature was plummeting under the clear sky. I could feel the earth's heat, the small bit of warmth it had gathered during the day, flowing back into the atmosphere, free of clouds. Back into space, back toward the sun.

"Did you ask Donna out?"

"We went to dinner," Walter said. "At Kingfisher Inn."

Martha had been on vacation, he told me. A different waitress was there. She didn't know his system: she didn't understand that when he was confused he pointed to the picture of the food he wanted. He kept pointing to a picture, but she wasn't looking at him. She was staring at her notepad, and he didn't know what to do. Donna ordered for him.

"I was embarrassed 'cause Donna had to help me."

I walked around the hilltop. The snow was rippled and folded like waves on a frozen lake.

Walter said that at the end of the dinner he tried to take his wallet out of his pocket to pay but it wasn't there. He'd left it at his apartment on the table next to the front door.

"It happens, Walt. I lost my wallet. Left it at your apartment—remember? It's not a big deal."

"But you and me weren't going on a date."

"I guess you've got a point."

"The waitress told me I had to wash dishes to pay for dinner."

"She was just joking, right?"

Walter hadn't understood that she was kidding, he said. When the waitress left he told Donna he had to go to the bathroom. He walked into the kitchen, rolled up his sleeves, got ready to wash dishes. The waitress came into the kitchen and asked him what he was doing. She laughed when he told her he was there to wash dishes. Then she whispered to the cook and he started laughing too. Walter ran out of the kitchen, back to the table.

"I must've looked mad or something, 'cause Donna asked me what was wrong. I told her what happened and she started laughing. I yelled at Donna. I told her it wasn't funny and shut up and never laugh at me again."

I looked past Walter at constellations I couldn't name, the stars pulsing like luminous life in a black ocean.

Donna cried when Walter yelled at her, he said. Not a lot, just small tears. Her eyes got wet and she wiped them with a paper napkin and they were both quiet. They sat there and didn't look at each other. People were staring at them, and nobody in the restaurant was saying anything. Then the waitress came over and patted Walter on his shoulder. She said she was just joking about washing dishes and he could bring the money in later to pay for dinner. He didn't say anything to Donna on the way home. When they got to her apartment she kissed Walter on his cheek.

"It's like her lips were the softest thing in the world," he said. "My heart hurt bad. I wanted to tell Donna I was sorry for yelling and I wanted to tell her how much I liked her and I wished she would keep kissing me. She went into her apartment and shut the door. I didn't say nothing."

I asked Walter if he'd talked to her since then. He said that when he heard her door open down the hall he looked through his peephole and watched her as she walked by.

"I see her red lips," he said. "And I imagine 'em kissing me. I want to open the door and tell her I'm sorry but I can't."

"Open the door next time."

"She knows I have a stupid fucking head now."

I thumped his back. "Come on, you've got to admit—it is kind of funny. You standing there with your sleeves rolled up, ready to wash dishes, while Donna thought you were in the bathroom."

"It's not funny! I fucked up."

"I don't think Donna was laughing at you. . . . Doesn't it seem a little funny now?"

Trees creaked as they contracted in the cold air; the sound, against the stillness of the mountains, was like cannon fire.

Walter was quiet awhile, then said, "Our dinner cost . . . 'bout twenty dollars. How many dishes would I have to wash to make twenty dollars?"

"Probably a couple hours' worth."

"Donna would've thought I was in the bathroom for a long time." Walter laughed, slowly at first, then in raspy waves. "She might've thought I fell down the toilet or something."

The lights of Alta glowed in the canyon below, cupped between mountains, shielded and safe. Thin clouds drifted across the moon, bright with the light of a vanished sun. For a long while we stood in silence. Finally Walter said, "Next time I'll ask Donna to have spaghetti at my apartment. I make spaghetti good."

I turned and looked at him. His face brightened as he tilted it skyward, his good eye steady, his sightless one drifting, not focused on the moon, itself an eye unblinking and blind. "I don't feel cold no more," he said. "It's like the moon's burning. Like it got so bright it caught on fire and now it's heating up the world."

We headed toward the lodge, powder squeaking beneath our snowshoes as we weaved between trees and walked through long shadows.

⇒ 12 ⇐

Into the Night

When we got back to the lodge we stopped by the bar, a dark and smoke-filled room covered with animal heads, football posters, and mining tools flaked with rust. Next to our table a rattlesnake skin was stretched flat and tacked to the wall. I ordered a beer, Walter had a Pepsi. We sipped our drinks and looked out a window at glowing mountains and clouds passing over the night. Walter stared, his eyelids sagging, his lips an open loop that dangled from his drooping face. I thought he was just tired.

Walter stood up. "Go . . . fishing," he muttered as he took a step and swayed. I jumped up, tried to grab him. He fell to the floor, thunking his head on an edge of a table. The crack of his plastic helmet against wood silenced the bar. Some came over to help, others backed away. Everyone stared.

"What happened?" a woman said as I knelt down next to Walter.

"He's having a seizure."

"Is he gonna be all right?" someone else asked.

"He'll be fine in a minute or so."

Walter had his arm wrapped around a chair with his hand clenching an armrest. I opened his hand, lowered him to the floor, turned him on his side. A convulsion raced the length of his body, making his arms and legs spasm.

"Don't just sit there," a man yelled. "Do something!"

The seizure had to run its course. There was nothing I could do to stop it.

A bartender kneeled down next to me and said, "What if he swallows his tongue? Shouldn't we stick something in his mouth?"

"That's an old wives' tale." I stood up and asked the bartender to help me clear a space. Walter started to convulse again. His back arched, his arms and legs twitched and trembled.

"Hold 'm still," a redfaced man said in a drunken slur. He broke through the circle of people and rolled up his sleeves as he stumbled toward Walter.

"Get him out of here," I said to the bartender, who jumped up and intercepted the drunk before he reached Walter, then walked him out of the bar. "Hold the son bitch down 'fore he 'splodes," the man shouted as he was shoved through the door.

Walter writhed a final time. He lifted his back off the ground and arched it, bridging himself like a yoga master; then he collapsed and went limp. I sat next to him, waiting for him to come out of it.

Walter coughed. Spit dripped from a corner of his mouth. I mopped it with my sleeve.

"I was . . ." Walter tried to sit up.

I told him to relax.

The people drifted away. They spoke words of encouragement to Walter and offered to help, then went back to drinking and talking, but in softer tones than they had before the seizure, as if by speaking too loudly they'd disturb Walter's recovery.

Walter tried to sit again; I caught him as he dropped his head toward the ground. I held him in a sitting position, and when he was ready I lifted his floppy body from the floor. He sighed and sank down, slumping himself into a chair. "I was fishing," he said in a voice that barely rose above the gurgle in his throat.

I told him he'd had a seizure.

Walter looked at me and tilted his head.

"Want to lie down?" I asked. "Want to go back to your room?"

"I'll stay here."

I noticed people looking at Walter, disguising their glances by pretending they were gazing out the window, into the night.

"Sorry," Walter said. "I look like I'm getting electrocuted or something when I have a seizure."

"Don't worry about it. You don't need to apologize."

He squinted at a wall next to our table, as if studying the woodgrain. "My dad used to yell at me when I had seizures. Before I started taking pills for 'em I used to have 'em all the time. My dad only hit me once in my whole life."

They'd been in a grocery store, in the aisle with pancake syrup, Walter said. He had a strong smell in his nose—the shaving cream his dad used. As though it were smeared all over his hands and chest. He knew a seizure was coming because right before they started he always smelled strange things. The grocery store was getting fuzzy and he felt his body growing light. He thought he might float away like a balloon, he told me.

He tried to fight off the seizure, but it came anyway. He must've fallen down, he said, because when he came out of it he was on the floor and there was sticky stuff all over his clothes. He'd knocked over syrup bottles. And there was blood, too. He'd forgotten to wear his helmet that day. His scalp split open when he hit the ground.

A store manager in a tie was standing over Walter, asking him if he was going to be okay. He smiled and asked what he could do to help, Walter said. His eyes looked scared but he kept smiling. Walter tried to sit up and answer him, but he was glued to the floor with blood and syrup, and he couldn't make his mouth talk. His dad kept apologizing to the manager, telling him it'd never happen again and he'd pay to get the mess cleaned up. The manager asked Walter if he needed an ambulance. Walter tried to say no, and his dad told him Walter would be fine, but he went and called for one anyway.

Walter said that the hospital let him out that afternoon, and when his dad drove him home he yelled. Told Walter he was sick of his seizures, told him he was tired of him having them in public and embarrassing him. Told Walter there was no way in hell he could afford to pay for an ambulance and stitches in his head. Walter's medical bills were already costing the family a fortune, and he had to mortgage the house, and he was afraid they'd lose it, and then where the hell were they going to live? Walter tried to apologize, but his dad kept yelling. When they pulled into their driveway he reached over and smacked Walter.

"On my cheek—that's where he hit me." Color drained from Walter's face as he touched his left cheek. He was still staring at the wall. After a few minutes, he said, "My dad put his head on the steering wheel. I couldn't see his face but I heard him crying."

I gulped my beer.

Walter tilted his head to the side, sliding his helmet across his greasy hair. "I touched my dad on his back. I thought he'd get mad and yell at me but he didn't. His back was sweaty and warm, and he let me leave my hand there. I couldn't hear him crying no more, but I could feel him crying with my hand."

Still Walter stared at the wall. His eyes were half closed and he was perfectly still. I looked past him, out the window.

"Haven't thought 'bout it in a long time," Walter said. "After a seizure I have weird memories." He looked away from the wall and stared at me. "What were your parents like?"

Fighting the urge to tell him I didn't remember, I took a long pull on my beer, then told Walter about my dad. He'd fought in Vietnam. He had wanted to go to college to be an architect. He was working in a lumberyard after high school to save up money. He thought his number was going to come up; he joined the Marines before he got drafted. After the war he went back to the lumberyard and got a job as a manager.

I finished my beer, glanced at Walter, then looked at the wall and kept talking. When I was a little boy I asked my dad about the war all the time. He told me stories about it when he was drinking. Sometimes when I sat in his lap I smelled gin on his breath—it smelled like pinesap. When I smelled the gin I knew he was going to tell me a story about Vietnam. First he'd make me promise not to tell my mom. Then I'd get excited and sit still and close my eyes and listen. He told me about villages in the jungle that were made from mud and straw. He told me about Vietnamese boys, smoothskinned and skinny as sticks. Boys he'd had to shoot. He told me about his buddy who'd been blown up by a landmine: one side of his body looked fine, the other side didn't have an arm or a leg. The stories scared me, but I always wanted to hear more. Sometimes my dad would stop in the middle of a story, right in the middle of a sentence, or even a word, and I knew he was done talking. And I knew better than to ask him to finish.

My dad and I went into the mountains together almost every weekend, I told Walter. Even on Sundays, which bothered my mom because she was a strict Catholic and wanted us in church. My dad told her the mountains were like church and he promised her we'd think about God when we were fishing or skiing. It was a joke between us: when we were making powder turns or catching trout on Sundays my dad would wink at me and say, "Son, you better be thinking about God right now."

"What was your mom like?" Walter asked.

I told Walter that she hadn't gone to college either, but she'd taught herself everything about philosophy, psychology, literature. The other waitresses at the restaurant where she worked made fun of her because she read on her breaks instead of smoking and gossiping, like they did.

I was staring at the wall next to the table, studying the woodgrain, as Walter had.

I told Walter about my basement fighting lessons, about how my dad had made me practice every day. My dad's arms were knotted with muscle and his hands were like iron from hitting the punching bag, I said. But when he combed his fingers through my mom's hair or hugged her, he was gentle, like he was afraid he'd break her.

My mom used to take me to her job when I was a little kid. I'd sit on a milk crate and drink Cokes and look at comic books. When I got bored I'd peek around the corner and watch her work. She smiled at her customers, but her face looked funny to me. It wasn't the way she looked at my dad.

Walter and I sat in silence, looking past each other, staring out the windows at the snowburied hills. They were patched with the shadows of trees, but no real darkness blackened the land, bright with the light of a bulging moon.

I went to the bar to get another beer. While I waited for the bartender I watched Walter. He sipped his Pepsi and looked out the window, pressing his face against it between drinks. The hair spilling from under his helmet left a greasy smear on the glass.

When I got back to the table I said, "Remember what you told me when you came out of that seizure?"

Walter said that before each seizure the world would disappear, but he could usually keep one thing, one thought, if he fought hard enough to hold on to it. He used to think about his family, he told me. When his mom died he started thinking about his dad—even after he stopped visiting, Walter kept thinking about him. But when he stopped calling, after a while Walter couldn't picture his face and he couldn't hold on to his voice when he had a seizure.

I swallowed a drink of beer and looked into the night. Beyond the lodge, moonbleached mountains seemed to glow from within, burning so bright they paled the stars above them.

"Sometimes it felt like I'd just float away from the world," Walter said. "I thought I might never come out of a seizure and then people would be glad that I was gone forever."

"You have a thought you can use now? Is that what the fishing was about?"

Walter nodded and told me that when he felt a seizure coming he thought about fishing. About letting the trout go. He remembered how

smooth they were. And he remembered how he could feel the life return-
ing to them as he held their bodies, and how when he loosed his fingers
and opened his hands they drifted toward slack places in the shallows,
places where they could rest and build back their strength before they
finned into the current and disappeared.

≈ 13 ≈

Desert

In northern Utah, the Green River knifes through stone, cutting canyons as it wanders toward a larger river. Walter and I dropped to our bellies and wiggled to an edge of one of those canyons, and we lay on a rock slab blown clean of snow and gazed at the waters below. Wind crackled along the canyon wall, a sound like freshly starched bedsheets fluttering in a breeze, and ravens rode the updraft, spiraling into the sky above.

"Vertigo Void," I said, pointing to a dot of red ink on a map I unfolded. "This is where the bartender told us to go."

The bartender at the lodge who'd helped Walter when he had a seizure had started talking to us when things slowed down in the bar later that night. He got excited when Walter told him he was a flyfisherman. Got really excited when I told him what a good caster Walter was and how he released all the fish he caught. The bartender told us about a place in the desert full of giant trout, a place where no one went in the winter; then he pulled a map from a shoebox under the bar, marked the route on it, and gave it to us.

We found an opening in a knot of bushes, and between mounds of snow we saw a footworn path in the flinty earth. I strapped snowshoes and ski poles to my backpack, then grabbed Walter's jacket as we hiked downhill. I held him steady, lifted him when he fell. Cap'n followed us, barking when Walter stumbled.

We stopped and looked down into the canyon, where the river flowed between corridors of trees. In a pool pinched off from the main current, trout glided through the water as if flying. There were no shadows below the fish, no bottom to the river. Just the shimmering green of its depths. Looking into the water was like gazing through sheets of glass, each layer absorbing more light, until the color near the bottom, buried under many thicknesses of glass, turned to jade.

"Is this the right way?" Walter asked, pointing at the path ahead: a narrow ledge of stone with a sharp rise above, a steep drop below.

I looked at the map, found another red dot. "Larry's Ledge," I said.

The bartender had told us that a guy named Larry got so excited when he saw all the trout in the river he stopped being careful, started to run, fell off the ledge and broke both his legs.

"Look," Walter said, pointing at the cliff face above us. A picture of a person with shoulders as wide as a pro football player's was carved in the rock. Wavy lines streamed from his hands and chest.

"I remember," Walter said. "Before my accident. Before I fell. There were pictures like that in the rock. I saw them."

"Pictures of what?"

Walter tilted his head, looked up at the symbol incised in stone. "For a second I remembered. But now they're gone."

"The Green River—isn't this where you had your accident?"

He nodded. "But it was on a different part. A whitewater part."

A breeze carried grains of sand, threw the grit in our faces, made us squint. Overhead, clouds bulked up like wet wool.

"Someday maybe I'll go back to where I fell," Walter said. "I want to see the pictures again."

For a few minutes neither of us said anything. I looked across the river, where rock towers rose from a scrim of haze like a cityscape, as if a civilization had sprung miraculously from the desert waste. Two ravens, big as eagles and shiny black, dropped out of a cloud, dove into the canyon.

We hiked through piles of talus, the loose stones wobbling beneath our boots and skittering downhill toward the canyon floor. Trees bearded with moss leaned over the water. Fingers of mist rose from the river, curling around the branches.

I smelled a foul eggstench as we walked along the riverbank. I stopped to look at the map. "Stinking Springs," I said, pointing to another red dot. "The bartender said that if we smelled sulfur when we got to the bottom of the canyon we were in the right place."

Walter wrinkled his nose and shrugged his shoulders.

"This is where we put on our snowshoes," I said. "We're supposed to hike upstream a mile or so." With my fingertip I traced the route on the map, the red line penned by the bartender. The next dot was near something called Tight Squeeze.

After we put on snowshoes we plowed through swirling drifts and stomped over banks of snow scabbed with ice. A sideways wind blew prickling flakes into our faces. Dust devils rose from patches of bare earth and swept across the snow, powdering it with red dirt.

We followed the river, gently curving, supple as a snake. I got ahead of Walter, stopped to wait for him by a cottonwood, its bony and snowcovered twigs like a witch's fingers dipped in white frosting. I saw something sticking out of the trunk. I walked over and took a look. A ballpoint pen. Above the pen, wedged in a crook between branches, was a running shoe.

When Walter caught me up, I pointed to the pen and the shoe and said, "Got a story to explain this?"

Walter sat down in the snow. He shut his eyes, opened them after a few minutes. "There was a curse here," he said. "The people who lived here were bad 'cause they hurt each other. An old witch who had special powers made the curse—if the people didn't stop being bad it would rain funny things. The people didn't care. They thought the witch was crazy. They kept being bad. So it rained shoes and pens all day and all night. There were shoes and pens everywhere, and the people were embarrassed 'cause they'd been so mean to each other. They picked up all the shoes and pens. But they left a few so they could remember and so they could show their children." He grinned. "How 'bout you, Mike? You got a story?"

I sat down in the snow, stared across the river at cliffs the color of cooked crab. I grabbed a pinecone, squeezed it until it dented my palm. When the wind paused there was the rumble of the river breaking against rocks and no other sound.

"Okay," I said. "I've got it. The pen is held in the tree by magic. Looks like it'd be easy to pull out but it's almost impossible. Only the right person can do it. And that person, the one who pulls the pen out, gets to make a wish. Many have tried but they've all failed. One guy camped out here for weeks, tried every morning. One day he climbed the tree; he thought that might help somehow. He got stuck halfway up— lodged his foot between branches and couldn't pull it out. The same magic that holds the pen in the tree held his shoe. He had to untie his shoe and leave it behind. He gave up and went home."

I spit on my hands, rubbed them together, then grabbed the pen and pretended to try to yank it from the tree.

"Let me try," said Walter. He reached for the pen with his right hand.

"Use your left, too."

Walter grabbed the pen with both hands, pulled it from the bark. "Looks like the pen I gave you," he said as he slipped it into a pocket.

When we reached Tight Squeeze, we took off our snowshoes and walked into a crack in the cliff, sucking in our stomachs and wiggling between the walls where they pinched together. Water dripped down rock, the plinking sound echoing in the narrow space. We passed through a dark tunnel, then stepped back into the sun, squinting against the light.

On the snowcrusted ground stood spires and domes—rock climbing into the sky and crumbling toward the earth like the ruins of an ancient village made of mud. And between pillars the river flowed, moving stone and soil toward a larger river, toward the sea.

"What is this place?" asked Walter.

I pulled open the map, flattening its accordion pleats. "Land's End,"

I said, pointing at the final red dot. "This is the place the bartender told us about. This is where he said trout are stacked up so thick you can't throw a rock into the river without hitting one."

We walked toward the water, passing under an arch, a span of brickred stone. On a snowbank at the water's edge, tiny black insects wiggled and crawled. I kneeled down and studied them.

"That's a lot of bugs," Walter said, stooping next to me.

"Should be fish feeding on them," I said. "Should be—"

We both saw it at the same time: spreading rings covered the water and fins sliced the surface.

"Hungry fish," Walter whispered as we took out our gear and rigged up. We worked in silence, racing to get ready before the hatch ended.

When Walter had his rod together and his vest on, he kneeled down and stared at the insects. "Tiny black midges," he said. He bent over, pinched one of the bugs, lifted it from the snow. "I don't got nothing this small in my flybox."

I clicked open a box and handed it to Walter.

"You got lots of little ones," he said, pulling one of the flies from the foam liner.

I wanted to be able to tie as good as my dad, I told Walter. In high school I got some books, taught myself. My dad was going to teach me. Told me he would when I was older.

"But he died?"

"He never got around to it."

In the shadow under a red rock, on the withered root of a juniper bush, I sat down and told Walter about my dad tying flies. The art of the common man: that's what he'd called it. I'd sit for hours next to him in the basement, watching him attach a vise to the edge of his workbench, helping him open boxes of feather and fur. Peacock herl—a thin and iridescent feather barb—that was my favorite. I'd hold a clump of it to the light, twirling it, watching it shimmer. When my dad got ready to tie he'd put on reading glasses; I'd laugh and call him an old man. He'd clamp a hook the size of his pinkie fingernail in the vise. Then he'd anchor the peacock herl and wind it around the shank of the hook. Too little pressure and it unwound, too much and it snapped apart.

From the juniper bush I plucked a berry. I rolled it between my fingers like a ball bearing, then sniffed it, inhaling its ginlike stink. I flicked it into the river. Through clear water the blue berry drifted. A trout swam around it, sucked it into its mouth, then spat it out. And before it sank into the seagreen depths and disappeared, another fish circled the berry, nipped at it, let it go.

Walter sat down next to me.

My mom had found an old display case in a thrift store, I told him. She stripped the wood and refinished it, cleaned the glass, made a tiny label for each compartment. She was going to put the best examples of each pattern my dad tied in the case and hang it above his workbench for a Christmas present. But when my mom went through the drawers on his workbench, she couldn't find any flies. He'd sold them and used the money to buy my mom a camera; she'd been talking about taking up photography.

"So the present didn't work out too good?" Walter said.

My dad tied more flies, I told him. He kept one of each pattern and put them in the cabinet.

I jammed my hand into a patch of snow, clawed into the ground below, lifted a handful of dust, as soft and smeary as ash. Let it filter between my fingers.

After a few minutes Walter said, "You know what these bugs are?" He pinched the tiny body of a midge, held it up for me to see.

"They're midges."

"Nope," Walter said. "Each one's a memory and they float down the river. The trout—they rise up to the top of the water and take a look at each one. If it's a good memory the trout don't eat it. If it's a bad memory they eat it up and then no one has to remember it no more."

"How about what I just told you? Are the trout going to eat that?"

"What happened to the case with the flies in it?" Walter asked.

I told him it was at my house. Promised him I'd show him the next time Nora and I had him over for dinner.

Walter walked to the water's edge and began to cast; I sat and watched. He kept his line in the air as long as he could, letting his rod flex forward and curl back like a willow branch bending in the wind. The sun crept above cliffs, and from the narrow strip of sky above, light poured into the canyon. In the warm sun Walter caught fish after fish; rainbow trout sipped his flies from the surface of the water, then rocketed into the air when they felt the hooks. Snow melted beneath his feet; the banks collapsed, turned to slush, slipped into the flow of the river.

"I can see fish rising over there," Walter said, pointing upstream, where the river bottlenecked between cliffs. "But I don't know how to get there."

I walked over to take a look. The riverbank dropped off, and there was no way to avoid it: a crag rose on one side, deep water flowed on the other. I inched toward its corniced edge, reaching my ski pole ahead of me, probing the thin and curling lip of snow. A chunk broke off, tumbled down a chute, landed about ten feet below.

"That's a bunch of fish," said Walter, pointing his rod at a pod of trout feeding in a calm eddy. "Can we get down there?"

"We'll have to throw our rods like javelins."

"Throw our rods?"

"So we don't break them when we slide down. My dad and I used to do it. If you throw the rod just right, its handle will land first and stick in the snow." I grabbed the middle of my rod, tilted the handle up, then threw it. The butt of the handgrip speared into the snow; the rod stuck upright like a flimsy flagpole, its shaft vibrating. Walter threw his rod; it landed safely, handle first.

"Not bad for a first timer," I said. "Ready for an avalanche?" We walked toward the drop-off. The snow settled with a loud whumping sound, and cracks shot across its surface. We took another step and the cornice collapsed; we went down a chute like a playground slide, landed at the bottom in a pile of icy debris. Cap'n tripped and rolled down the slope, snow clumping to his fur, making him as bulky as a bear. He jumped up and shook himself, flinging snow through the air.

Walter grabbed his rod, walked to the river's edge. "See that fish rising out there?" he said, pointing to a long trout holding just below the surface, lifting its head to pull insects from the top of the water every few seconds. "I'm gonna catch it."

I stood up and rummaged through the pockets on my vest, found what I was looking for. In a metal flybox that my father had given me on my twelfth birthday, I kept flies he'd tied. I pulled a Griffith's gnat from the box, handed it to Walter. Its peacock herl body shimmered in the sun. "It looks like a cluster of midges to the fish," I said. "Give it a try."

Walter took the fly, held it with his trembling left hand, tied it to his leader with his right. The fish rose and slurped. It was as predictable as the tick of a Swiss watch: every four seconds its head poked above the water.

Walter dabbed the fly with floatant, blew on it, studied the trout— its head rising above the river, then dipping below. "I'll show you how it's done," he said. He pulled out line, began to false cast—away from the fish so he wouldn't spook it. When the line was the right length, Walter dropped it onto the water. The fly settled on the surface as gently as a feather landing, and the current swung it downstream, in front of the fish. The trout's glossy jaws and black eyes rose above the river as it sucked down the fly. Walter raised his rod, set the hook. A rainbow trout long as my arm shot out of the water, arched above the river, sank back in. And then it dove. Walter's reel zinged as the trout pulled out line. The silvery fish flashed below the surface, then disappeared into the heavy green at the bottom of a pool. Walter tightened the drag on the reel, but still it hissed as line stripped off the whirling spool.

Suddenly Walter's line wasn't taut and straight; it lay in limp spirals on the river. We both knew what had happened but neither of us said a word. Walter lowered his rod, let it drop to his side. Let his line coil and spin serpentlike on the water.

Walter spoke first: "Sorry I lost your fly."

"That was a damn big fish. One of the biggest rainbows I've ever seen."

"I shouldn't have tightened the drag," Walter said. "I should've let it pull out all the line."

"I don't think I could've landed that fish. It was too big. Too mean."

"I'll never be able to hook it again. Now it's smart. It's not gonna make that mistake again. It's not gonna eat my flies no more."

I thumped Walter's back. "You'll catch other trout that big. And next time you'll know. Next time you'll let out the line."

Walter sat down on the bank, stared at the river. "Look," he said after a few minutes. "Mayflies."

The insects' tiny wings glimmered in the sun as they rose from the river. Walter laid down his rod, then reached into a shallow channel of the stream. One hand dipped into the water, scooping up mayflies; his other hand held his helmet in place, kept it from slipping over his eyes. Beyond Walter lay a pool, a deep hole where the stream eddied. And in that circling water I saw the heads and tails of trout as they fed deliberately, rhythmically. The fish rose, sipping mayflies that slipped through his fingers and drifted toward the pool.

I walked next to Walter. He lifted his hand, showed me the mayflies on the tips of his fingers. A smile curled his lips. "What do you call these?" he asked.

I let one of the mayflies crawl onto my hand. "Blue wing olive," I said as the insect flew away.

"They're everywhere like fog," Walter said. He grabbed his rod, tied a mayfly imitation onto his leader, then cast his line back and forth, and dropped the fly on the water in front of a fish. With a splashy rise it broke the surface and gulped the fly. And while Walter set the hook and fought the fish, mayflies covered the sun and dimmed the light, as if a cloud had passed over the sky and turned day to night.

≈14≈

Spam

All the fish we caught that day we released unharmed. Except for one.

Walter hooked another big rainbow. Shaped like a football, it wasn't as long as the one that had broken off earlier, but it was just as heavy. Walter cranked open the drag on his reel and let the fish spool out line. It porpoised above the water, then dove to the bottom of the river, swimming into the main flow and following the current downstream. When finally it tired and stopped stripping line from the reel, the fish was almost a hundred yards away. Walter had to drag its bulky body upstream, against the current; it was exhausted by the time Walter netted it. He kneeled and scooped it up, his net so full of fish it seemed stretched to the point of breaking.

"I let you have all the line you wanted," Walter said as he cradled the fat belly of the trout in his left hand and pinched the fly with a pair of forceps. "I'm gonna let you go now."

"What's the matter?" I asked after a few minutes. Walter was still holding the fish, still trying to pull the hook out.

"He keeps closing his snout. I can't get the fly."

I kneeled down next to Walter, offered to help.

"I can do it," he yelled. "I can let my own fish go!"

As Walter pried open the trout's jaws and gripped the hook with his forceps, the fish flopped. It slipped from his hand as the hook popped from its jaw. Walter reached for the fish; it pumped its tail, swam away.

"I didn't get to make it strong again," Walter said.

"That thing had some serious teeth. You get cut?"

"Not too bad." Walter held his hand out, wiped the blood away. Red dots marked his fingertips—tiny punctures from the trout's teeth.

"That's your proof that you caught a big fish," I said. "You can show the bartender your battle scars."

In the middle of the pool a fish floated toward the surface, turned over when it reached the top of the water. Its slabby sides were slashed with red. A fat rainbow trout. The fish Walter had caught.

"If it don't have its strength back before it gets in the current, that trout's in big trouble," Walter said.

We watched the fish; it limply floated, then flopped, then floated again, drifting toward the edge of the pool, toward the rush of the main current. The trout curled its body: became a circle, like a dog chasing its tail.

"It's getting some strength back," I said. "It might make it."

The fish heaved itself above the water, landed with a slapping splash, and then floated farther away. It drifted into the seam, bubbling like champagne, between the circling pool and the racing current.

Two bodies splashed in the river: first Walter's, then Cap'n's. Cap'n barked as he paddled behind Walter, who sloshed through the pool, toward the floating fish. I dropped my rod, went in after Walter.

"Walt, stop," I yelled. "The water's deep. You're going to go in above your waders!"

He was up to his knees. He took another step; the river rose to his chest, and his waders ballooned full of water. The instant before I reached him he fell. He started swimming, grabbed on to Cap'n, hugged his shaggy body. I slipped, swam next to Walter and Cap'n, grabbed Walter's shirt with one hand, a clump of Cap'n's fur with the other. Swimming as one, a soggy dog and two bluefaced men with clacking teeth paddled toward shore, thrashing through the icy water like shipwreck survivors heading toward land.

"What the hell?" I said after we'd crawled from the river. "What were you doing?"

Walter's chattering teeth sounded like gravel rattling in a glass.

"Were you trying to kill yourself?" Cap'n whimpered and nuzzled Walter. I screamed: "Were you trying to get us all killed?"

Walter ignored me. He turned and looked toward the river, where his fish still floated in the foamy seam, caught between current and pool. Walter was convulsing with chills. A breeze swept the river and surged over us. I fought a spasm of cold by moving: I grabbed a snowshoe and used its edge to scrape snow and push it into a pile the size of a refrigerator. I packed the loose flakes by smacking the pile with the flat of the shoe; then I used its broad tip as a shovel and tunneled into the mound.

A half hour later, when I had a snowcave hollowed out, I dragged Walter inside the sheltering space. Cap'n howled and whimpered and climbed on top of Walter. I peeled Cap'n away, ripped Walter's waders and soggy clothes off. Stripped him down to his underwear, then lit a candle. I rummaged through my backpack, found an aluminum survival blanket, wrapped it around Walter until he looked like a giant burrito covered in tinfoil. I plugged the entrance to the cave, left small holes for air, lit another candle.

I had made better snowcaves; it wasn't textbook, but it worked. Within a couple minutes it was hot as a sauna. I stopped shivering, my teeth stopped chattering. Walter's cheeks turned from bonewhite to red. For a few minutes neither of us said anything. We just absorbed the warmth. The emergency blanket covering Walter glowed like aluminum foil in a campfire.

"How'd you learn to do that?" asked Walter. "Who taught you how to make a snowhouse?"

I told him my dad had showed me when we were skiing in the backcountry. He had explained that snow was one of the best insulators in the world. Said it might save my life someday.

"This is my fault," said Walter. "I messed up big time."

"What the hell's wrong with you? Did you forget it's the middle of winter?"

"I wanted to help the fish." Walter fell silent for several minutes. As wind wafted through an airhole, the candleflames gently flapped. Shadows flicked across the walls of the cave. "Pulse control," Walter finally said. "That's what the doctors call it."

"Impulse control?"

"My stupid head doesn't have good 'pulse control. Sometimes I do things before I think 'bout them."

"Nora says I'm impulsive. She tells me I should make better decisions. Says I should plan things out." I rubbed my hands together. "Hey, you hungry?"

Walter pulled a soggy energy bar from his pocket, offered it to me.

"I got something better," I said, pulling a can of Spam from my pack. I peeled back the lid, ate a piece of the slick and mottled meat, then handed the can to Walter.

"Looks like dogfood," he said. He scooped out a piece, gulped it down, licked his greasy fingers. Cap'n crawled next to him and sniffed. Walter fed him a chunk.

We found a waterbottle, passed it back and forth, took turns sipping from it.

"When I was in a coma it was like being dead. Kinda like this snowcave."

Water dripped from the roof onto the candles. Their flames hissed and popped, then flared straight and bright when the dripping stopped. "What did you say?"

"I died once," Walter said. "It wasn't so bad."

In the silence that followed I watched the naked candleflames, steady in the still air. Then I crawled toward the entrance of the cave, put my ear next to an airhole. Outside, the wind fumed. Pricking flakes of snow drifted through the hole, stung my cheek.

"What was the coma like?" I asked.

"Kinda like a seizure." After a few minutes: "My parents still liked me, and my girlfriend—she liked me too. It was before they knew my head was fucked up. I thought 'bout them when I was in the coma and it wasn't so bad."

I glanced at Walter, looked away. I listened to his breathing as I studied the walls of the cave. The heat from the candles and our bodies was melting the rough walls, smoothing them.

Walter clapped his hands. "I got lots to think 'bout now," he said. "I got a friend who don't care that I do stupid stuff."

I kicked him; the foil blanket crackled. "Don't be so sure about that. Next time I might leave you in the river."

Walter put his head next to Cap'n, who lifted a shaggy brow and opened one eye. His snowsleeked fur shined in the candlelight. Walter said: "Mike don't care that we're broken, Cap'n."

I stared at the glistening walls of the cave, lost track of time.

Walter pulled me from my trance: "Do you remember any more 'bout your dad? More stuff like what you told me today?"

I watched him, then went back to staring at the snow. I told him that I used to spy on my parents when I was a little boy. I'd sneak out of my room at night, creep down the hallway, and peek around the corner into the living room so I could watch my mom and dad when they were playing cards. They'd sit on the couch and drink beer from bottles. My mom always tucked her legs under her, my dad always put his feet up on the coffee table. My dad didn't say much around strangers, but when he was with my mom he never stopped talking.

I kicked at the floor of the cave, punched the heel of my boot into the snow. After a few minutes I told Walter about the last time I'd seen my dad. He'd been in the kitchen, talking to my mom about dinner that night, about barbecuing. He said he needed to run to the store to get some charcoal. He grabbed keys and a pair of sunglasses from the kitchen table, a coat from a hook next to the door. A tan coat that he wore when he went birdhunting.

"What else do you remember about your dad?"

I remembered a Vietnam story about one of his buddies who'd caught fire, I said to Walter. My dad told me the story one night when my mom was asleep and he'd finished off a flask of gin. I remembered how sweaty he was; it sheeted off him like shower water. It was cold in the house. I had on thick pajamas with feet in them. He told me his friend had been in charge of keeping a trash fire going. They were in a tent walled with sandbags, listening to the radio, smoking cigarettes and drinking whiskey from metal cups. The tent door was open, and they could see the dump where the trash was burning. His friend went outside, got a can of gasoline, and shook it to let a stream of fuel fall on the fire; it had died down to a few coals, a little smoke. Flames shot up the stream of gas, into the can. It exploded and the guy caught fire and started screaming. My dad ran out of the tent, rolled him on the ground. He put out the flames, but the skin on the guy's arms melted like candlewax, my dad told me.

"You better let the trout eat that memory up," Walter said. "I'll bet your dad wanted the trout to eat that one too."

Neither of us said anything. The candles burned down to dripping stubs. Wax pooled on the snow.

After a while I told Walter about my mom's funeral. I remembered shoes pinching my toes. A social worker had guessed my size. She was wrong: the shoes were too tight.

"You had a social worker? Like Nancy?"

"Sure, same thing."

Walter's gurgling laughter bounced off the walls of the snowcave; it sounded like water pushing through clogged drainpipes. "Was yours mean like mine? You remember weird stuff—just like me. Do you got a broken head, Mike?"

I ate a chunk of Spam, then wiped my hand across my mouth and laughed.

When we crawled from our snowcave in the early dawn, the air was heavy and damp. Grainy light filtered through the gray—the promise of sun hovering above. On a rockface above the river, a desert sheep stepped from the mist. Its head bowing from the freight it carried, its enormous horns like coiled nautilus shells, the ram reached its nimble hooves onto a ledge. As Walter and I watched, as if the sheep were multiplying, another stepped from behind it. And from under a flank of the second sheep poked the head of a lamb. For an instant the animals seemed a three-headed monster, as if some fabled beast had been born from the fog.

Walter pointed at the sheep and laughed. He stopped laughing when I handed him a can of Spam. "More Spam?" he said, kicking the snow. "We have to eat this crap for breakfast?"

"This isn't Spam," I said.

Walter took the can, scooped out a chunk of pink and greasy meat, and examined it. "Looks like Spam to me."

"It's prime rib."

Walter tilted his head, stared at the slippery chunk between his fingers.

I grabbed a rubbery clump, closed my eyes. Popped it into my mouth, chewing slowly, licking my lips. "Delicious," I said.

Walter closed his eyes, ate a piece of Spam, his gullet pumping as he swallowed. "Just like prime rib," he said, rubbing his belly. Cap'n hopped around him and barked.

A few stray snowflakes wandered the sky, dissolving when they touched the river. We climbed the slope we'd avalanched the day before;

then we hiked downstream. At Tight Squeeze we took off our snowshoes, pushed through the tunnel, popped out on the other side. I got through first and sat down to wait for Walter, resting against the trunk of a ponderosa pine, rubbing my hand over the thick plates of bark that armored it against bug and blight and fire, time its only assassin.

Across the canyon a coyote yelped. Others joined it, howling above me. Their wailing song echoed across the river, then disappeared in the gray and soggy sky. A hole opened in the fog, and on a far rim of the canyon stood three trees blacked by lightning, dark and twisted shapes like apparitions in the mist. The foghole opened, and domes of particolored rock appeared. I remembered what the bartender had said about them when he'd shown me the route on the map: the domes were what remained of ancient tides. The comings and goings of a vanished sea, each bright layer marking a different era.

Walter squeezed through the tunnel, sat down next to me. Cap'n joined us. The sun was a pale place in the leaden sky, nothing more. Rock towers the color of bleached bone rose from the fog.

"What do you think those towers are?" Walter asked.

"Maybe people from an ancient civilization used them. When someone died, they'd climb a tower in the rain."

"Why in the rain?" Walter asked.

"The towers would get slippery as dog snot when they were wet. Carrying a body up was dangerous. But the people believed that the challenge honored the dead. When they reached the top they shouted their favorite memories of the person who'd died. And they left the body at the top of the column for birds to pick apart. They thought that was better than putting it in the ground for worms to eat."

I looked at Walter. "You got a story?"

"I'll try to think of one."

We followed a trail of stone ledges, like a staircase climbing out of sight, into the cloudcover above. When we reached Larry's Ledge, we saw the sun, a pale disk.

"There's another one," said Walter, pointing at the cliff above us.

Another petroglyph: etched in the patina of the mineral-blackened rock was a white spiral.

Walter traced the spiral in the air with a fingertip. "I know what those towers are," he said, turning toward the stone columns on the canyon rim. "A man and a woman had a son. Then the woman fell down and hit her head and died. The man—he was so sad he didn't know what to do. He started stacking up rocks, and pretty soon he'd made a big pile of rocks, and before he knew it he was building a tower. He tried to stop but he got sad 'cause he missed his wife so much, and his heart cracked open like a broke melon. He couldn't stand it, so he started building the tower again. And when he finished that tower he made another one.

"The son—he thought his dad was crazy. He didn't want to help build towers that did nothing. He wanted to travel round the world and see lots of things and get rich. The son left. The man kept building towers. He grew a long beard, and his back bent over from carrying so many heavy rocks.

"One day the son came back home to his dad. The son had seen lots of things in the world, and most of them scared him or made him angry. Building towers didn't seem so crazy anymore. He started helping his dad. When his dad died the son kept building towers."

When he finished the story, Walter folded his arms across his chest and smiled.

We climbed above Larry's Ledge, above the fog, where the sky blued and sunlight slanted between fir trees. Spiderwebs coated with moisture sparkled in the gathering brightness.

At the top of the canyon we crawled to the edge of Vertigo Void and stared beneath us. Pebbles slipped from the ledge and spilled over. Mounds of rock rose from the mist below like the backs of breaching whales, like petrified seacreatures from a time when all before us had been underwater. And like the last trickling of that ancient sea, the river flowed, its water clear where it ran over beds of gravel, green where it pooled. Somewhere in that river a rainbow trout swam with my father's fly lodged in its jaw. And in a bubbly seam between circling water and surging current floated another fish. A dying trout that had almost cost us our lives. As a gap opened in the mist, on the canyon floor far below I saw a pile of snow: the shelter where we'd spent the night. Then the hole closed, and like a slow fade in a film the scene dissolved into fog.

Walter, lying next to me, said, "Was I right 'bout the towers?"

I took off my baseball cap, put it on backward so the wind couldn't tear it from my head. "It was a good story, Walt. A damn good story." My voice faded into a windgust rushing up the canyon wall.

After a few minutes Walter said, "I want to try again with Donna. Think she'll give me another chance?"

"Next time you hear her in the hallway, open your door and ask her."

Walter said, "You're lucky. Nora gives you lots of chances."

From the fog below rose tiny curls of mist, like the fingers of babies. As I sat at the edge of the canyon and listened to the wind, the sun slipped out from behind a cloud, coppering Cap'n and edging Walter's helmet with light. They walked toward the truck, Cap'n hopping next to Walter and barking, rubbing his hand with his rumpled head.

≈15≈

Upside Down

A month passed after Walter and I left Utah and returned to Wyoming. One afternoon, under skies cold and clear, we put on snowshoes and hiked away from town, into hills crusted with brittle snow. For almost two weeks the temperature in the Kingfisher valley had dropped to twenty or thirty below zero; but in the mountains it was warm enough to wear a T-shirt. An inversion: that's what the meteorologists called it—cold air sinking and pooling in the basin of the valley, warm air rising up to the mountaintops.

"You were right," Walter said as we walked away from my truck. "Donna gave me another chance."

I caught Walter up, hit him with my ski pole. "Did you go out with her again?"

"I opened my door when she was walking down the hall. I told her sorry for yelling at her."

At the top of a hill we paused to rest. After he caught his breath, in a voice raspy from the cold air, Walter explained what had happened. He told Donna that if they didn't go out, then he wouldn't do something stupid in a restaurant and get embarrassed, but if he cooked at home he might start a fire. Donna said Walter could make dinner and she'd take her chances with the apartment burning down. When she came over for their date, she brought Walter a present. It was covered with Christmas paper that had Santas and candy canes on it. She said she knew Christmas was over but that was the only wrapping paper she had.

Walter stopped talking. Through a blue and windless sky streamed sunlight. Ice crystals in the air sparkled like insect wings. "So what was the present?" I asked.

"A fire 'stinguisher. Donna asked if I already had one and I said no."

"Even though you did? So you wouldn't hurt her feelings?"

"We really didn't have one." A cloud of steam escaped Walter's mouth like a dialogue balloon in a cartoon.

I reminded him that Nancy had bought him a fire extinguisher.

Walter raised his parka collar and pulled down the earflaps on the wool hat he was wearing under his helmet. "Nancy taught Mitch how to use it and he did. He squirted the toaster with the 'stinguisher when he burned his toast. It wasn't really on fire but there was lots of smoke."

"Why didn't you tell me? We could have gotten it recharged."

"Mitch didn't know you could fill it again. He thought when it was empty you throw it away like a pop can."

"He threw it in the trash?"

"He tied it to his bike with shoelaces. Then he rode to the recycling center and put it in one of the bins."

Walter told Donna the fire extinguisher was the best present he'd ever gotten, he said to me. Better than the flyrod I'd given him, better than his dad's checks. He told Donna about his dad, about how good he was at building things. Walter showed Donna his birthday check at the end of their date. He had taken it to the library and copied it before he cashed it. He showed Donna the copy, showed her where it said "Happy Birthday" on the memo line. Then he showed her his photo album.

I looked at Walter. His lashes and brows were crusted white with frost. "The one with pictures of Kmart in it?" I asked.

"The one with pictures of how I used to be. I wanted Donna to know I didn't always have a fucked-up head."

We climbed the next hill, rising above the valley, above the cold air. We were high enough that the gridwork of the town below looked as small and orderly as computer circuitry.

"It's warm up here," Walter said. He stopped to take off his parka and tie it around his waist. "Warm up high, cold down low. Usually it's the other way around. It's upside down."

"It's an inversion," I said.

Walter started walking again. The snow beneath his snowshoes squeaked like Styrofoam. " 'Cause warm air rises and cold air sinks when there aren't no storms to mix the air up," he said. "I remember that. A teacher in science class taught us 'bout . . . meteors."

"Meteorology?"

"I wanted to be a meteorist." Walter stopped next to a stump that wore a hat of snow. "I wanted to be a lot of things. Now I put labels on boxes at Kmart and stock their shelves."

I looked below us, into the valley, where car engines groaned in the cold, where snowy streets polished by car tires gleamed like rivers of ice, where woodsmoke hung in the air, trapped by the inversion. After a few minutes: "So what did Donna say about the album?"

Walter told me that Donna didn't care about any of that. She said she liked him the way he was, and she said look at her—she wasn't exactly Miss America.

"Ever since Donna broke her head she eats too much," Walter said. "She sees food and it makes her hungry and she eats it 'cause her 'pulse control is broken and she can't help it. She used to be skinny before her accident, and she had pictures of when she was skinny, but one day she was looking at them and she got so mad she cut them up with scissors."

I noticed a stone, a chunk of granite shaped like a lopsided heart. I bent down, pried it from the crusty snow.

"What's that?" Walter asked.

"Remember Nora's rock collection?"

"She's got them everywhere. All over your house. Even in the bathroom."

He was right: from a few stones on our mantelpiece, Nora's collection had grown to hundreds of rocks that now covered every windowsill in our house, dotted our garden, spilled out of bowls and buckets in our closets.

The past spring when I was fishing I'd found a rock shaped like a heart along a streambank. I stuffed it into a pocket on my fishing vest, forgot to give it to Nora when I got home. A few days later I saw another one: a stone shaped like a heart. I didn't tell Nora and I started looking for more. Including that one, I'd found eight. I slipped it into my jacket pocket.

"When I've got nine, one for every year since we met, I'm going to give them to Nora."

Walter tilted his head and squinted his good eye at me. "I want to give Donna something like that. What'd be a good present for her?"

"You have to figure it out."

Walter turned toward the sun, riding low on the horizon. "You met Donna before, Mike. Did you like her?"

"She seemed nice."

"She's not real pretty, is she?"

The sun slipped behind an evergreen. Its branches blazed and sparkled like the limbs of a Christmas tree covered with tinsel and lights. "I don't know her as well as you do, Walt."

"I don't care that she eats too much. I told her that and I believe it, too. She gave me a present. Nobody's given me a present in a long time."

"What about that flyrod I gave you?"

"You're just my friend. Now I got a girlfriend." He clapped a hand against his leg. "A girlfriend who gives me presents."

At the edges of the valley, smoke gathered, blocking our view of homes and cars; through gaps in the yellow fog we glimpsed broken images of the world below, an unreal town. After a few minutes Walter said, "Hey, Mike, now that Donna's my girlfriend I can't ask Nora out on a date."

"That's good—we're back together." I started walking again, following a trail up the next hill, climbing higher into the mountains, into the warmth above.

"Are you still fighting with her?" Walter asked as he walked behind me.

"Sometimes. But not as much as before." I pulled an itchy wool hat off my head, stuffed it in my pocket. "I started telling her that stuff about my parents that I told you."

Mountains rising from the floor of the valley to the roof of the sky unfolded in pleats of lavender and orange. In town, westfacing windows blazed bright, as if houses, in answer to the dying sun, held tiny suns of their own—miniature stars that ignited in the dusk.

I started walking again, following the warmth, climbing higher. After a few minutes I felt Walter's ski pole poke my leg. "Hey, Mike?"

I stopped walking.

"Now that I finally got a girlfriend, and now that you aren't arguing with Nora all the time, think we'll still be friends?"

Turning to face Walter, I raised my ski pole. In the failing light of that winter's afternoon I challenged him to a duel, and on a snowy slope two friends clacked their poles together, locking them in swordplay, battling like knights of old.

We stayed up high, enjoying the warmth as color drained from the sky. Stars winked in the blackening night as we made our way down, back to town, back to the stinging cold. Beams of light borne on icy crystals rose from streetlights. The lightbeams shot into the sky like lasers, seemed to reach the stars above.

"I know what I can give Donna," Walter said as he climbed into my truck and shut the door. In the stillness of the night, the creaking of cold metal was like a gunshot in a chapel. "A flyfishing lesson," Walter said. "That's what I do good, and I could teach Donna how to do it."

The thermometer in my truck read twenty-five below zero. I started the engine and blasted the heater; then I grabbed a down sleeping bag from behind my seat and wrapped the puffy bag around Walter, bundling him up for the cold ride home.

As I drove onto the highway, spackled with ice and humped with windrows of drifting snow, I glanced at Walter. His sleepy eyelids drooped shut a moment; then he opened them and said, "I know why the snower broke."

"The what?"

"The thing that makes snow fall out of the sky—the snower."

"It hasn't worked in Wyoming in almost a month. Maybe it needs a tune-up."

"Remember the old lady who lives in the sky and makes the stars? And when people get married and love each other the stars fall down like snow?"

I nodded.

"Nobody loved each other enough this month in Kingfisher—that's the problem. That's why the snower don't work." Walter thumped his chest. "But I'm gonna make it work."

"You're going to fix the snower?"

Walter grinned. "The old lady in the sky—she's gonna be happy. I'll love Donna so much that the old lady's gonna make all the stars fall down." His eyelids shut; he slumped into his seat and pulled the sleeping bag around his shoulders. And before he drifted to sleep, he said, "It's gonna be a great big storm. You'll see, Mike. I'll show you how it's done."

PART THREE

16

Coconut

Spring came to Kingfisher. At first the snowpack thawed from within; as the days grew warmer and rain leaked from the soggy sky, wandering streams furrowed the snow's surface, flowing in silvery channels that branched and laced together. Chunks of snow peeled off mountainsides and rolled downhill, melting to slush, then to puddles. Branches shook themselves free of ice and sprouted new buds. Green ribbons of grass sprang from the gray earth. Wildflowers raged, their blossoms growing so heavy they sagged toward the ground. Streams crashed down from mountains, filling rivers until they ran bloated and brown; and when the floodwaters dropped, high in the cottonwoods hung clumps of river rubble: sticks and trash nested in the crooks of branches, reminders of the flood. Reminders of how far the waters had swelled.

One afternoon in April, I went to a bar with a couple friends from college who were in town to ski, but after downing a few beers and listening to stories about how their lives hadn't turned out as they'd expected, I got bored and left. I drove to Walter's and walked through the front yard, mud squishing beneath my boots, lilac shrubs tangling around my legs, their purple flowers reeking.

"Come in," Walter shouted after a few minutes of knocking.

I stomped the mud from my boots, then made my way toward a commotion in the kitchen. Mitch was kneeling on top of a counter, holding a wingtip shoe. Walter reached into the sink. Something thumped against its metal sides. I stepped closer. Mitch raised the shoe above his head.

In the center of the sink, resting in the drain, was a coconut that Walter had propped upright like a football perched on a tee. "We can't get this thing open," he said.

"So you're beating it with a shoe?"

"Yeah, yeah," said Mitch. "Hit it hard with a shoe." He raised the shoe higher and squinted at the coconut like a marksman lining up rifle sights on a target. He took a deep breath.

"Hold on a minute," I said.

Air squeaked from Mitch's mouth and his body went limp. He dropped the shoe.

"What else have you tried?"

They had tried using a wrench, Walter said. Then they stuck it in the doorjamb and slammed the door. Mitch kept slamming it, over and over.

"Yeah, yeah," said Mitch, clapping his hands. "Slammed the door hard."

The door started to crack, Walter explained. And the coconut didn't break and their neighbors pounded on the wall and yelled at them to shut up.

Mitch: "Yeah, yeah. Mad neighbors."

I sat down, stretched my arms behind my back. "Try anything else?"

"Mitch hit it with a Wiffle ball bat," Walter said.

I leaned back in the chair. "And?"

"The bat bent."

"Stupid plastic," said Mitch.

"Mitch wanted to hit it with a golf club."

"Yeah, yeah. Golf club won't bend. It's strong metal, not stupid plastic."

"I didn't think that was a good idea," said Walter. "I stopped him."

"The voice of reason. What else? Any other schemes to get it open?"

"You'll like this one," Walter said, kicking my chair. "It's about you."

I nodded, waited for him to continue.

"We thought if we drove a car over the coconut, that might open it. We were gonna call you 'cause you got a big truck but we didn't want to bother you. We used our bikes instead."

I put my hands out, palms up. "And?"

"When my front tire hit the coconut, my bike didn't roll over it like I thought it would. It just stopped and I fell off."

Mitch burst into squeaky laughter.

"At least I tried, Mitch. You didn't even try."

Mitch laughed harder.

"Want to see what happened when I fell?" Walter said. He rolled up his shirtsleeve, revealing an elbow scraped raw. It was covered, but not with gauze and tape: at least a dozen Band-Aids were lined up across it in a neat row.

"Mitch did that. He fixed me up. We used lots of soap. It hurt like hell but we used it anyway."

Mitch grinned and raised the shoe again.

I jumped out of my chair. "Hold on, I've got a better idea."

I lifted the coconut from the sink, found a groove in the shell. "See this?" I said. "They make this notch in the shell so it'll split apart."

"Who puts it there?" Walter asked as he ran his finger along the notch, circling the coconut.

I shrugged my shoulders. "The people who grow them? The people who sell the coconuts?"

Walter tilted his head. "Seems like they'd be too busy growing the coconuts and picking 'em to put notches in 'em too. Somebody should thank 'em. Maybe we should write 'em a letter, Mitch."

Mitch climbed down from the counter and brushed his fingers over the notch as if stroking a baby's head. Then he took the coconut from me and held it in his arms. Cradled it.

"We'll need a hammer and screwdriver," I said.

Mitch handed the coconut back to me, then shuffled toward his room. A few minutes later he came back into the kitchen, grinning, carrying a toolbox.

I grabbed a screwdriver, jabbed it into an eye of the coconut. Drained the thin and watery milk into a coffee cup. Then we went out back, set the coconut on the cement patio, and circled around it. I put the business end of the screwdriver in the groove and raised the hammer. "Tell you what," I said, nodding toward Walter. "Why don't you do it."

"Hold the screwdriver *and* swing the hammer? I can't do both!"

"Mitch can hold the screwdriver."

I handed the hammer to Walter, the screwdriver to Mitch.

"Trust me, Mitch?" Walter asked as he raised the hammer.

"Yeah, yeah. Hit it hard."

Mitch was grinning and staring, a look of Christmas morning anticipation on his face.

Walter brought the hammer down. It was a good, clean blow; the coconut split apart, revealing the pearly meat within. Walter and Mitch each grabbed a section of the hairy shell. As if raising a sacrifice heavenward, Walter lifted up his chunk of husk, a brown smudge against the gray and dripping sky.

⌐

That evening I sat with Walter at his kitchen table, watching him put together the border of a puzzle. Mitch had gone to work.

The kitchen was spotless: dishes put away, counters freshly scrubbed, floor gleaming with wax.

"Your place looks good," I said. "Want to clean mine?"

"I'm not gonna do it for you. You got to learn how to do it yourself." He smacked the table and shouted: "Now we're even!"

I laughed and said, "Since when do you actually clean this place? I think this is the first time I've ever seen the floor." I slid my boot across the shiny linoleum.

"I don't mind a messy house, but Donna—she likes a clean house."

Walter told me they were going on dates all the time. Sometimes they went to Kingfisher Inn, sometimes they went to his apartment. And Walter had given Donna her present: a flyfishing lesson.

Mitch had helped him make a coupon, he explained. They used construction paper and Magic Markers to make a coupon that said, "Good for one free flyfishing lesson with Walter." Donna told Walter it was a good present.

I asked Walter if she'd liked fishing.

He studied the puzzle, shifting pieces around the table. "She told me to forget that I used to be a football player," he said. " 'Cause lots of people can play football, but not everyone can cast a flyrod as good as I do. I told her I had to practice every day and make my stupid left hand work before I could get good at it." Walter glanced at me and grinned. "Donna said she was proud of me."

"Did you give her a casting lesson?"

"She was a natural. She had good form—I told her that. When she gets embarrassed her cheeks don't get red but her neck turns red like a tomato."

Walter said that Donna hadn't caught any fish because she refused to put a fly on—she didn't want to hurt a fish's mouth with a hook. But she liked looking for bugs. She turned over rocks and found nymphs underneath them, and when there was a stonefly hatch she snatched at the air, trapping them in her hands. She told Walter that when they went fishing together she could figure out what insects were in the river and tell him which flies to use.

Walter rearranged puzzle pieces, then said, "Last night Donna got mad at me."

The bathroom door had been open a crack, he told me. He saw Donna's shadow bouncing around on the wall inside. He walked on his tiptoes like a burglar and peeked in. She was looking at her butt in the mirror on the wall. She kept moving around and squeezing her butt cheeks. Walter said he couldn't help it: he laughed. Donna ran out of the bathroom and tackled him and said she hated her big fat ass and Walter was mean to laugh at her. She told him that before she had her accident, when her impulse control worked, she didn't eat too much and she used to have a butt like a movie star's.

"I told her movie stars were too skinny and I liked her butt better," Walter said. "Then she wasn't mad at me no more."

I kicked his foot. "You definitely said the right thing."

Walter went back to working on the puzzle. After a few minutes he said, "We might get married someday."

"You just started dating."

Walter dropped a puzzle piece and swung around to look at me. "Is that too fast, Mike? How long should I wait?"

"I can't decide that. You have to figure it out."

Walter leaned back in his chair and smiled, tracing an empty place in the puzzle border with his fingertip. "I can talk to Donna so good. I can tell her things and she knows what I mean. And when I try to kiss her she kisses me back. And she says I make her feel good. She thinks I'm funny, too."

"Funny looking?"

Walter took a swing at me and missed.

"You're getting stronger," I said. "Now we have to work on your aim." Walter got up from his chair, landed a left jab on my shoulder, then sat back down.

"Much better," I said.

"I don't want no babies but Donna does. I can't have 'em anyway 'cause my mom and dad made me get a . . ."

"A vasectomy?"

"That's it—a 'sectomy."

"You know what it means?"

"Means I can't make babies no more." Walter was quiet a moment, then said, "Getting married makes me scared." Walter stopped shuffling puzzle pieces, looked up at me. "I don't want no divorce. I don't like that. . . . If I don't get married, then I can't get divorced."

"You'll probably like being married to Donna."

"There you go again—always telling me what to do." He turned away, went back to working on his puzzle.

"You asked her out on a date even though you were scared. And then you asked her out again after you made a mistake on your first date."

Walter was quiet a moment. He picked up a puzzle piece, dropped it back on the table. He cocked his head to the side. "Love isn't gentle. It's scary." Walter picked the piece back up, tried to jam it into a slot that was too small. He yelled: "Shit!" Threw the piece onto the floor, smacked the top of the table, kicked one of its legs, put his face in his hands. After a few minutes he raised his head and looked at me. "When I get scared, I do what you said, Mike. I think 'bout good things. Like Donna's red lips and kissing 'em—when my lips are dry and hers aren't and she lets me kiss 'em and it feels good . . . and I think 'bout her hair—when it's tangled and I pull my fingers through it and get the knots out and I do it just right, not too hard, and she likes it."

Before I left that night, Walter asked me to remove a splinter from his thumb. He had tried to use his left hand to get it out with tweezers, he told me, but he couldn't hold the tweezers steady. Donna wouldn't touch it; she was afraid she'd hurt him. And Mitch told Walter he could fix cuts with Band-Aids but he couldn't fix splinters.

I held Walter's hand under a lamp. Far beneath his skin, in the meat of his thumb, a brown sliver was buried.

"It's a good one," I said. "It's deep."

I sat down on a folding metal chair, plastered with bumper stickers. "What's the deal with these stickers?" I yelled into the bathroom, where Walter rummaged through cabinets in search of peroxide.

"The DJ at the radio station gave 'em to Mitch. I think they look stupid all over our chair, but Mitch likes 'em." Walter walked out of the bathroom with a bottle of mouthwash.

"Peroxide, Walter. Not mouthwash."

"Oh yeah, peroxide." He stood still, staring at the floor.

"Remember what you need to find?"

"Mouthwash?"

"No, peroxide."

"Right. Peroxide." He walked back into the bathroom. Cabinet doors clicked open and slammed shut.

He walked out of the bathroom emptyhanded. "My memory's shit today. I keep thinking 'bout Donna. Maybe love makes you dumber." Walter thumped his helmet. "What am I looking for?"

"Peroxide."

"Peroxide, peroxide, peroxide," Walter repeated. "Write it for me." He grabbed a notebook from his backpocket and tossed it to me. I pulled a pen from the metal spiral that bound the pages, flipped to a clean one, and wrote "peroxide" in large block letters. I stuck the pen back in the spiral, tossed the notebook to Walter.

He studied the word a moment, frowned, walked back into the bathroom. He returned, smiling, holding a brown bottle of peroxide. He set it on the table next to me; then he pulled his pad from his pocket and crossed off the word I'd written with a bold slash of the pen.

I swabbed Walter's finger with peroxide, dipped a pin into the bottle, and began to poke under his skin.

"I'm tough," he said. "It won't hurt me."

I probed deeper; Walter sat still, staring straight ahead, over my shoulder.

The pin finally reached deep enough—touched the sliver. Walter flinched. He took a deep breath. "I'm fine."

After loosening the splinter, thin and brown, I gripped it with tweezers, pulled it from his thumb, held it to the light. "The operation was a success," I said.

"I'm gonna live?"

"We don't even have to amputate."

I poured some peroxide into the rift in Walter's thumb. Sudsy beads gently fizzed as they dripped onto the chair, then fell to the floor. They made a puddle that sparkled on the linoleum under the glow of a fluorescent light. I listened to the hum of the refrigerator. Stared into Walter's eyes, his blind one drifting, his good one gazing back at me.

"Remember that duct tape you gave me?" I said.

"And a pen. I gave you a pen, too."

I told Walter that the duct tape may have saved my life. When I was skiing in the backcountry earlier that week I'd fallen and cut my wrist on a rock. I had his roll of duct tape in my pack; I ripped off thin strips of tape and pressed them to the cut, pulling its edges together to slow the bleeding, to seal the wound. When I finally got to the emergency room, a doctor told me the cut was already healing and there was no need for stitches. I showed Walter the ragged scar across my wrist.

"How come you didn't use Band-Aids?" Walter asked. He rolled up his sleeve and again showed me Mitch's patchwork on his scraped forearm.

"I didn't have my first aid kit. I forgot to pack it the night before."

"That's not safety first."

And after I cut myself, I made another mistake, I told Walter. A big one. Instead of going down the mountain and getting help, I went back up so I could ski again.

"You went up instead of down?"

"If I'd lost any more blood I would've been in real trouble. Thank God for the duct tape. And the Australians."

"What Australians?" Walter asked.

"Two Australians on the mountain helped me out. Drove me to the hospital."

"What were people from Australia doing on a mountain in Wyoming?"

"They gave me their address before they dropped me off. We could write and ask them. They live in California."

Walter tilted his head. "Australians from California?"

"The man's skin was so black it was bright," I said. "I think they might have been Australian Aborigines."

"What's a . . . bornagie?"

"Native people. The people who were in a place first."

"Like Indians?" Walter tilted his head. "What were Australian Indians from California doing climbing a mountain in Wyoming?" Walter shook his head. "I'm gonna tell Mitch what you did. He's gonna talk to you 'bout safety first."

"Maybe we could just keep it between us, Walt."

"No way. I'm telling Mitch and he's gonna talk to you. Don't try to get out of it."

I laughed, punched him in the shoulder. He hit me back with his left. His punch was firm.

"Not bad. You've been working that left side, haven't you."

"I've been hitting the couch every day. Mitch still won't let me practice on him. I ask him but he says no."

"Tell you what—I've got an extra punching bag in my basement."

My dad had given it to me when I was a boy. It was covered with bloodstains and mildew, and the canvas was worn so smooth it was slick. But I could clean it up and give it to Walter. He could use it to strengthen his left side.

"You're gonna give me a real punching bag so I don't have to hit my couch?" he asked.

"And so you don't have to hit Mitch."

Walter frowned. "If you're giving that to me, what's my part of the deal? What do I have to do?"

"Nothing. You've given me plenty."

"Like the duct tape that fixed your cut? And the pen I gave you?"

I laughed. "Exactly."

He was quiet a moment, then said, "You know when you were bleeding and you went up the mountain instead of down? Maybe it's like that time I got out of your truck and went up to the wild horse. I don't know why I did it. I don't know why I forgot safety first. . . . I knew it was a crazy thing but I did it anyway."

"That's right, Horse Tamer. We both forgot safety first."

"Sometimes it's good to forget safety first," Walter said. "But don't tell Nancy I said that."

Walter went back to working on his puzzle; then he tilted his head and stared at me. "Hey, what happened to Cap'n? Can I keep him?"

"Think you're ready for that?"

"I think I can take care of him." He worked on his puzzle a few minutes, then looked at me and said, "Remember when we went fishing at the place the bartender told us 'bout and there was a pen stuck in a tree? Remember how I pulled it out and I got to make a wish? I wished that you and me would always be friends. You haven't been around too much and I thought maybe you were mad 'bout me swimming in the river in winter."

"That reminds me," I said. I reached into my backpack, pulled out a T-shirt with a can of Spam painted on it.

"Where did you get that?" Walter asked.

"Nora made it for you. In college she used to airbrush things on T-shirts and sell them at concerts. Now she just does it for fun."

Walter took the shirt, held it up, grinned. "It'll make me remember when we fished in the secret spot in the desert and made an avalanche and slept in an igloo and ate Spam for breakfast."

"She made another one for you," I said as I reached into the backpack and pulled out a sweatshirt. I held it up for him to see. In the center of the sweatshirt was a silver circle, a roll of duct tape

"Nora made these just for me?" Walter said, touching his chest with his clenched left hand. Red splotches bloomed on his cheeks.

≈17≈

The Water Beneath

A few days later, when it finally stopped raining, Walter and I went in search of a stream I'd overheard some people talking about in a flyfishing shop. They had said it was difficult to find, almost hidden, but worth looking for. It was rich with trout, they'd said. Crammed full of fish.

As we drove down a twisting gravel road, sliding around bends, clouds pulled apart overhead and sunlight leaked through. I turned onto a washboarded road. My truck jerked over ruts, bounced through water-filled potholes. Grasslands and sagebrush plains stretched out ahead. I opened a map, then tossed it on the floor when I realized the roads we were traveling weren't marked on it. I tried to remember the directions I'd overheard, but after hitting a few dead ends and turning around and backtracking, I was thoroughly lost.

"I don't see water," I said. "All I see is sagebrush and these damn roads. They go everywhere. And nowhere."

Walter, slumped in his seat, stared out the windshield. "You said there's a lot of fish there?"

I stopped my truck at a crossroads. "That's what I heard. So many trout that at the end of the day your arm hurts from fighting them and reeling them in."

"Let's keep looking. We found those lakes with fancy fish in 'em."

Walter stared straight ahead. "And we found the secret spot in the desert that the bartender told us 'bout. Try that road over there." He pointed to a rutted mud path.

Calling it a road was a bit of a stretch. And I didn't see any sign of a stream. Just sagebrush. But I shifted into fourwheel drive and went where Walter pointed; we climbed sand dunes and sloshed through mudpuddles until we reached a clearing in the sagebrush near a collapsed barn.

"This might be it," I said. "I remember hearing something about parking next to an old barn. There should be a trail on the north side of the clearing."

I jumped out and took a bearing from the sun, then walked to the northern end of the barn to have a look. Heading into a tangle of sagebrush was a faint trail. I went back to the truck and told Walter. We stuffed our gear into backpacks, then headed down the path.

"I told you," Walter said.

The plain stretched in all directions, the world ringed by the flat horizon only. "I don't see any sign of water," I said. I toed at a bootprint pressed into the mud, then kicked a rock, sent it scuttering across the ground. "We should at least be able to see trees lining the edge of the stream, even if we can't see the water." I kicked a ragged clump of sagebrush. Scraped my bare leg. When I reached down to rub the blood from a cut, I saw a yellow caterpillar inching across a stick. Covering its back were dozens of orange and black dots.

"That must be smart," Walter said, pointing at the caterpillar. "With all those eyes it can see everything in the world. I'll bet it knows where the water's at."

We hiked for half an hour along the trail and found no hint of the stream. Footprints from people disappeared, replaced by the marks of animals—hoofprints and pawprints. Clods of mud spotted our bare legs like leopard skin. Walter's breath grew fast and wheezy. He tripped over a boulder and stumbled; I grabbed the back of his shirt to steady him. Ants marched in a black line over a dry crust of mud.

"Don't overdo it," I said. "You don't want to have a seizure."

Walter stepped over the line of ants, into a puddle. Mud splashed up, freckling his face. "I think we're getting close."

I turned around, scanned the landscape: fields of scraggly bushes, no trees, no sign of water. The outlines of mountain ranges were etched in the haze of the horizons, the mountains so faint they looked more like images in a dreamscape than like true peaks of stone. "You think we're getting close, huh?"

In a dry whisper: "I know we are."

I stepped over the line of ants and we hiked on, trudging through the silvergreen monotony of sagebrush. We lost the trail, backtracked and found it. Walter wheezed and panted. He stumbled every few steps. In a crackly voice he said, "The grasshoppers are like puddles. Every time I take a step, they jump and scatter all over the place. They splash like water."

"Think it's time to turn back?"

Walter ignored me and kept walking. As he pushed through bushes his boot caught on a branch; he crumpled and fell to the side. I reached out to grab him but missed. A bush cushioned his fall as he dropped to the ground.

"You okay?" I asked, standing over him.

He stared up into the sky. "Fine," he yelled. "I'm fine!"

I sat down next to him. Rows of clouds fanned out overhead, then joined in the distance, vanishing behind hills humped and bald. As if some void on the horizon were drawing the clouds toward it and sucking them from the sky.

"My stupid fucking head," Walter said after a few minutes. "I could see my foot catching in that bush and I tried to pull it out but I couldn't make my leg move."

His voice was small against the empty plain.

I reached over, squeezed his shoulder, and looked at his shirt—the Spam T-shirt Nora had made him. "Come on," I said. "Let's go back to the truck. We'll find somewhere else to fish. It's my fault. I shouldn't have brought you."

Walter pulled away from me. "You shouldn't have brought me with my fucked-up head," he said quietly. "You should have brought one of your other friends instead of me. That's what you mean."

"That's not what I meant at all." My voice died in the silence.

We sat and said nothing. There was no breeze to rustle the sagebrush. All was still. I lay down, resting my head against a flat rock, staring up at the sky.

"Ready?" I finally said when the wind kicked up.

"I'm not going back. I'm gonna find that river." Walter spoke softly, but with a firmness that told me there was nothing I could say to change his mind. He stood up and continued down the path; I followed, almost smacking into his back when he skidded to a stop. Moving next to him, I saw.

A gap in the earth held a stream hedged by cottonwoods. The current had knifed into the soft dirt of the plain, cutting a ravine that hid the water and the trees surrounding it. Only at the edge did the stream appear: even a few feet back there was nothing but the monotony of sagebrush and no sound of water—uninterrupted flatness and the windy silence of the plain.

Where the water turned a bend it gently rippled, glinting in the sun. It wasn't a mountain stream that crashed down from above, cascading toward valleys. It was a spring creek: an upwelling of water from within the earth that meandered and pooled, curling and looping across the plain like a carelessly dropped rope. The fish shadows drifting through the shallows hinted at a bounty of trout. In a sluggish pool cut off from the main current I saw motion. A stirring in the springfed depths, like something struggling to rise.

"We did it!" Walter yelled, bending over to pick up a rock. He flung it into the stream. Fish darted away as it shattered the calm water. "I scared the trout. Now they'll be too afraid to eat our flies."

I grabbed a rock and chucked it toward the stream. "We can fish a different stretch." Ripples spread away from the disturbance, then melted back into the water.

Walter pushed a boulder with both hands, rolling it downhill toward the stream. Water geysered into the air. We took turns throwing and rolling rocks, and from the edge of the ravine we listened to them kerplooshing and kerplunking in the water below. We whooped and yelled into the still sky.

"Maybe we're the first people to ever see this stream," Walter said, pausing between throws.

"Could be," I said as I chucked a round baseball of a stone as high as I could. When it hit the water a column spouted into the air.

"We're like explorers," said Walter. "Like on *National Geographic.*" He picked up a flat stone with his right hand and whizzed it toward a pool below. It skimmed the surface, skipped a few times before it sank. He grabbed a rock with his left hand and threw it, then pointed at the water. "We discovered this." He dropped a rock, stared into the ravine. "Little Snake," he said after a moment. "I want to call it Little Snake."

"Why Little Snake?"

"The water's shiny and smooth like snakeskin. . . . And the stream winds and twists, just like a snake. . . . It looks a little like the Snake River in Jackson. Remember when I caught Slashback? Remember when it snowed from the trees?"

"We name this stream Little Snake," I yelled.

"Little Snake!" said Walter. With head backflung, arms raised, and fisted hands shaking at the sky, he looked like an ecstatic worshiper performing a primitive prayer, the way ancient people had thanked gods in a time before churches. Sunlight bounced off Walter's helmet. His voice hung in the stillness before scattering across the sagebrush and sinking below, toward the water; and drifting above, into the cloudstreaked sky.

We hiked into the ravine, stumbling toward the riverbottom on a slithery path. I held the back of Walter's shirt, kept him steady. The last twenty feet of trail were so steep we had to sit down and slide. Stones broke free from the loose grip of the slope and bounced beside us as we tobogganed down. Dirt cascaded with us, and we landed in a soily heap at the edge of the water.

"You think we can get back out?" Walter asked. "What if we have to stay here?"

I looked behind us at the ravine wall, steep and crumbly and tall. A pandemonium of plants surrounded us. "Maybe this stream is the fountain of youth," I said. "We can live here forever. We'll drink pure water and feast on trout and never feel pain and never get old. Never die."

"Maybe it'll fix my head," said Walter, as he waded through a patch of leafy ferns that looked like giant bracken from a time when the earth had shuddered beneath dinosaur feet. He reached out and pulled something from a log, then held it up for me to see: a fly with bushy brown hackle. A classic fly pattern, one of my father's favorites. A pattern I hadn't tied in years.

"Okay," I said, "so maybe somebody was here before us. And maybe it isn't paradise. But it's still our stream. It's still Little Snake. And I bet we'll catch some damn fine fish here."

We pushed through bushes toward a brook. Blue forget-me-nots covered the ground: a mat of color, solid and bright. Above the flowers hundreds of damselflies hovered and darted. A blue fog, teeming with life.

"That looks fake," Walter said. "There's too much blue. Blue flowers, blue bugs, blue everywhere. Looks like somebody painted it."

We followed the brook, schools of silver minnows darting ahead of us. The water was so clear that only where it bubbled or rippled did it look like water: the minnows seemed to float through air. We hiked over a rich tangle of grass, found the main channel of the stream, then walked toward a pool, its bed cobbled with waterworn stones as round and smooth as eggs. Rising trout spread rings across the water as they slurped insects. Walter and I knelt in the shade of a cottonwood to watch. A smack punctured the silence as a fish sucked something from the top of the stream. The trout's head and then its tail, silvery in the sunlight, broke the surface; then the fish turned to shadow and sank back into the green pool.

"Hungry trout," Walter whispered.

"There's a hatch going on." I pulled a bug from my shirt as I walked across the windsculpted sand of the shore. "Caddis," I said, holding the fluttering bug, tent-winged and tan, for Walter to see. Another bug lifted off the stream, bounced in the breeze. I reached into the water and shuffled rocks; to their mossy undersides clung caddisworms—larva that lived in silken cases covered with tiny bits of stick and stone.

Walter started rigging his rod—the bamboo rod my father had made, the one I'd given Walter.

He joined the rod, twisting the male and female sections together. I took it from him and cast it back and forth, feeling the evenness of the stroke—a smoothness of motion not found in storebought rods made of synthetic materials. With one hand I gripped the cigarshaped leather handle, polished by use; my other hand glided over the shiny bamboo. I pinched one of the ferrules: metal bands that stopped the slender shaft from splitting. I rubbed the slick finish covering the wraps of thread bonding guides to rod. Everything was intact—still sturdy after so many years.

Walter brushed a finger along the handgrip. "How'd your dad make such a good rod?"

I handed it back to Walter, told him about the work that had gone into crafting it. Every night for almost a month I had crept down the basement steps, sliding my hands along the splintery rail. I learned which boards creaked and stretched my legs across them so my dad wouldn't know I was coming down to watch. A lightbulb hung bare in a corner of the basement. I could smell the dust that settled on it and heated up. I hid in the shadows, watching my dad as he split a bamboo cane, peeling it apart and bonding the strips together with glue.

I remembered watching my dad's hands, I told Walter. The wrinkled seams of his knuckles smelled dryly of sawdust and stank of varnish when he came up from his basement workshop, then poured a glass of gin and put me on his lap to tell me stories. I had stared at those hands and tried to imagine them holding an M-16 in Vietnam. He seemed so gentle: the way he peeled apart the bamboo cane and carefully put the pieces together. It didn't make sense. I didn't understand how my dad could have killed people in a jungle on the other side of the world. How the finger touching that bamboo could have pulled tight a trigger and sent a bullet into some boy's brain.

Walter shook his head. "Don't think 'bout that too much."

When Walter finished rigging, he tied on a fly, a caddis imitation made of bristly elk hair. He crept from under the tree to the water's edge and cast toward a rising fish. The trout ignored the fly as it drifted by.

I rigged up, moved downstream from Walter, made a few casts. Fish were feeding all around me—there was a frenzy of rises—but none took my fly.

"Any luck?" I asked after a few minutes.

Walter shrugged his shoulders. "Nothing. I got a caddis on and I'm casting good with this rod. I don't get it."

I propped my rod against a bush, waded through a mat of moss fringing the stream, and scooped at the water as insects floated by. Weeds swayed in the current like kelp in an ocean. My feet stirred clouds of silt that billowed in the clear water and rose to the surface. Mayflies flew from the water and lifted into the air, their wings sparkling in the sunlight.

When I bent down and stared at the water, I saw mayflies struggling to escape their nymphal husks. Some had shucked off their skins and pushed through the film covering the stream. With upright wings, the adult mayflies floated like tiny sailboats, bouncing across the water as wind stirred the air. Adrift on the current, they were waiting for their wings to stiffen so they could fly away to mate and die, far from hungry trout.

I plucked one of the mayflies from the top of the water. Its palegreen body wiggled between my fingertips; its flimsy wings and slender tails trembled in a breeze. I dropped it on the water, watched it float downstream. A trout sucked it from the surface as it passed a grassy bank.

"They're feeding on PMD's," I yelled to Walter. "Pale morning dun. A kind of mayfly."

"There's a cloud of 'em over here," Walter said. "They rise off the water real slow like steam."

"You have a fly to match them?"

Walter pulled a box from his vest and opened it. "I got one that's the right color," he said. "But it's too big."

I walked over to him, opened my flybox. Gave him a good match. Found one for myself and tied it on. I walked back downstream, cast beyond a rising fish. The current swung my fly in front of it; the fly disappeared, slurped under by the trout. I lifted my rod, set the hook. Felt the weight and pressure at the other end.

"Got one," I said.

"Me too," Walter yelled. "I got a good one!"

The fish were feeding fast and furious and we'd found the right fly. Spreading rings scarred the water; fins and tails sliced it. There was the slurping of insects being sucked under and an occasional plunk when a fish landed after jumping from the water, chasing a mayfly as it lifted off the stream. Almost every cast caught a fish.

"Look," Walter yelled. "The bugs are changing. They're getting bigger!" He spun around, arms held high as he pointed at clouds of mayflies.

I scooped one off the water and let it crawl along my hand. Walter was right: it wasn't a tiny PMD; it was a green drake, big and dark. I found two flies that matched the real thing—wriggling on the tip of my finger, trying to spread its wings, struggling to rise.

Walter walked toward me, sloshing through the stream. Their wings glinting in the sun, mayflies covered him in a bright mist.

Our first casts after tying on the new patterns we each caught a trout. Big, hungry fish that chomped our flies as though angry at them. After I released my trout I watched Walter. With wet hands he cradled a fish, swishing its head and gills in the current to revive it, granting it life.

A few hours later, suddenly, as though a switch had been flipped off, the fish stopped rising. The hatch had ended. No more riseforms of feeding trout marred the water, glassy and sparkling dully in the light of the weakening sun. Dusk was near; I'd lost track of time.

I broke down my rod and packed my gear, then walked around a bend in the stream while I waited for Walter. Against a sandy beach littered with driftwood lapped a pool of water—water the color of light shining through a greenglass bottle. With the blue sky stretching overhead and the sun low but still hot, it seemed I'd stepped out of Wyoming, onto a beach in the Bahamas.

I walked into the foam at the edge of the river, dropped to my knees in scalloped sand littered with mayfly husks. I picked one of the molted skins up. It was split down the middle, as if the mayfly had unzipped it to crawl out, like taking off a jacket. It was hollow inside. Empty. I pinched it between my fingers, watched the thin sheath crinkle and crack.

I speared my fingers into the beach, then lifted my hands and studied the sand: tan grains flecked with red and green stone and white specks of bone. I shook the clumps from my skin, let the wet heaviness ooze between my fingers, let it slough away. I watched it cloud the water, watched the blackness spread. When it settled I could see a round and shiny rock. I grabbed it, pulled it from the sand. It had been buffed smooth as a gemstone. I stuck it in my pocket, saving it to give to Nora.

As we walked away from the stream, Walter said, "How many fish did you catch today?"

"Not sure," I said. "I lost count. How about you?"

"I caught a lot. My arm hurts from fighting 'em."

A heron flew by, its wings softly thumping as it passed. It glided in front of the sun, turned to silhouette. With wings as long as a man's armspan, it looked like a pterodactyl in the Wyoming sky.

Walter was quiet a moment, then said, "Don't tell anyone 'bout Little Snake. We discovered it. It's ours."

"I doubt I could give anyone directions here. We're going to have a hell of a time finding the road back to the highway." I was quiet a moment as I listened to my boots squish mud. "There aren't any maps for the roads around here. Our only clue if we come back is going to be that barn."

"This might be the only time we get to fish here?"

"Maybe we'll try to find it and not be able to."

Walter turned and looked behind him; I glanced over my shoulder. The stream gleamed in the long rays of sun that spilled into the ravine. We scrambled toward the top, slipping in loose dirt, dislodging stones. We disturbed a deer—a doe. She trotted away, her legs silently bucking the air as she slipped into the tarry shadows of trees. A sandpiper hopped along the river's edge, picking the ground for bugs with its needlethin beak.

At the top of the ravine we stopped to rest. Stenciled against the sky was a faraway mountain, and on its summit, like a plume of volcanic ash, hung a gray cloud. The riverbottom blackened as the last light of day crept up the ravine walls; the stream turned to a vague shape in the darkness below. Walter stood up, spreading his shadow over the stream and across the plain. He laughed his gurgling laugh, then raised his arms and flapped them like a bird, casting a shadow black and winged. A giant raven.

"Little Snake," Walter said. "Little Snake," he repeated. And again: "Little Snake." As if by naming it he could keep it from fading, from dissolving in darkness.

A breeze blew; for a moment there was the rushing air and no other sound. When the wind settled, the burbling of the stream rose to our ears.

"Maybe next time we can go further," Walter said. "Maybe we can go around the next bend. I wonder if it's full of fish there."

"I took a look while you were breaking down your rod."

"Was it a good place?"

"It looked like a tropical beach. It had everything but palm trees."

Walter stared below, into the hidden watershed. I looked at the ground beside me. In the sandy soil were stamped footprints of birds, three-toed and faint.

"We'll find the stream again," Walter said. "I know we'll be back."

Beneath a bush I saw something yellow. I hooked it with a stick, dragged it into the light. A dead bird.

With his boot, Walter nudged the limp body and said, "Looks like he broke more than his head."

We stared at the bird, tiny and yellow; then we headed into the sagebrush, racing the creeping dusk as we followed the path toward the truck. Bats flew crookedly in the gloom, and stars winked like whitehot eyes in the coming night. After a few minutes I stopped and looked behind me. The ravine was gone, its water hidden below the flatness of the plain. All I could see was sagebrush, the darting bats, the stars above.

I almost smacked into Walter when I turned back to the path and started walking; he was bent over, studying something. I moved next to him, leaned over and looked. A black beetle, its wings splitting apart and snapping shut, climbed the stem of a columbine and crawled behind a white fold in the flower.

"Its wings open and close like a camera shutter," I said.

Walter fingered the petals apart and let the beetle drop into his cupped palm. "That's what it is—a camera. Aliens got worried and sent tiny cameras that look like beetles to spy on us."

I shoved him. "Why are the aliens so worried about us?"

"They were gonna come help us and make us smart. But one day they were watching our news on their spaceship TV, and the news said that more people get divorced than stay married. The aliens thought they might be wasting their time trying to help us. So they decided to wait and spy on us and see what the hell's going on down here." Walter opened his hand. The beetle dropped onto a petal and then slid down, disappearing into a paperwhite crease of the flower.

⇒18⇐

Wilderness

When we started hiking again, we passed a Forest Service sign that said we were crossing a boundary and entering a wilderness area. Vines climbed the post, bushes blocked the sign. I hadn't noticed it on the way in. I stopped and stared. Rust rimmed its edges, bulletholes puckered its center. Beyond the sign lay a pond furred with moss. Scraps of mist curled over the water.

Walter grabbed my shoulder and pointed ahead on the path. "Look," he whispered.

In a parkland of meadows and widespaced trees, elk stood with heads held high, staring at us. A bull moved to the front of the group; antlerless cows clustered behind him. When the wind died the world grew still and silent. In a woodsy place next to the path, a bonepile reflected light filtering through branches. Clouds like horses' manes stretched across the evening sky.

"Let's go," I said. "It'll be dark soon."

Walter shuffled a few steps forward, toward the elk. The herd trotted away, all animals moving as one. Then they stopped and turned to watch us. The bull thrust his head back and bugled: a trumpeting noise, alternating between squeaky and throaty, that echoed off faraway hills. From his flared nostrils and gaping mouth steam puffed into the cool air.

He stopped bugling, dropped his head, tossed it from side to side. His crown of antlers, with broad beams and pointy tines, scraped his muscled sides. The bull's movement spread through the other animals as a ripple passes over water. Together they turned and ran, their white rumps bright in the fading light. Then they stopped, turning to face us farther down the trail. And the pattern repeated: we walked down the path; the elk startled, ran, stopped to regroup. As if we were herding them across the plain, toward the truck.

Suddenly the herd turned and ran toward us. The antlered elk stopped and looked away. The cows watched us, pawing the ground, shuffling around the bull. A breeze carried their gamy stench.

Walter pointed toward a forested ridge. At its crest, silhouetted against the sky, stood a huge doglike animal. "Coyote?" Walter asked.

"Looks like a wolf, but there aren't supposed to be any around here."

Walter shook his head. "One time when my dad was watching football with his friends I heard him say he saw pawprints when he was out hunting. He thought they were from wolves. He said he hated them 'cause they kill elk. He said he'd shoot a wolf if he ever saw one."

The doglike shape turned and slinked away; it slipped between the shadows of trees, passed from sight. The bull elk bugled. From the path, toward a stand of timber it ran, its royal spread of antlers blending into a tangle of trees. The cows followed, their long legs kicking as they disappeared into the woods, endless and black.

"Wonder why the wolf let us see him," Walter said. "He must've wanted us to know he's here."

Walter grabbed a shirt out of his backpack—the sweatshirt with a roll of duct tape airbrushed on it that Nora had made him. He pulled it on, got stuck with it halfway down his arms. I helped him wriggle into it; then we followed the path to the ridge where the animal had stood. Walter dropped to his knees, stared at the ground. He stretched out his hand and put it next to a print embossed in the mud. It was the same size as his hand. He stood up, walked off the path toward a wall of trees, its top a sawtoothed edge that cut the sky.

"That's a wolf," Walter said. "And I'm gonna find it."

I grabbed his arm. "Don't be ridiculous. You're talking about a wolf. It's not like that wild horse you chased after. It's a predator. It kills."

"They eat people?"

"Wolves don't attack people for no reason. But it's stupid to go chasing after one."

Walter pulled away from me. I followed him between scattered trees and beyond that, into thick timber. "I don't know where you get these ideas of yours," I said. "Horse taming, wolf tracking. What's next—alligator wrestling?"

He ignored me and kept walking. As we passed into a small clearing, birds lifted off the ground: an explosion of noise and motion. Sage grouse. They looked like plump camouflaged chickens as they landed and ran clumsily through the brush.

"Crazy birds almost gave me a heart attack," Walter said.

Staring at the place in the bushes where the birds had disappeared, I remembered walking along a streambank with my dad. I was little—probably eight or nine. When we got to the top of a hill, we jumped some sage grouse. Their flapping wings were loud as gunshots. I grabbed my dad and hugged his leg. I told him I'd been so scared I thought my heart would quit. I started to apologize for being afraid; I thought that was what he wanted. He stopped me. Told me he'd been scared too: the noise had reminded him of a landmine exploding in Vietnam, he said. A mine he'd been in charge of finding but missed. A mine that had blown up his friend, turned him to shreds of flesh and puddles of blood. It was the only time my dad ever told me a Vietnam story sober.

I kicked at some grass, told Walter what I remembered.

He thumped my back. "You gotta let the trout eat that memory up." He started walking toward the trees, then stopped and stared into a stand of pines, shadowy with the coming night. The soft cooing of turtledoves drifted from the woods. He stepped from the light of the clearing into the inky forest. I followed him in. There was no path: tangles of deadfall covered the ground. Walter climbed over a downed tree; I hopped over and grabbed his shirt, steadying him as he wobbled. A twig snapped somewhere deep in the woods. I thought I saw movement between shadows.

"See that?" Walter whispered. "That's our wolf. He wants us to know he's here."

"Maybe he's telling us to get the hell away."

Walter tripped over another dead tree; its rotten bark sheared off as he rubbed against it. A spiderweb wrapped around my head as I ducked under a branch. I spat it out of my mouth, clawed it from my face.

Blackness surrounded us; the light of the sagebrush plain, fading quickly, was a dimming beacon beyond the forest. Walter stopped and sat down on a log. He coughed and wheezed. I sat down next to him. The ground below us was a mat of pinecones and needles, springy as a trampoline.

"What're you supposed to do if you see a wolf?" Walter asked.

"Don't follow it. That's probably rule number one."

"What if you're face-to-face with one? What should you do?"

"Nora knows more about them than I do. I'm no expert, but I think you'd have to be careful not to be threatening. You wouldn't want to corner it. You'd want to back away slowly—no sudden movements. Let it know you're not dangerous, and keep your eyes down and try to look submissive, I guess."

Walter slid off the log and stood up. He sank into the cushiony ground—seemed to shrink.

"We're running out of light," I said. "Pretty soon we won't be able to see the edge of the woods. Won't be able to find our way back."

"Do you have a flashlight?" Walter asked.

I shook my head.

"You didn't bring one?"

"If I'd known we were going to chase wolves through dark forests, I would've been sure to pack one."

Walter started walking again.

I grabbed his shirt. "Come on, Walt. Be reasonable."

"I just—"

There was sudden noise; the air vibrated with the fastflapping beat of wings. Something brushed the top of my head.

"More crazy birds," Walter said.

My chest was pounding so hard I was sure my heart would pop like a squeezed blister. I turned to watch the birds, black shapes passing into the night.

"Bats?" Walter asked.

"They fly too smoothly. They're ravens, I think."

Walter said, "I had a dream 'bout ravens once. Right after my accident, when I was out of the coma, I dreamed that a flock of ravens picked me to pieces. Tore my body apart. They flew in different directions with the pieces and scattered 'em all over the place."

"Sounds like a scary dream."

"It didn't end so badly. The ravens flew around and found all the pieces. Then they put 'em back together. But I looked weird. My parts were all mixed up."

I could barely make out the light at the edge of the forest. "You can tell me all about it back at the truck, Birdman." I put my hand on his shoulder.

"My dad told me something 'bout ravens," he said.

"Tell me back at the truck."

"He said they travel with wolves. They feed on the animals wolves kill—they get the leftovers. And the wolves like the ravens 'cause they lead 'em to prey. They circle over elk and deer to show the wolves where they are."

"Interesting, Walt. Tell you what: we'll talk about it when we get back to the truck." I pulled his arm.

He yanked away from my grip. "I want to keep going."

I looked behind me. The light was fading fast. "Don't be ridiculous."

But Walter wasn't listening; he had already walked on, slaloming between trees as he moved further into the dark wood. I crept behind him, steadying him as he slipped on rocks and tripped over logs. We reached a thicket that looked like handcrafted basketry, as if a forest gnome had woven the bushes together.

"Looks like we'll have to turn back," I said.

Walter dropped to his knees.

I pointed at the plaitwork of branches. "You can't get through that."

"It's not so thick down low. Come on, Mike, we'll crawl like wolves."

Walter wiggled through the bramble, pushing branches away with his helmet. I grabbed his legs and held them. "This is ridiculous!" I yanked on his legs, tried to pull him back from the bushes. He squirmed against my grip. "Walter, knock it off!" He kicked his legs; one of them slipped free and his boot glanced off my face. I tasted blood, metallic and salty, as I pressed a hand to my stinging lip. "Goddamnit, Walter! What the hell's wrong with you?" I let go of his other leg and walked around, kicking at branches bristling with pine needles. "If you want to chase after wolves you can do it on your own. I've had enough." I stomped off through the woods, heard myself say, "I wish you'd quit being so fucking stupid." I punched a tree, felt my hand shred against its bark, as abrasive as a cheese grater. I stuck my torn and swelling knuckles into my mouth as I paced in circles, walking off the rest of my anger. Walter had disappeared behind the bushes. I dropped down and followed him through. Thorns tugged at my clothes, scratched my skin. I closed my eyes as I struggled against tangled twigs that held me like a net. With a final heave I burst through.

I opened my eyes. I was in a place free of trees and brush, covered with moss. Walter was walking across the clearing. At the base of a slope was a rock wall, and in that wall was a gap that looked like the entrance to a cave. Starlight leaked through an opening in the forest canopy. The moon was hidden behind trees. In the center of the clearing was a boulder webbed with cracks, as if it had been dropped from a great height, or struck by lightning. Moss greenly caulked the seams of the rock, and in one wide crack a tree was rooted. A tiny tree, erratic and perfect, like a bonsai. As if the clearing were a garden, fenced with bushes and carpeted plush with moss, where a hermit in the dark of the forest cultivated strange plantlife.

I saw a huge pawprint, pressed into a patch of mud and filled with rainwater. Next to the print something gleamed. I kneeled down, parted a tuft of grass, saw a bone. I noticed them all around: bones halfburied, hidden by grass and moss. Before me was a headless elk skeleton, grass growing tall between its slatted ribs.

Walter walked across the clearing, through the bonestrewn grass, toward a skull. As he bent down to touch it, I heard a muffled sound like puppies whimpering. He grabbed the skull and tried to yank it from the earth. The ground next to him sloped, dropping toward the cave. As the skull popped free, Walter tottered and fell. Slid on his belly down a steep and grassy hill, landed in front of the cave.

"You all right?" I said as I ran across the clearing.

No answer.

"*Walter!*"

I saw him as I reached the edge of the slope. He was lying facedown.

"Walter?"

I slid down the hill. Landed next to him. I touched his neck, felt for a pulse. Still he hadn't moved.

"Did you hear the pups?" he whispered, as if being careful not to disturb something better left sleeping.

"Are you hurt?"

"I think the wolf's a mom wolf. I heard her pups. They sounded like little dogs."

"Why didn't you answer me?"

He rolled over, his good eye fixing on me, his sightless one wandering, as if trying to focus on something in the sky. As if searching for the absent moon. "I did just like you said. I was quiet and I didn't make no sudden movements. I sat real still so the mom wolf would know I wasn't gonna hurt her or her puppies. When I looked into the cave I saw lots of wolf eyes. Little bright eyes and one pair of big green eyes."

I looked into the cave, saw blackness only. "Now can we get the hell out of here?"

Walter stood up, used the palm of his hand to wipe blood from a scratch on his cheek. "I did just like you said. 'Cept for one thing. I had the wolf cornered. Had it trapped in the cave 'cause I was blocking the entrance.... Unless the cave has a backdoor. Maybe that's why the wolf didn't attack me. We should try to find the backdoor. It might be on the other side."

"Walter!"

"You're boring sometimes, Mike."

I helped him up the slope. We crossed the boneyard, grass and moss growing from the earth that humped above buried carcasses. In front of the thicket we dropped to our hands and knees, and as we pushed through, I heard the muffled yelping sound again.

The forest was a dark jumble. There was no light, no sign of the edge of the woods. "I have no idea where we are," I said. The adrenaline of my anger and fear had drained away. I asked Walter if he had heard what I'd said before I crawled through the bushes. He told me he had.

"Look," I said, "you're going to get yourself seriously hurt one of these days. You frustrate the hell out of me sometimes."

He tilted his head, stared at me a moment. "You seem pretty stupid to me sometimes, Mike."

We fell silent. There was the distant croak of frogs and no other sound.

"We better get out of here," I said after a few minutes.

"I can find the way out. I'll show you." Walter slithered over a log, then ducked under some branches, weaving his way through the forest. I heard a twig snap behind us and turned to look. I saw nothing but sensed something was watching us. Walter led; I walked behind him, helping him get his balance when he stumbled over deadfall and slipped on mossy stones.

Ahead, gray light filtered through the trees, and a sickle moon cut a bright slash in the sky, dimming the stars around it. Walter looked at me and grinned. "Told you I'd find the way."

As we walked away from the trees, onto the sagecovered plain, I said, "What did you want with that skull, anyway?"

Walter held up something small and white.

"A tooth?"

"Not just any old tooth. It's an elk's eyetooth. They're made out of ivory. They're like mini tusks."

"Ivory?"

"My dad taught me that," said Walter. "He keeps the eyeteeth from all the elk he kills in a cigarbox. He can pick any tooth out of the box and tell you exactly which elk it came from. He'll tell you how big the elk was, how long he stalked it, what gun he used to shoot it."

Walter handed me the tooth. I rubbed it between my fingers. It was smooth as soap.

We found the path and stepped onto it.

"I'm gonna put the tooth on a necklace," Walter said. "Or maybe I'll put it on a ring and wear it all the time. It'll remind me of the wolf."

I handed the tooth back to Walter, feeling its cool smoothness pass into his hand, warm and leathery. We walked under the stars. The trail glowed in the light of a lean moon, skinny but bright.

"I've decided something," Walter said as we neared the truck. "I'm gonna marry Donna."

"You didn't sound so sure about it yesterday."

"Just now I decided."

"You nervous about it?"

"Even more scared than when I saw the wolf eyes back there."

We stepped over stagnant puddles, choked with algae. From a patch of clover came the buzzing of bees, their hum like a radio show with the volume turned too low to make out words. We hiked through flinty rubble. The stones sparked when they rubbed together.

"I'm scared like shit to marry Donna," Walter said. He stopped, turned to look at me. Stars prickled whitely in the sky above. "Donna told me she loves me. It might not work out too good but maybe it will." He shrugged his shoulders. "That's good enough to try, I guess."

PART FOUR

≈19≈

Lex

It was the middle of July. The sun, burning in a hazy sky, heated the air by late morning. Clouds bulged and blackened, covering the valley with shadows; and between the shadows, where sun reached the earth, patches of ground shined like lamplit windows. Almost every afternoon, dry thunder echoed in the mountains and clouds swelled, but on the darkening earth below only drizzle fell. Leaves hung limp from thirsty plants, and their dry stems hummed in the wind. Lightning strikes sparked fires and breeze provoked the flames; the scant rain did nothing to slow them. Either firefighters doused them or the fires burned themselves down to nothing. Wildfires rioted in distant valleys; Kingfisher had so far been spared. The flames and smokeplumes could be seen only from the tops of mountains, but traces of the fires were everywhere. Haze scummed the sky like pollution in a city. And you could taste the soot: it was as salty as a seabreeze.

One dry and smoky afternoon Walter called me. "Don't let her take my bike away. It's all I got. Please—"

"Slow down," I said.

Walter calmed down, the story came out. When he finished, I called Nancy. A man had stopped by her office that afternoon to tell her that Walter had been swerving his bike all over the road and had almost gotten hit by a UPS truck. Nancy had fielded comments and complaints about Walter's driving for years, and she'd finally reached a decision: he had to stop riding his bike. It was a matter of safety, she told me. A matter of common sense. She wasn't going to sit by and do nothing while he got himself in a wreck.

After I got off the phone with Nancy I called Walter back.

"Sounds like you almost got killed today."

"I always wear my helmet."

"That's not going to help you if you get hit by a truck. What about taking the bus around town?"

"I never understand those stupid bus schedules."

He had a point: deciphering a Kingfisher bus schedule was more complicated than calculus. "What about walking?" I asked. "It'd be good exercise."

"How would you like it if somebody took your truck away?"

"Aren't you worried about getting hurt?"

"My life would be shit without the bike. Everything got taken away. I want to keep one thing."

I was quiet a moment. "Look, Walt, Nancy understands that—"

"She's gonna let me keep it? I promise to be careful! Thank—"

"Hold on. You have to get your dad to sign a release form saying it's okay for you to keep it."

"But he won't even talk to me."

"He's still your legal guardian."

"How am I gonna get him to sign the form?"

"We'll ask him."

"That's crazy," Walter yelled. His voice crackled in the phone. I pulled the receiver away from my ear.

"You want to keep the bike?" I said. "Getting your dad to sign the form—that's the only way."

A few days later we drove from Kingfisher, away from roads that wound among mountains, onto a highway that stretched across the flat and spreading plains of central Wyoming. The everpresent wind lifted dustclouds that hovered over the sagebrush like a biblical plague, like a strange and destructive weather system born not of water but of dirt.

"What did my dad say on the phone?" Walter asked. "Does he want to see me?"

I hesitated a moment. "He didn't want us to come."

"But he let us anyway?"

A mass of rainclouds billowed above the dust on the horizon ahead of us. "I can't lie to you, Walt. I offered him money. I thought it was the only way he'd agree to look the form over."

"Did he say he'd sign it?"

I started to say something, stopped. A tumbleweed wheeled across the road. After a moment: "He told me we could come see him and he'd look the form over—that's all. He didn't agree to sign it."

"What're we gonna do? He's gotta sign it for me to keep my bike."

"You'll have to talk him into it."

Across the flatness of the prairie, clouds drifted and bulged. There was the steady throb of the truck engine and the hum of rubber as tires slapped asphalt. Tiny hailstones scratched against the windshield.

Walter said, "I wonder how come he'd let you pay for us to see him and show him the form but he wouldn't just sign it. We could've mailed it to him."

"Maybe he's afraid of letting you do something that could get you hurt. I think he wants us to explain in person what it means, why it's important. I think he's worried about you."

"He's got a weird way of showing it."

A seam of lightning opened in the sky. I blinked to clear the afterimage from my eyes. Rain fell as a light mist, then thickened. Plump drops smacked the truck; water smeared in waves across the windshield.

"It was nice of you to pay your money to help me out," Walter said.

"Forget it. I didn't earn it."

Lightning flashed, showing distant mountains quivering and lurching behind sheets of rain. As if the storm were creating the peaks, shaping them as it tugged at the plains, pulling the earth skyward in points of stone.

Walter was quiet a few minutes, then said, "Are you and Nora mad at each other?"

I looked away from the road, at Walter's face, his right eye riveted on me.

" 'Cause when I saw you and Nora last week it seemed like you were mad at each other."

I stared out the windshield, focused on the road. "Is it that obvious?"

"When I broke my head it got hard for me to understand what people are saying—my ears hear words, but when people talk too fast my brain don't know what they mean. So I look at their faces. Their faces tell me what they mean."

Gusts of wind moved across the sagebrush like waves on a lake. I sped up the windshield wipers as water rippled down the glass. I looked over at Walter, then past him.

We'd driven out of the storm by the time we reached the town where Walter's father lived. The sun was low and bright in the afternoon sky. Trailers and sagging houses covered treeless hillsides strewn with mine tailings, showing naked bedrock where the earth had been stripped bare. Oil pumps worked up and down like giant sewing machines stitching the ground.

Walter gave me vague directions to his dad's house; we circled through town a few times before finding it: a doublewide trailer on a plot at the edge of the prairie. As we walked toward the front door, pieces of crumpled paper blew past us. Sprigs of dead grass tufted up from the baldish lawn like failed hair implants.

Lex, Walter's father, was a thickbodied man with grease in the creases of his hands and black gunk under his fingernails. His T-shirt stuck to his chest like Saran Wrap. After shaking my hand, without looking at Walter, he said, "Go outside, son. Need to talk to Mike."

Walter went outside and wandered across the yard, stopping at a shed with a coyote pelt hanging from its door. I followed Lex into the living room. He dropped onto a couch, clicked on the TV, and scrolled through the stations until he found a football game. I didn't think it was football season; I wondered if the game was being rebroadcast. I sat down in a chair with white puffs of stuffing sneaking through the seams.

"Who's your favorite team?" Lex asked.

"I'm not much of a fan."

"Play any football when you were a kid?"

I shook my head.

"See that trophy up there," Lex said, pointing to a bookshelf. The pictures and books surrounding it were felted with dust. The trophy gleamed as if Lex had polished it just before I walked through the door. He said, "We were state champs my junior year in high school. Coulda played real college ball, but busted my knee in practice two weeks before the season started my senior year. Spent the whole goddamned season on the bench. Didn't get no scholarship offers. Ended up at a community college. Played a season for 'em."

Lex grunted. "We lost every single game. Didn't even have a coach for most of the games—he left after our first couple losses. I didn't go back to college the next year. Couldn't stand bein' part of such a pathetic team. And without football, there wasn't nothin' there for me."

The voice of an announcer on TV rose to a highpitched wail. Lex and I looked away from each other, stared at the screen.

"Was strollin' down memory lane," Lex said. "Missed the goddamned touchdown." He smacked his open hand on the arm of the couch as he watched the instant replay. The announcers argued about whether the receiver had had both his feet inbounds when he caught the pass. The scene played again, this time in slow motion.

"Whadaya think, Mike? Looks like his left foot ain't in. See—right there!" Lex jumped up from the couch, pointed at the screen. Plopped back down and stared at me.

I said nothing.

"I'll be goddamned," Lex said. "You don't like football, do you."

"I really don't."

We stared at each other.

There was a pause on TV as a break began. In the silence that came before the commercial, Lex said, "You gay?"

I laughed a few times, tried to stop but couldn't. My laughter blended with a blaring beer commercial. I said, "Are you kidding me? You think because I don't like football I might be gay?"

"Why do you spend so much time with my son?"

"What exactly are you asking me?"

"I don't know no decent guys that don't like football. What'm I supposed to think? You like any sports?"

"I ski and mountain bike, if that helps."

"Those ain't sports. Not real ones, anyway."

"How do you define a sport?"

"This is my goddamned house," Lex roared. "Don't get smart with me." He glared at me a moment, then said, "You like girls or not?"

"Love 'em, Lex."

He started to rise from his seat. Sat back down. Neither of us said anything for a few minutes. Finally, Lex said, "You got a girlfriend?"

"I'm married."

Lex's face softened. He smiled. His teeth were white as chalk against his grimy skin. He smacked the armrest of the couch; a puff of dust floated into the air. I watched the particles spiraling in a shaft of light that crept between drawn curtains. Lex laughed—a chesty sound releasing tension—then said,

"Well that's a relief." He stood up and walked toward the kitchen, thumping me on the back as he passed. Almost knocked the wind out of me. "Had me worried for a minute there," he said, and again he laughed.

I heard a refrigerator door open, then Lex's voice—muffled, as if his head were in the refrigerator: "Don't tell me—you just drink natural shit, right? Got some orange juice. You wanna glass?"

"I'd rather have a beer."

"Well now—you like women and beer," Lex said as he came out of the kitchen and handed me a cold can of Budweiser. "Guess we'll get along just fine after all."

He sank back into the couch and we stared at the TV. A band was playing in the center of the football field.

"Hate these halftime shows," Lex said as he hit the mute button on the remote. The band marched on, silently.

Neither of us said anything for a few minutes. I cleared my throat, the noise as loud as if I'd shouted. Lex finally said, "You probably think I'm a bad person 'cause I don't keep in touch with Walter."

"I didn't come here to judge you."

"I did the best I could with him after he had his accident. Wasn't easy." After a pause: "Did the goddamned best I could."

For a few minutes, silence.

"I'll be payin' off that boy's medical bills forever," Lex said in a tired voice. "I'm over a hundred thousand dollars in debt. Before we got Walter on Social Security and Medicaid, insurance paid a lot of them bills—hell, most of 'em—but there was still plenty left over. Some of them specialists he had to see? Insurance wouldn't cover 'em. I'd take my boy to see one doctor, that doctor'd send us to see another one—and that doctor'd send us somewhere else." Lex pounded the arm of the couch. "They got a fuckin' racket goin'! By the time it was all over I was a hundred grand in the hole. Any idea what that means for a guy like me? I work at an autoparts store. Got promoted to manager few years back. And that's 'bout as good a job as I'll ever get. Make monthly payments on them medical bills, but it's all interest, hardly any principal. I'll be in my grave before that debt's paid off. . . . That's why I took that money from you. It ain't for me. It's to help pay them bills."

Lex stared at the floor, squinting at the carpet, ragged and stained. He was quiet a moment, then looked up and continued: "Wife died few years back. Walter probably told you."

I nodded.

Lex looked me in the eye. Looked away. "Just a little lump on her breast. No bigger'n the tip of my pinkie." He held his finger up; we both stared at it. "Always teased her when she did them breast self-exams in the shower," he said. "Told her I'd be happy to do 'em for her. Hell, I squeezed her titties all the time, anyway." He tried to smile. "When she found the lump she was real worried. Wanted to go to the doctor right away. Wanted me to take her the same day she found it."

Lex fell silent. We stared at the TV, watched the band marching without sound, their instruments gleaming in the sun of some faraway city.

"Told her not to worry 'bout it," Lex said. "Told her we already owed them doctors and hospitals everything. Didn't need to be rackin' up more debt. . . . Guess I just couldn't see how somethin' so small could be so dangerous. Didn't look like cancer to me. Didn't feel like cancer. Not that I had any idea what a tumor should look like or feel like—guess I just didn't want to believe it really was cancer."

Lex fell silent a few minutes, then said, "She finally talked me into lettin' her see a doctor—'bout a month later. . . . It was so far advanced they couldn't stop it. Tried chemo but it didn't help. Just slowed it down a little. Couldn't be stopped, they said. I asked the doctor if it would've made any difference if she'd come in a month earlier. He said probably not. But there was a chance it might've. . . . A chance it might've—I gotta live with that."

Lex paused, then looked me in the eye and said, "Right after the funeral I stopped callin' Walter. Don't know why—just did. He's my boy and

I love him, but I just can't see him or talk to him no more. I can't look at him or hear his voice without thinkin' 'bout who he was. Who he should be now."

Lex stared into the TV. The band marched on, zigzagging across the field like an army of insects.

"What the hell you come here for anyway?" he asked. "You said somethin' 'bout Walter wantin' to keep his bike? Somethin' 'bout his social worker tryin' to take it away?"

"You know Nancy, his caseworker?"

"A real bitch from what I remember. She's so goddamned scared that boy'll get hurt she'd lock him up to keep him safe."

"She means well."

"That why she don't want him to ride his bike?"

"She's afraid he'll get in a wreck."

"And he wants to keep it?" Lex asked.

I nodded.

"Can he get around without it? Don't they got buses in Kingfisher?"

I looked at Lex. Met his eyes. "He can take buses or walk to get around town, but it's not the same."

"What the hell's the difference long as he gets where he needs to go?" Lex asked. He frowned. "Is it dangerous? I never seen it."

"It's a big fourwheeled rig. He can't ride it on sidewalks—takes up too much space. Has to ride it on the roads. Most locals are patient with him and give him room. But he could get hit—especially by a tourist cruising around, not paying attention."

Lex looked in the direction of the TV, but past it. "What's the paper?" he asked. "You said I need to sign a paper if he's gonna keep the bike?"

I pulled the form from my pocket, unfolded it, handed it to Lex. He snatched it from my hand.

"If you sign this, Walter can keep the bike," I said. "If you don't, Nancy'll take it away."

"That simple, huh?"

"That's how it is."

Lex put on a pair of crooked reading glasses and studied the form. Squinted at it. "Says right here I'd be takin' responsibility for whatever happens."

"That's right."

"If I sign this, and Walter keeps the bike and gets in a wreck, know what that'll do? I already got enough guilt to last me." Lex took off his glasses, dropped the paper on the couch next to him. "Does it really mean that much to Walter to keep the bike?"

"Why don't you ask him," I said.

I went outside, found Walter sitting on a stack of cinderblocks. He was staring at a car, its sides bare of paint and its windows blasted opaque by windblown grit.

"When I was a little boy my dad and I used to drive this car around," Walter said. "I got to sit on his lap and steer. We'd drive with the radio up loud but we'd slow down and turn the radio off when we got near our driveway so my mom wouldn't get mad. My dad said he was gonna give it to me when I grew up so I could drive it."

Sunlight leaked through the trees, and an afternoon breeze cooled the air. A honeybee buzzed around Walter, circling his helmet.

"What happened in there?" he asked.

"We talked."

" 'Bout me?"

"About a lot of things."

"Is he gonna let me keep the bike?"

"You need to go see him."

"Think he'll say no?"

"Talk to him, Walt."

"What should I say?"

"Tell him what the bike means to you. Just tell him what you told me."

I sat on the stack of cinderblocks and waited, watching plastic bags flag off a barbwire fence. A paperscrap blew across my feet and lifted into the air; it hovered ghostlike, caught in crosscurrents of wind. By the time Walter came out of the house, shadows oozed across the ground like motor oil, and nighthawks circled and swooped, plucking insects from the violet sky.

"My dad wants to see you before we leave," Walter said.

As I stepped into the kitchen, I heard Lex yell: "Grab us a couple a cold ones."

I pulled two Budweisers from the fridge, took them into the living room. The TV was off. I stopped at the edge of the room and stared into the shadows. As my pupils opened in the dark, I saw Lex sitting on the couch, back bent, head slumped forward. I opened a beer, handed it to him. He grabbed the can and took a gulp, then turned on a lamp. A pool of light illuminated his face, red and swollen. I sat down.

"So hard to see him like he is," Lex said in a scratchy voice. "I just keep thinkin' 'bout how he should be 'stead of how he really is."

Lex stood up, and from the shelf that held his football trophy, he grabbed a picture. Dropped it in my lap. It was a shot of Walter in a football uniform. He was kneeling in the grass, his helmet cradled under his arm. His hair was cropped close in a crewcut.

"My boy was a helluva running back. Broke some of the rushing records at his school. Woulda made the high school team no problem. Bet he woulda gone to college on a scholarship. . . . Always said them whitewater rafting trips was too dangerous. Tried to talk him out of goin' the summer it happened. I tried, but he wouldn't listen. My boy always did have a stubborn streak."

I laughed and said, "Well that hasn't changed. He's still stubborn as hell. When Walter decides he wants to do something he does it."

We fell silent a moment. Through an open window I heard crickets clicking in the dusk.

Lex took the picture back, stared at it. "This is my son. This is Walter. I don't know who that is." He pointed into the kitchen, toward the backyard; then he threw the picture against a wall. Glass sparkled as it exploded, sprinkling the carpet and furniture. "I don't know who that goddamned freak is! He's not my son."

Lex dropped onto the couch, buried his face in cupped hands.

After a few minutes I said, "Did Walter tell you he learned how to flyfish?"

Lex looked up. "I remember his doctor givin' him a flyrod when he was in the hospital."

"He taught himself how to cast. Practiced every day for a whole summer. When the weather got bad he went inside an empty warehouse. He told me he asked some guy in a flyfishing shop to help him learn. The guy told him he'd never be able to do it. He can cast better than me now, and I've been at it my whole life."

Lex said nothing.

"You like to fish?" I asked.

"Use a spinnin' rod. Not much of a flyfisherman."

"Maybe you could go on a trip with me and Walt sometime."

Lex dropped his head back into his hands.

I said, "You know, you're right: the Walter in that picture's gone. There's a different person in his place. But I think he's worth getting to know. And he's probably no more fucked up than the rest of us, Lex. You and me—we just hide it better."

"You don't know a goddamned thing about me," Lex said in a muffled voice, hands squeezed tight against his face, his palms like slabs of ham, his fingers fat as sausages.

As I stood to leave, Lex handed me the form for the bike. I stuffed it into my pocket without looking at it. My shoes crunched crumbs of glass as I walked through the house. I stepped outside, shut the door. Sunlight slanted across the yard, dust motes catching the brief light. They whorled and gleamed like galaxies, then vanished in the dusk.

Walter was in the truck, waiting, when I climbed in. "Well?" he said.

I turned the key and revved the gas. "Well what?"

"Did he sign the paper or not?"

I pulled the form from my pocket, switched on the domelight. The truck trembled under the thrum of the engine. I unfolded the paper. At the bottom, scrawled in tiny letters, was Lex's signature.

≈20≈

Safety First

A few days later Nancy called to say that Walter had been fired from his job and had crashed his bike into a car. The woman in the Lexus he'd hit had told Nancy that Walter was flying down a hill, out of control, riding in the middle of the road. Nancy said that Walter was in her office and wanted to talk to me.

Walter, wearing his Spam T-shirt, was staring out the window when I got there, and didn't look at me as I walked in. Nancy stood to shake my hand; she was short enough that I could look down on her part, where undyed roots showed darkly under silvery blond hair. She shut the door, blocking the noise outside her office. In the sudden silence that followed, I heard the faint rasping of Walter's breath. Nancy dropped into her chair and pressed her hands to her desk, then tapped the tips of her short square fingers on its top. She glanced at me before opening a manila file and reading two reports: a police account of Walter's bike accident and his termination notice from Kmart.

Walter said nothing; he pulled at his shirt, knotting it in his balled left fist. When Nancy finished reading, the three of us sat in silence. Nancy looked at me. I glanced at Walter. He was staring out the window.

Finally, Nancy said, "What's going on, Walter?"

He turned from the window, tilted his head, and looked at Nancy.

His helmet shifted and slipped a few inches down the greasy dome of his hair.

"Stealing at work, driving your bike like a maniac—that's not like you. That's not the Walter I know."

He lifted his shoulders, let them sag.

"You were doing so well. You were getting good performance reviews at Kmart, you had a girlfriend, you were talking about marriage. What happened?"

"Two guys that I work with . . . worked with . . . they made fun of me."

"They teased you?"

Walter fell silent a few minutes; finally he explained what had happened. He'd been getting a candy bar from a vending machine, he told us. He heard people talking in the breakroom, arguing about whose turn it was to work with him. They flipped a coin. Walter heard it land. "Heads," one of them said. Then Walter heard the guy say he should've picked tails because he hated working with the retard, hated his helmet, hated the way he tilted his head, hated his laugh.

When Bob—the guy who'd lost the bet—met Walter at the pharmacy and they started to open boxes and to stock the shelves with aspirin bottles, Bob pretended he was happy to be working with Walter. He kept telling him jokes.

"Dirty jokes 'bout penises and stuff," Walter said. "When he finished a joke he'd laugh and smack me on the back. I kept staring at him, and I tried not to tilt my head like he said he hated, and I tried to clear my throat before I laughed, but he wouldn't look at me."

Walter stared outside. Above the mountains hovered bulbous clouds, like giant heads of cauliflower. Rays of sunlight slanted past them, brightening their puffy edges.

"I'm sorry that happened," Nancy said. "But I still don't understand why you stole . . . what was it . . . a CD."

Walter told us that when he got done stocking and was on his break, he went into the music department and put a CD in his coatpocket. The alarm went off when he went home at the end of the day.

"You didn't know there was one of those security strips on it?" I asked.

Walter shrugged his shoulders.

Nancy said, "That's just not like you, Walter."

He tilted his head and stared at her. "Maybe you don't know me so good."

Nancy squinched her eyes. She was quiet a few minutes; then in a small and tired voice she said, "What about the wreck? What happened there? The woman you hit said you were riding right down the center of the road, totally out of control."

Again he shrugged his shoulders. "Guess I was going too fast."

"She said something else, Walter. It's not in the police report. It's something she told me in confidence. Something that really worries me. She said the last thing she saw before she swerved off the road was your face. She said she saw it clearly and can't forget it. She said you were smiling."

Walter looked away. "Maybe she imagined that."

"She was sure of it. She said you looked calm. Almost happy."

"Why would I be happy to wreck my bike?"

Nancy leaned across her desk. "You tell me—why would that make you happy?"

Walter glanced at me, looked away. Shadows moved across the office floor like spilled ink. After a few minutes he said, "I won't steal nothing at my next job. And I'll be more careful on my bike. I promise."

Nancy sighed, then asked Walter to step outside so she could talk to me in private. Walter stumbled as he passed my chair; he put his hand on my shoulder to steady himself. Through my shirt I felt the heat in his fingertips.

"What do you make of that?" Nancy asked after Walter left her office and shut the door.

"There's something he's not telling us. People making fun of him—

that's never been a big deal for Walt. He's strong that way. I don't buy his story."

"I don't either," Nancy said. "Will he tell you what's really going on?"

"He might."

"Will you tell me what he says? I want to understand what happened. I want to help him, Mike."

As she rose to shake my hand, Nancy formed her lips into a tiny, puckered butthole of a mouth, then spat out air. "I never should've agreed to let Walter keep the bike if his father signed the form. To be honest, I didn't think you'd be able to pull it off. Didn't think his father would lift a finger to do something for Walter. He probably did it just to spite me."

"I'm not so sure about that. But I'm glad he signed it. I'm glad Walter has the bike."

"You're kidding, right?"

"It's all he has, Nancy."

"He was lucky this time. He could get killed."

"Walter understands that every time he rides that thing he's taking a risk."

Nancy gave a disgusted grunt. "And you think he's capable of making that choice?" She shook her head and looked away from me. "You know, I could just tear up that form and take the bike away. I could do that right now."

"At least think about it first. Think about what it'll do to him. He believes it's the only thing he has left that hasn't been taken from him."

"If I let him keep the bike and he gets in a wreck . . . I take pride in my safety record with my clients. I've always placed their security above everything else. Jesus," Nancy said, shaking her head. She plopped back down in her chair, scooted it away from her desk, then stretched out her legs and laced her fingers together. "When I was studying for my master's in social work I was taught to follow rules and policies. The safety of the clients above all else—that's what the professors said was the most important thing. 'Emotions have a place in social work, but it is not a promi-

nent one.' Those were some of the last words I heard before I graduated."
Nancy looked at me and blinked hard.

⌒

"I messed up, huh?" Walter said. We were driving away from town,
toward mountains. I stuck my head out the window. It was raining somewhere: I smelled wet pine on the wind.

"You made some mistakes."

"Are you mad at me?"

"It's your life, Walt."

We drove in silence toward low lumps of hills, close to mountains, far
from town. At the end of the road we parked, then walked toward a canyon.
We sat down on a boulder under the gray and swirling sky, bloated with the
moisture of a growing storm. The wind carried spits of rain.

"Want to tell me what really happened?" I said.

Walter looked at me, tilted his head.

"I don't believe that you got fired from your job and crashed your
bike because some guy made fun of you. That's bullshit."

He said nothing, looked away. He opened his backpack and pulled
out the sweatshirt Nora had airbrushed. With a hooked finger he traced
the outline of the duct tape roll. "Does Nora know I got fired?" he asked.

"I haven't told her."

He took off his helmet and put the sweatshirt on; I helped him stuff
his arms into it and pull it over his head.

Through a gap in the clouds a patch of clear sky opened and the sun
blinked, a bright pupil in an eye of blue.

"I'm scared, Mike." Clouds covered the sky, blocked the sun. Walter
frowned and said, "You never seem scared."

"I hide it well."

"Bullshit. You don't got nothing to be afraid of." He fell silent a moment, then said, "Tell me what you're scared of. Then I'll tell you what really happened."

"Are you making a deal?"

"Tell me first, then I'll tell you."

"Nora's pregnant, Walt. I'm going to be a father. . . . I'm afraid to bring a baby into a world that might take its parents away. I don't want my child to have to grow up without parents, to have to go through what I went through." I looked into the black yawn of the canyon and said, "I'm scared my child will be someone else I care about that the world can kill. That's what I'm really afraid of."

I looked at Walter. He stared back.

"Does that make sense?"

He laughed. "I didn't understand what you said. But I looked at your face and your mouth twitched. When you talk 'bout your parents your mouth twitches."

"I guess I didn't explain very well," I said. "Want me to try again?"

"You told the truth. That was your part of the deal."

From the bruised and soggy sky a shaft of light fell onto a canyon rim. Trees and boulders glowed as if a searchlight were passing over them. Then clouds bulked up, and as quickly as it had appeared, the light was gone.

"Now it's time for my part of the deal," said Walter.

"You don't have to tell me if you don't want to."

"I don't break deals."

Light escaped the storm: this time not in a beam; it leaked from the edges of the sky. The stormlight seemed of another spectrum entirely, of another sun.

Walter looked at me. "I was scared for Mitch. Who's gonna help Mitch find the things that he hides so people can't steal 'em?"

"Are you afraid for Mitch or for yourself?"

"If I marry Donna and move out of my apartment, then I won't have Mitch to tell me when I'm burning dinner."

"Donna can help you with that."

Walter stared at me. "I thought if I got fired then Nancy wouldn't let me get married." He looked away. After a few moments he told me he'd been mad when Nancy didn't stop him from getting married. He started riding his bike around, going faster and faster. He saw a hill and pedaled as hard as he could, and he knew it was dangerous but he didn't care. He heard the wind, and the world was a blur, and he was going so fast he forgot about everything. And he felt better than he had in a long time, he told me.

Before his accident he'd spent a couple weeks riding his mountain bike in the desert around Moab, he said. He was careful, following his friends who knew the trails, who had ridden there before. But on the last day of the trip he called his girlfriend and they got in a fight on the phone; he went off on his own and rode so fast he forgot about their argument.

Walter said, "Nancy don't understand. All she cares 'bout is safety first."

The canyon was black and calm and strangely bright.

Walter looked at me and said, "If I marry Donna I don't know how it'll work out."

"Nobody ever does."

"But Donna and me—if we're gonna make a lot of mistakes with our broken heads, then maybe we shouldn't get married." Walter kicked a rock. It rolled through the dust. "Look at you: you fight with Nora all the time. You shouldn't tell me what to do."

"You're right, Walt. I've made a mess of my marriage. I'm not trying to talk you into marrying Donna. I'm just trying to find out what you really want."

Waves of light broke through the clouds and glowed in the canyon and around us. Every bush and boulder seemed to brighten, absorbing the light, then scattering it back into the blackness of the storm.

"I was mad 'bout Donna when I crashed my bike. 'Bout her broken head. You know how it happened?"

Walter told me that Donna had been driving her car when she was sixteen. Her parents had given her the car for her birthday. A drunk driver hit her.

Walter said, "The other day after we finished dinner and we were sitting on the couch, Donna told me that after her accident she used to wish every single day that she'd died instead of having to live with a broken head. She told me she still thought that sometimes, but since she met me she didn't think 'bout it so much anymore."

The light that had found its way through the clouds disappeared, and a mist began to fall. Wind thrashed the sky, slanting thin drops of rain.

Walter said, "When I was a boy my parents took me to church and they told me there was God and I believed it. I don't believe it no more. I don't care if I go to hell like they said I would in church. I don't believe in no God that lets things like that happen. He should just kill people like me and Donna 'stead of letting us live. . . . He lets us come back but he don't tell us why and nobody in the world wants us back anyway. My dad signed that form for my bike but he wouldn't look at me. I stared at his face when he was talking and I knew he wished I would've died."

The wind kicked up, scattering crisp leaves that crackled like cellophane.

After a few minutes Walter said, "Are you gonna tell Nancy what I told you?"

"Do you want me to?"

"Nancy's not my friend like you are, but she's always helped me. I don't know how to explain it to her. You tell her what I mean."

"I'll do my best."

"Do you promise? Is it a deal?"

I nodded that it was.

We sat quietly, looking out at the canyon, a dark gap splitting parched and smoking hills, where wildfire had burned. Walter said, "Did you forget what yesterday was? It was my birthday."

"Shit, Walt. I'm terrible at remembering stuff like that."

He tilted his head. Stared at me. "Know what, though? I don't care that it was my birthday. 'Cause my birthday's the day I was born."

I waited. . . . "And?"

"And when I was born I was somebody else. I was a different Walter. That Walter was smart and played football and his dad liked him."

I watched him as he stared into the canyon, rain spattering his helmet. "What do you think about celebrating the day you came out of your coma after the accident?" I asked.

"Why would I celebrate my accident?"

"The day you woke up from that coma the new Walter was born. And the new Walter is one hell of a fisherman. He deserves a celebration."

Walter was quiet for a few minutes. "Can we have a birthday party for the new Walter?"

"Tell you what: we'll call it your 'rebirthday party.'"

In a sudden blast of wind, rain lashed the earth. We walked away from the canyon, our footfalls silenced by the beating drops. It was the first wet storm in months. The moisture would be enough, I hoped, to slow the wildfires.

We tried to outrun the storm, but wind battered us, rain stung our eyes, and mud greased the ground. We stumbled like drunks; when the trail grew steep we sat down and slid. At the bottom of a hill we ducked under trees, but they offered no protection from the lashing wind, the pelting rain. As we reached the truck the storm exploded: lightning forked the sky, thunder boomed off canyon walls, plump raindrops poured down.

Soaked and laughing, Walter and I paused before climbing into the truck. We pressed our backs against the slippery metal and let water wash over us. We stared straight up, eyes blinded by rain, mouths open to catch the drops. With safety so close, it was easy to be brave, easy to challenge the storm.

After I dropped Walter off, I stopped by Nancy's office. I told her what he'd said—used my own words, tried to help her understand.

"Why can't he tell me those things himself?" Nancy asked. "Why can't he talk to me?"

"You're good at your job," I said. "And Walter knows you worry about him."

"But?"

"Try being his friend, too, for christsakes."

Nancy thumped her desk; piles of paper trembled. "I told you—that goes against everything I was taught. I have to leave emotion out of it. My relationship with Walter is professional. I'm not supposed to be his friend; I'm his caseworker."

"I think you can be both."

Again she hit her desk. "There are professional boundaries that have to be maintained, Mike. Do you understand what that *means*? Do you understand my *responsibilities*?"

"Look, I didn't study social work in college and I don't know shit about professional boundaries. I don't even have a job. But what I do know is that Walter doesn't just need your services as a social worker. He's more than that."

Nancy clenched her mouth, then spat out air. She threw her hands up, sank into her chair.

I took a few breaths, looked into her eyes. "Take him out of town somewhere—he's more comfortable away from a lot of people. Go for a walk with him and talk to him. Be honest—he respects that more than anything else. And listen to him. Really *listen* to what he's saying. Show him you don't just care about his health and his finances—show him you care about who he is. Let him know he has something to offer you. Let him know he's not just some pathetic disabled guy. Let him know he matters. . . . That's where it starts. That's where you'll gain his trust. And once you have that you'll have his friendship. And when you have that you'll not only have given him what he really needs—if you're lucky you'll take something for yourself. And if you're as empty and fucked up as I am, you won't understand how you've found it or why you have it, and you'll know you don't deserve it, but you'll thank God, or the world or whatever, every fucking day of your life . . . "

I realized I was shouting. "I got carried away." I stared outside. Raindrops bore into the ground, drummed against the roof. I wiped my eyes—realized I was crying. "I don't think I've cried in front of anyone since my mom died," I said.

After a few minutes Nancy looked up from her desk, met my eyes. "When was that?"

"I was fifteen."

In a tired voice: "That's a long time."

I stared out at the parking lot, at the raindrops popping against it. "I shouldn't dump my problems on you."

"Are you going to be okay, Mike?"

We looked away from each other. I didn't volunteer any more information and Nancy didn't ask.

"Did you decide about the bike?" I finally said.

"You know how awful I'd feel if he got in another wreck?"

"We've been through that."

Nancy sighed. "You're right. I'm stalling."

"You think if he got hurt it wouldn't haunt me the rest of my life?" I started to stand. "I'd never forgive myself if he got in a serious wreck. But it would be even worse to take his bike away. To us it's just a bike, but to him it means a hell of a lot more. It's one of the only things that hasn't been taken away from him."

We fell silent for several minutes. I looked away from the window, at Nancy's face.

"I could get disciplined for this," she said. "If he gets hurt and there's an investigation I could be in big trouble with my supervisor."

"Maybe we'll run into each other at the unemployment office."

Nancy smiled and walked around her desk to put out her hand. I shook it, but it felt too formal. I opened my arms and we hugged. Her breasts pressed against my chest, and through the fabric of our shirts I felt her warmth. As Nancy held me I looked over her shoulder and watched the rain. Watched the drops making tiny splashes as they dimpled puddles.

That storm slowed the wildfires. It cleaned the air of its campfire stink and scrubbed the haze from the sky. But the next few weeks brought waterless storms with lightning and no rain. In shimmering waves, puddles evaporated until the earth lay dry and brittle under a withering sun. Wind stoked smoldering fires, and lightning cut the sky, seeking trees to strike, turning wood to flame. And again the wildfires burned.

≈ 21 ≈

Release

The phone rang at 3:30 the next morning, yanking me from a dream.

"This is Lex, Walter's dad. . . . Remember me?"

I rubbed my eyes. "You're a tough one to forget."

"Look, Mike, I was kinda rough on you the other day." He was slurring. "But I gotta look out for my boy. Didn't have no idea what type person you were. . . . Gotta watch out for Walter."

I kissed Nora on her head, smelled her hair, then carried the phone into the kitchen so I wouldn't wake her. "You been drinking, Lex?"

"Been sittin' here all afternoon and all night. Didn't go to work today. I started drinkin' and that got me thinkin' . . . which drove me to more drinkin'!" Lex bellowed out a laugh; I had to pull the phone away from my ear. "You hear that—I'm a poet. A goddamned poet!"

I grabbed the clock. Studied it. "It's three thirty in the morning. *Three-thirty in the fucking morning, Lex!*"

Silence.

"Why did you call?"

More silence.

"Lex, why are you calling me?"

In a shaking voice: "Guess I wanted to say sorry. Sorry for givin' you a hard time. . . . I 'preciate what you do for my boy. 'Preciate you helpin'

Walter. . . . You must think I'm a real piece a work. I go years without talkin' to Walter, then go and tell you I gotta watch out for him."

I didn't say anything.

After a few moments: "I send him checks. He tell you that? Every birthday and every Christmas I send him a check. . . . Don't got much money, but I give him some anyway. Try to help him out a little. Give my boy a little money to buy himself somethin' nice."

"I know you do."

"It's hard. It's . . . goddamned hard. I'm lookin' at his football picture right now. The one I showed you."

"The one you smashed?"

"I framed it again. Put a real good frame round it. Made it myself."

There was silence on both ends.

"Mike, I wanna go flyfishin' with my son. I want my boy to show me."

I yawned, then said, "Walter and I just found a stream. It's tough to get there—confusing drive, long hike—but it's worth it."

Lex laughed. "Think I can catch me a trout with one of them fancy flyrods?"

"Walter'll teach you. He'll help you catch one."

"He's good, huh?"

"Tell you what: give me a call during the day. We'll work out the details."

"Just one more question, Mike. You guys keep them fish you catch or you throw 'em back?"

"Can't this wait till morning?"

"I been wonderin' 'bout that. For some reason I been thinkin' 'bout it all day."

"We let them go."

Lex grunted. "Never understood that. Never could figure out why a fella'd go to the trouble of catchin' a fish, then throw it back in the river. Why let 'em go? Why put the damn thing right back where you got it 'stead of eatin' it?"

"Walter can explain it better than I can. Ask him."

After hanging up the phone, I went back into the bedroom and pulled a sheet over Nora's bare toes, then climbed into bed and curled up next to her, resting my forehead against her back. I tried to quiet my mind, but sleep wouldn't come; something kept me awake—something Lex had said.

"Why let 'em go?" echoed in my head.

It was tied to something else, something I hadn't thought about in a long time. I clawed at the pillows, struggled against the sheets. And then I remembered: something Walter had said to Nora the first time they met. Nora had asked Walter why he put the fish he caught back into the river, why he let them go.

"When I had my accident I was in a coma and it felt like I was dead," he said to Nora. "I couldn't talk, couldn't move, couldn't do nothing. But then I woke up. I was broken but I got to come back 'cause something let me go."

~22~

Learning to Cast

A week later, I watched Walter's father pace along a streambank. We had agreed to meet at Island Park on the Henry's Fork, a river in Idaho, one of Walter's favorites.

"Thanks for coming," Lex said as he shook my hand. Forearms corded with muscle and brailed with veins hung bare from his shirt-sleeves. Lex turned to his son, and avoiding his eyes, he offered to shake. Walter took his dad's meaty hand and limply gripped it. Lex told us he'd taken extra time off work and had gotten there the day before. He'd set up a camp, then done some exploring and found what he thought would be a good place to fish.

In silence we stood, staring at the river. Against the bank below us water puddled, the stream slowing and circling as it bumped against the shore. Wind fell out of the day and all was silent and still. The moon shrank as it cleared hills and climbed an indigo sky, where the brightest stars burned above. Beneath us the earth was warm; stones that had shored up dayheat now leaked it into the coming night. From the river rose clouds of insects, and with them a fog—two gray mists, one living, one not. The real fog spread, rolling over fields. And above the fog insects flew, a cloud of life lifting over the dead vapor, a million wings in constant whirl, catching the last bit of light. Light not of the sun, fallen behind hills, but a stubborn glow that clung to day. When that glow faded the insects vanished, like sparks from a campfire that burn and then pale to ash as they drift into the night.

Lex turned to Walter and asked him if he had an extra flyrod he could use.

Walter looked at the ground. "Why did you come here?"

"Mike tells me you're a helluva fisherman. I'd like to see for myself."

"I wrote you letters 'bout fishing. You never wrote me back."

With the toe of a workboot, Lex scuffed the ground. "Look, son, I want to start over. That's why I'm here. I want to—"

"You stopped talking to me after Mom died. Why?"

"Guess I screwed up. I never was the sharpest tool in the shed." Lex tried to smile; he looked like he was opening his mouth for dental surgery. He reached out, held his son's shoulder. "So are you gonna teach your old man how to fish?"

Walter pulled away from Lex, took a step back. "You didn't talk to me for years. You didn't answer my letters. And now you want me to teach you how to fish? How come?"

Lex tried to laugh. "Well, I guess I could've had Mike show me, but he says you're better than him. Thought I'd have the expert show me how to do it." He fell silent. The stream spoke softly, and there were no other sounds.

Walter tilted his head and stared at his dad. "I don't know if I want to teach you. I'll have to think 'bout it. I'll decide in the morning." He walked to a flat and grassy place where we'd dropped our tents and piled our gear. He shook his tent from a carrying sack, started to put one of the poles together. Lex walked over, offered to help.

"I can do it," Walter said, keeping his back to his dad. He fumbled the pole, dropped it into the dust at his feet. Lex bent down to pick it up. Walter snatched it from him. "I can do it by myself," he yelled. "I don't need your help!"

Lex took a step back and watched. When Walter had put the last pole together and slipped it into its sleeve, popping the tent into a dome-shape, Lex said, "Look, son, I'm sorry. I didn't—"

"I'll talk to you tomorrow," Walter said as he stuck stakes through the grommets at the corners of the tent and drove them into the ground with the heel of his boot. He crawled into the tent and zipped shut the door. "I don't know if I want to teach someone who won't even write me back how to fish."

"Maybe I shouldn't've come," Lex said to me. "Maybe this was a big mistake." He turned away, then wandered toward his tent as fog rolled and lifted off the river, covering the moon. I moved through mist, following Lex over the fogslicked grass. There were no trees, no rocks—only the grass below me. Wet blades clung to my bare legs. I yelled to Lex, he called back. I kept walking, adjusting my course, aiming toward his voice as I stepped through the wet grass, the milky fog.

And then he appeared, a dark shape distant in the mist. Several more steps and I saw his face. One more step and he was close enough to touch. "You're not really going to leave, are you?" I said, my voice muffled by the quilted fog.

"Walter's right to be mad. I don't blame the boy a bit." He looked down at the ground. "What kind of man turns his back on his son? What kind of man gives up on his boy that easy?"

"Give him some time to think. Try again in the morning."

Lex rubbed the palms of his hands over his balding head. "Don't know why he'd feel any different in the morning. That boy hates me and he should."

"He wanted to come." I stared through the mist, tried to meet Lex's eyes. "He doesn't hate you. He wants to give you another chance."

He spat into the grass. "I'm not so sure about that."

"That's what he told me. He misses you."

"I should leave the boy alone. I already pained him enough." He walked away.

I yelled into the mist, into the blank place where he'd disappeared: "So that's how it is? You take one chance and it doesn't work out so you give up and go home? You're going to quit Walter just like that? 'What kind of man gives up on his boy that easy?'—isn't that what you just said, Lex?"

He reappeared in the mist, walking toward me. Stopped when he was a few feet away. He grabbed my forearm, shook me. Through lips stretched tight he said, "I already hurt him enough. He's my boy. You don't know a goddamned thing about it. Just because you go fishin' with him don't make you an expert." He visegripped his fingers into my skin, pressed them into the muscle beneath. "You get along with your dad?" he shouted.

I rotated my wrist to break Lex's hold. He tried to grab me tighter, but I twisted out of his clutching hand and took a step back.

"Does your dad tell you how sorry he is when he screws up?" He lunged toward me. I stepped to the side, watched him stumble. He spun around and grabbed at me; I ducked his reaching arm, my movement automatic, born of muscle memory from years of basement fighting lessons. As Lex fell forward, his boots stuttered over a knobby root; his legs hinged under him and he dropped to his knees.

He stood up and turned to face me. I stared at him and said, "My dad died when I was thirteen."

Lex stood still, didn't reach for me again.

"When he was alive he wasn't much of a talker. He didn't tell me he was sorry but he did show me." I looked at Lex a moment, tried to see his eyes through the mist, but they were just dark places, like holes in a mask. I said, "I'm no expert on fathers and sons but I'll tell you what I do know, Lex. You're going to fuck up even worse if you leave. If you quit Walt now, there's no going back. He won't give you another chance. You know how scared he was about coming here? He already thinks you hate him."

Lex was silent a few minutes. He wiped the back of his hand across his face, snuffed his nose a few times, said, "Look at me, cryin' like a little girl." He stepped toward me, moved close enough that I could see his dripping eyes. He stared past me, into the fog. "So what the hell do I say to him? How do I tell him I was wrong?"

"I don't think it matters so much what you say. Words don't make a lot of sense to Walt, and they don't mean much to me."

He kicked at the ground, glanced at me. "So what do I do?"

"Show him, Lex. Show Walt you care about him by sticking around and trying again tomorrow. Show him by not giving up."

He nodded a few times. "Would it make a difference if I told you I was sorry for grabbin' at you? I don't know what got into me."

"Just be here tomorrow."

He nodded, turned and walked away.

I headed back toward camp, rubbing my boots along the ground to feel for bumps and dips before I slowly stepped, and I zombied my arms straight out, reaching into the mist, feeling no obstacles, only its wetness. When I got to our camp, I put together the stove and attached a fuel bottle to it, dumped the cookware out of a stuffsack, then squatted in front of Walter's tent. "You hungry?" I asked. "Is pasta okay?"

"I don't want dinner."

I stared through the mesh, into the dark cave of the tent. The nylon floor crackled as Walter shifted around inside. "I don't understand why he's here," he said. "Do you think he's really sorry for not writing me back? For not talking to me?"

"You have to decide that."

"Is he gonna be here in the morning?"

"I think he will be."

After a few minutes Walter unzipped the door, crawled from his tent, helped me make a fire. We gathered dry limbs that littered the ground, snapped them apart and piled them inside the stones of a fire ring. I dumped stovefuel on the sticks. Some splashed on my hands; I rubbed my fingers in the dirt to scrub the stink from them, then wiped them clean on my shirt.

Walter said, "In Boy Scouts we had to start a campfire with just twigs and one match."

"I never was a Boy Scout." I flicked a match onto the fuelsoaked pile of wood. Flames whooshed up. Their cloven tips tongued blackened stones, and light flooded the campsite, covering Walter's face with a pale mask, turning his eyes to orange balls, bright as the sparking wood. I reached into a stuffsack and pulled out a can of Spam. Peeled back the lid, handed it to Walter. He looked in the can, looked at me, said pasta didn't sound so bad after all.

While I started the stove and lidded a pot of water to boil, firelight drained from the campsite, unmasking Walter's face, showing darkened eyehollows and curves of mouth angry or sad, changing as light flicked back and forth, brightening and then dulling and then flaring again as the fire settled into a steady burn.

"You're on dish duty," I said when I finished eating. "A chef doesn't have to clean up."

"I gotta wash all the dishes?" Walter said, spooning up the last of his soggy noodles and sticky sauce, grimacing as though it were foul medicine when he fed it into his mouth and chewed.

I looked at the cookware. "A pot, two bowls, two spoons. I think you can handle it."

Walter tilted his head. "Is this a joke like when the waitress said I had to wash dishes 'cause I couldn't pay for dinner?"

"This is no joke," I said, laughing as I used my foot to push the pot toward Walter.

He picked it up, grabbed a soapy scrubpad, grinned. "You being a chef—now that's a good joke."

In the morning, my breath boiling in the chill air and my fingers crimping with cold, I looked out from my tent at plants pearled with moisture. I burrowed into my sleeping bag and watched the river as I tried to fall back asleep. Against boulders and cliffs water shaped itself, and into dirt banks it cut, trenching the soft loam. The morning warmth began burning fog away, and through the thinning gray I glimpsed the sun. Its brightness dulled by mist, it was a pale yellow hole. Like the opening of a tunnel leading to a place beyond the gray.

I crawled from my tent and looked at Walter, asleep in his tent: chest lifting and falling, mouth hanging open, his tongue poking out. On his head was a red stockingcap; next to him lay his helmet.

Over the murmur of the stream I heard a slapping sound, a loose sole flapping against a boot. I gazed upriver and saw a dark shape. Like a developing picture, the shape turned into a person, and from the grainy mist stepped Lex. "We going fishin' today?" he asked.

"Walt's still sleeping."

Ducks rose from the river, lifting off the water as one. Then they scattered into the wind like a handful of confetti tossed in front of a fan.

"When you two are ready, if you want to, head over to my camp. I made pancakes."

"Pancakes?" Walter said, sticking his head out of his tent and rubbing balled hands against sleepy eyes. "I'll be over in a minute."

Lex crouched down in front of Walter's tent, smiled. "You don't mind eatin' with your old man?"

"If your cooking's better than Mike's then I don't mind."

After breakfast we rinsed our dishes in the stream and headed out, following Lex. We traveled a paved road that turned to gravel, then to dirt, and then to nothing, passing through tangled bushgrowth and through bogs that made sucking sounds when we pulled our boots from the mud. We wandered into a stand of lodgepole pines, their trunks as straight and bare as matchsticks. Then we turned back toward the river and picked up a path, a gametrail tamped into a carpet of moss. We pushed through a jungle of willows, and before us was the stream, fast and frothing. Foothills rolled toward mountains, purple swellings against the sky. Edging the river was a grassy bank. We stood and watched the water pass while a circling wind blew. Wind that seemed to have no source, no destination. A senseless swirl.

"What is this place?" Walter asked.

"I found it yesterday," said Lex. "I could see trout swimmin' around."

"Did you fish here?"

"Was waitin' for you to show me how to use one of them flyrods. Left my spinnin' rod at home."

I sat down on a smooth heap of stone.

"You plan to keep any fish today?" Lex asked as Walter joined together the halves of his bamboo rod. "Maybe a couple for dinner?"

Walter glanced at him. "We got Spam. We don't need any fish."

"You're the boss," Lex said. "Show me how this thing works." He took the rod from Walter, and gripping the handle with both hands as though it were a baseball bat, he swung it back and forth.

Walter pulled the rod away from him. "If you want a lesson, you gotta tell me something first. You gotta explain why you stopped talking to me. I didn't do nothing wrong."

"No, son, you didn't." Lex's Adam's apple pumped twice as he swallowed. He looked away and told Walter what he'd told me about his wife, about his guilt; then he stared at Walter and said, "I didn't come here to make excuses. What I did was wrong. I can't explain why I stopped talkin' to you because I don't understand it myself. I came here to start over. I came here to tell you I was sorry. And to ask you for another chance."

When Lex finished talking, the wind and the water were the only sounds. After a few minutes Walter nodded. He gave the rod back to Lex and showed him how to hold it, molding Lex's fingers over the handgrip, polished smooth by my father's hand and mine. The rod like some storied scepter: its transfer between generations a rite, the secrets of its use rooted not in the courage to kill but in the strength to let go.

"You gonna join us?" Lex asked me as they walked toward the

water's edge.

I told him I'd watch.

Lex took a step toward Walter, who scraped dirt into a pile with his bootsole. Lex tucked the rod under his arm, took another step, reached into his pocket, pulled out a flybox. Walter lifted his eyes from the ground, looked at his dad.

"Got this last night when I went into town," Lex said. He clicked open the box, held it toward Walter for him to see. "Guy at a fishin' shop told me these here are all the best kind. One of every fly you'll ever need on this river." He laughed and said, "Goddamn, these flies are dear. I've never paid so much for things so small." As he handed the box to Walter, a windgust pulled a fly from the foam liner of the box, tumbled it across the ground. Lex chased after it a few steps, reaching and grabbing, then laughed and let the wind take it. "See that—damn breeze just blew away two bucks. That's how much that piece of feather on a hook cost me. I got to learn how to tie them things myself instead of buyin' 'em in stores."

"Mike ties good flies," Walter said. "His dad was gonna show him how but he died so Mike taught himself how to do it."

Lex stared at me a moment, then asked if I'd teach him. I nodded, told him I'd be glad to.

In the morning warmth, on a grassy bank, I sat and watched them. Walter showed Lex how to cast, and then they moved into the river. Lex grabbed Walter's arm, helped him climb atop a stone that stuck above the water like a giant turtle shell. Lex found a rock of his own to stand on, and they took turns casting toward a riffle that churned into white riverfoam. In that quick race of current swam rainbow trout, some small and hungry, gulping any fly that drifted past, others big and wary, rising to get a closer look at a fly and then sinking back, disappearing beneath the frothy surface like a thing imagined.

I had been there before. I'd caught the little fish, brought them to my net and released them. And I had seen the big ones, their silvery sides flashing and then disappearing in the bubbly water. The place hadn't looked familiar until we reached the bank of the river; I had come to it a different way. Years ago I'd followed the river upstream, walking against the current, fishing until light dropped out of the day; and where father and son now stood before me, I'd made a few casts, caught a couple small fish, and then turned back and waded downriver to my camp. I hadn't told Lex I'd been there and I wouldn't tell him. The place was his. And his son's.

I watched them cast, watched the river go by as the morning slipped into a drowsy noon. I drifted to sleep, and when I woke, shadows lay long and sprawling across the grass. Birds flew over the river, dipping low to catch insects on the water. And the two men cast, whooping when trout rose to their flies. I got up and stretched, walked to the river's edge. In a pool against the bank the stream stood still; the water lay calm and dark, and on its surface bubbles bulged and popped. Beyond the pool ran trembling current, white with foam. As a fish lifted its head to inhale Lex's fly, his shouting rose above the noise of the stream. I closed my eyes and listened to the muddled soundscape.

When we finally headed back, shadows blackened the ground and distant mountains melted into graying sky. The dropping sun showed strange contours on the rockfaces around us. As if the few minutes of low light at dusk revealed the world, and the bright of day and the black of night hid the true shape of things.

When the sky turned to full dark, like miners going into a coal pit, we put headlamps on and followed the lightbeams. Through tangled junglegrowth, through meadow and through forest we hiked, tripping over rocks and slipping on roots, using our headlamps to guide us in the gloom. When we crossed a boggy place, our boots made sucking sounds in the mud, and our footprints vanished as though erased by magic.

We left the bog and passed between pines. Against the starry sky their trunks were black slashes, like slits opening in the night. As we weaved between trees our headlamps lit the trunks, showing brown bark and treewounds leaking amber sap. Past the forest we picked up a path faintly worn and followed it to the dual ruts of a road, its potholes green with pondslime. The road improved, its ruts shallowing to faint dips. Finally the dirt turned to gravel, then to pavement. Starlight reflected off tarred ribs of buckled blacktop. We found the riverbank and followed it toward our camps as the moon bumped above the horizon, dark craters and shadowed valleys showing on its face.

When we reached Walter's tent he unzipped the door, started to crawl in.

"Goodnight, son," said Lex. He turned and walked the path toward his camp, his body a black shape against the sky. "You're a good fisherman, just like Mike here told me. I'm proud of you."

"Hey, Dad?" said Walter.

Lex stopped walking.

"Dad?"

Lex turned, his silhouette shifting against the night.

"Maybe you can move your tent down here. You can camp next to us if you want."

"You don't mind camping next to your old man?"

Walter said, "If you do all the cooking I'll let you. Make pancakes again. Those were good."

Lex moved on, his laughter fading as he passed over a rise and disappeared. And then there was only the sky above, the light of the moon falling on the ground where a moment before Lex had stood. I climbed into my tent, crawled into my sleeping bag. A while later I heard Lex come back. Heard Walter offer to hold a light for him while he set up his tent. The sound of the river was with me when I fell asleep and it was with me in my dreams.

PART FIVE

≈23≈

Rebirthday

In the third week of August, on the day Walter had risen from his coma to begin his new life, I took him out for dinner at Kingfisher Inn. Martha, his favorite waitress, made him a special sundae—so big and covered with goodies and goo that he sat and picked at it for an hour, pacing himself, but still couldn't finish it.

After dinner we went to his apartment. Mitch was there, waiting for us. He ran at Walter as soon as he walked in, got right in his face. "Have a secret. Can't tell you." Mitch giggled. He rubbed his hands, rocked on his feet.

Nancy knocked on the half-open door, let herself in. She smiled at me, then grabbed Walter and hugged him. Not a light hug—she really squeezed him.

"What was that for?" Walter asked. "We always shake hands."

"It's your rebirthday, Walt. You deserve a hug."

"What did you call me?"

Nancy shrugged her shoulders. "Walt?"

He tilted his head. "Mike calls me that."

"Do you mind if I call you that?" Nancy winked at me.

"Are you still gonna be my caseworker? You don't let me do stupid stuff. . . . You're not leaving me, are you?"

"I'm still your caseworker. But I'd like to be your friend, too."

Walter stared at her, said nothing.

"Is that okay? Can we be friends?"

"Can you be Mitch's friend, too? Mitch don't got a lot of friends."

Nancy laughed and walked toward Mitch, arms out. "Of course."

Mitch stood there, giggling, staring at Nancy's breasts, shifting beneath her sweater. When she hugged him his giggles turned to a full bellylaugh and his glasses slipped down his face.

"Why don't you tell Mike what you do at the fish hatchery?" Nancy said.

"Feed the fish. Hungry fish."

"But what're the most important parts of your job?"

Mitch looked at his feet. He was quiet a moment. Then he looked up and peered at us through his glasses, perched crookedly on his face. "Feed the fish?"

"How about sweeping the floors and emptying the trash?" Nancy said.

Mitch grinned and clapped his hands. "Hungry fish."

Nancy laughed. "Okay. We'll work on that. Here, Walt, this is for you." She handed him a box wrapped in newspaper. The funny pages.

"Look, Mitch," Walter said. "It's got our favorite on it—'Family Circus.' "

"There's a present inside."

"A present?"

"You have to open it."

Walter tore off the newspaper, handed it to Mitch. "Keep this, Mitch. We'll read 'Family Circus' later." They started laughing.

When Walter settled down, he opened the box and pulled out a bike headlight. He stood there, holding the light, staring at Nancy.

She said, "I figured I could give you something to help you stay safe."

"You're letting me keep my bike?"

"I'm letting you decide. You think about it. You tell—"

"I'll keep it!"

Nancy scrunched up her mouth. I tried to make eye contact, tried to thank her with my smile. But she stared away, out the window, shaking her head so slightly I might have imagined it.

Walter said, "What's my surprise, Mitch?"

"Yeah, yeah. A secret." Mitch clapped his hands. "Mike knows."

"Go look in your room," I said.

Walter headed to his bedroom; Nancy, Mitch, and I followed.

"What?" Walter turned in a circle, threw up his arms. "What's the big secret?"

"Right there." I pointed to the wall opposite his bed.

"A sheet? That's my surprise?" There was a bedsheet covering something. He went over to it. Lifted the sheet, peered underneath. Smiled and tore it off, revealing an aquarium.

"How'd this get here?"

"Mitch and I set it up when you were out with Donna today," I said.

Walter kneeled down and pressed his face to the aquarium. His breath fogged the glass.

"We've talked about how you might be able to adopt Cap'n someday. I thought the fish—"

"But I'm taking care of myself better now. Maybe I can have Cap'n soon?"

"What do you think?" I asked Nancy.

"Let's start with fish first and see how that goes." Nancy kneeled down next to Walter, stared into the aquarium. "Maybe we'll move on to a hamster if this works out. Then we'll talk about a dog. Who's this Cap'n, anyway?"

"Cap'n's broken but he's a good dog."

"And you want to adopt him?"

Walter nodded. "I'm gonna try real hard to take care of the fish." He stared into the water. "I hope I don't forget to feed 'em. Hope my broken head don't mess up."

Mitch patted Walter on his back and said, "Hungry fish."

"We can make a chart," I said. "We'll put it on the refrigerator to remind you. And you can mark it each time you feed them so you don't forget and feed them too many times."

"Fat fish," Mitch said. "Feed the fish too much they get fat."

Nancy told us she needed to leave; she had some paperwork to catch up on. Walter thanked her for his present as she left.

I stared into the aquarium, following a group of neon tetras that swam together, moving as one.

"When we go fishing we just see trout feeding on top," Walter said after a few minutes. "We don't see what they do underneath. Now I can know what happens inside the water. . . . I like that one." He pointed at an angelfish as it glided by, its fins feathering in the water. "Hey, Mike," Walter said. "Think we should put trout in here so we can catch 'em with our flyrods?" His gurgling laughter blended with the sound of water spilling from the aquarium filter.

Mitch shuffled into the room, cradling a bundle wrapped in toilet paper.

"You're giving me a mummy?" Walter asked as he took the bundle from Mitch.

Mitch clapped his hands and grinned so hard I thought his glasses would pop off his face. "I made it for you, Walter," he said.

Walter grabbed an end of paper and unwound it. A few minutes later a pile of toilet paper—it looked like Mitch had used an entire roll—lay at Walter's feet. And in his hands Walter held a clay mask with a narrow face and a nose long and twisted. Feathers clung to the clay.

"It's a birdman." Mitch clapped his hands. "A birdman mask for your birthday, Walter."

I kneeled down and stared into the aquarium. Followed the fish, lost myself in the water.

"What're you thinking 'bout, Mike?" Walter asked a few minutes later. He kneeled down next to me.

I told Walter that my mom had bought an aquarium the Christmas after my dad died. She said we needed a pet around the house to keep us company. She wanted a puppy but couldn't get away from her job long enough to come home and feed it, and I was at school all day, so she settled for fish.

I remembered sitting in front of the aquarium, next to my mom, rubbing her feet. She'd worked the night before—Christmas Eve. She said she'd wanted to stay home with me, but we needed the tips. She started to tell me about a customer she'd had, some drunk who kept making her take his eggs back to the kitchen. First they were too soft, then too hard. Like he was some kind of egg connoisseur: stumbling drunk, but an expert on the art of egg preparation. She was telling me about how he kept her running for almost an hour, left a handful of change for a tip—mostly pennies. Then she stopped in the middle of a sentence. She combed her fingers through my hair and pressed my cheek. She rubbed my skin, looked at her fingertip, asked me if I was wearing makeup.

Walter said, "You put on makeup for Christmas?"

I was trying to hide a bruise from her, I told Walter. I'd gotten in a fight and I didn't want her to know. The kid I'd fought with—his name was Stewart. He was a football player with nice clothes, all the best brands. He'd been after me for months, trying to get a rise out of me, calling me trailer trash, calling me the Kmart Kid because I wore such shitty clothes. He had bulging arms and chiseled abs, spent every afternoon at football practice or in the gym. Some of the kids in school said he took steroids.

One day when I passed Stewart in the hall, he told me he'd seen my mom working at Howard Johnson's. Said he'd sat at one of her tables and she'd come on to him. Told me the trailer trash bitch had a nice ass. I told him where to meet me after school let out. Spent the rest of the day going from class to class in a fog. His size didn't register; his arms were twice as big as mine, but that didn't matter. Losing the fight, getting hurt—I didn't think about those things.

My father had taught me about limits, about when to stop before I really hurt someone. He'd shown me how to give out just enough pain to stop an attack, to defend myself. When I had Stewart on the ground I gripped his windpipe. Closed it. Watched his face turn purple. Studied the fear in his eyes. Felt him spasm. Choked the thought of my mom's ass out of him, then let him go.

When I told my mom what had happened, she asked me if I thought my dad would have approved of me getting in fights at school. I said he would have been proud of me—why else would he have taught me how to fight?

She told me he'd seen so much in Vietnam and there was a lot I didn't understand. A lot he didn't tell me. She told me that the Marines had taught my dad how to kill and got him ready for war. But he had to work a lot harder to learn how to fight. And she didn't think he enjoyed it that much. She thought he was doing it for me. So he could teach his boy things that would keep him safe.

I looked into the aquarium, not watching the fish, just staring through the water. With a filter to clean it and a heater to keep its temperature constant, the aquarium was without seasons—without spring floods, when rivers fill with silt and their gravels clack below; without summer clearing, when the waters retreat and warm; without droughty autumn flows, when stilled pools are painted by leaves of saffron and bushes red as blood; without sluggish winter currents, when channels clog and fish sleep beneath the ice. After a few minutes I told Walter that later that Christmas Day I had asked my mom about the guy who'd hit my dad: the man who'd run a stop sign, broadsided his car, killed him on impact. She said she would talk about it once, and she made me promise never to ask her about it again.

I felt wet trickles on my cheek, realized I was crying.

Walter said, "You don't have to talk 'bout it if you don't want to."

I tasted salt as the wetness touched my lips, dribbled onto my tongue. I stared through the aquarium water, as transparent as the glass that held it. Water without hidden places, without the seagreen holes of trout rivers—places where the fish flash like chrome when they rise, then fade to shadow as they drop toward the river's floor.

I told Walter that a county prosecutor had called my mom a few days after my dad's funeral. Asked if she wanted to press charges: reckless endangerment, maybe manslaughter. The prosecutor said he was on the fence about whether to pursue it. Told my mom she could sway him either way. She said first she had to talk to the guy—to Mr. Jind.

I pressed a fingertip against the cool glass of the aquarium.

She met him at Denny's, I told Walter. She'd thought about calling him but decided she had to see his face. I asked her what kind of name Jind was. She thought it might be Indian. Maybe Pakistani. She said it didn't matter.

Sitting on the couch, her bare feet tucked under her, gazing at the aquarium—she looked so delicate. Like she had bones of glass. She told me that Mr. Jind had been messing with his stereo. Trying to find a radio station he liked. Didn't see the stop sign, went right through it. He was speeding—not a lot, just ten miles an hour over the limit. He saw my father's face right before he slammed into his car. Mr. Jind said my dad had looked surprised. Not scared, just surprised. It was that simple; that's what happened. She said it took Mr. Jind less than a minute to explain. He was done before the waitress brought their coffee. Mr. Jind didn't cry when he told her, didn't look sad, she said. Just sat there and stared. And that was it: after my mom left Denny's, she called the prosecutor, told him not to press charges. When I asked her why, she said she was afraid of becoming bitter. Becoming so bitter she couldn't start her life over: that's the thing that scared her most, she told me.

After a few minutes Walter looked away from the aquarium, stared at me. "You had a smart mom," he said.

$\approx$24$\approx$

Between the Boards

At the base of Snow King Mountain, seeds clumped in puffy globes had replaced yellow dandelion flowers. Walter picked one up and blew on it; tiny parachutes floated away. Cap'n chased the seeds, hopping and yelping, biting them as they fell from the sky.

"Sure you're ready for this?" I asked.

Walter scratched Cap'n's ears. "Think Cap'n'll be all right?"

"He's turned into a damn good hopper," I said. "He can hop faster than most dogs with four legs can walk."

Walter said, "I'm getting stronger 'cause I've been hiking all summer. I can make it to the top."

We hiked uphill, past a stable. Piles of dry horse manure stood in fossilized clumps. The road turned from gravel to dirt, chalky and crumbly, but sometimes smooth—pressed shiny and hard where bike tires had passed over it.

I pointed to a path that sidehilled through the woods instead of climbing toward the summit. "Want to try that trail?" I asked.

Cap'n stopped and panted, his tongue dangling from the side of his mouth. Walter paused and looked at me. "I'm gonna go all the way to the top."

"We can go a few times and build up to that," I said. "We can hike partway up today—then we'll go a little higher next time. In the fall we'll make it to the summit."

Walter turned away, started walking again.

I jogged a few steps to catch up with him. "You don't like that plan?" Cap'n hopped next to Walter, licking the salt from his sweaty arms. "We could take the ski lift up. It just costs a few bucks."

Without turning to look at me, his eyes on the path ahead, Walter said, "It's not the same. I gotta hike up and show you something at the top."

I threw my arms up. "What is it, Walt? Are there wild horses up there? Another wolf den?"

He ignored me, kept hiking.

We passed through sunlight and through shade. The path zigzagged up the mountain, cutting through stands of trees, dark and cool with shadow, and crossing open ski runs—where the delicious shade ended and there was only sun. Walter and I followed Cap'n into a crowded stand of pines, into cool shadows. Light filtered thinly through the branches, sap spiced the air, moist needles thatched the ground. Then the piney dark ended and we were back in the blasting heat.

Finally the road flattened: we'd reached the crest of the mountain. We stopped and rested, sucking water from our bottles, rinsing dust from our throats. The Grand Teton, as slim and sharp as an incisor, was red with alpenglow in the afternoon sky. The Gros Ventre Mountains, mellow in contrast to the Tetons, rolled along the eastern skyline. Somewhere past the Gros Ventres, Little Snake—the stream Walter and I had discovered—cleaved a dry plateau, and beneath the flatness it pushed water pure and clear.

On the open ridge where we stood, branches of pine trees flagged away from the wind like arms pointing to where the gusts blew. Walter wandered between the windpummeled trees, onto the deck at the top of the mountain; I followed him and stared at the wooden floor. Suddenly I realized where we were: the deck where Walter had been photographed with his mom and dad before his accident. Where his mom had dropped her earring through a gap in the boards. Where Walter and his dad had played "hot or cold," working together to find the earring. Where Walter's dad had hugged his wife and his son at the same time. Where the mountains had been lost in the haze of wildfires because the West was burning.

I remembered the picture: Walter's favorite photo, the one in the center of the last page of his album. The album he kept because it was painful to remember who he'd been, but sometimes he needed to because he believed that was all he had.

"This is what you wanted to show me?" I asked.

He nodded that it was.

I dropped down onto the deck, pressed my stomach and face to the wood, looked between the boards. Didn't see any earrings, but in the beams of light that cut through the floor, coins gleamed. I sat up and grinned, then started laughing. A guy dressed in plaid shorts and a cowboy hat walked around me, gave me plenty of space. Pulled his kids away from the guy laughing on the deck, peeking between the planks. I laughed like a lunatic. Shook my head, flung my sweat through the air. Watched tourists scatter.

"Don't worry 'bout him," Walter said to a woman wearing hotpink shorts. "My friend's crazy but he won't bite." Walter gave his gurgling laugh and the woman stepped away.

We walked off the deck, found two boulders to sit on. Walter said, "Last night I dreamed 'bout that time I was here with my mom and dad. But it was different 'cause you were here too."

From the top of a distant mountain, a column of smoke rose into the sky like a volcanic eruption, and flames crept down timbered slopes like lava. Up north toward Yellowstone, the Absaroka Mountains were blue with the haze from wildfires. Fires burning in faraway valleys, consuming trees and plants and grass. Turning fuel to ash.

"In my dream you got to meet my mom," Walter said. "She liked you."

"Did I like her?"

He nodded.

Aspen leaves trembled in a burst of wind; pulpy raindrops brushed my skin.

"Your parents were there too," Walter said. "You never showed me no pictures of them, but they looked like how you told me. Your dad was big and strong and he didn't talk too much, and he was scared about Vietnam but he wasn't mean. And your mom smiled at your dad all the time and she read books and was smart. We all ate sandwiches and drank Pepsis on the deck."

"That's a hell of a dream."

"Ever since I broke my head I have weird dreams. The other night I couldn't sleep 'cause I was thinking 'bout how I was gonna ask Donna to marry me. I want to do it good and not make no mistakes, and I got nervous and stayed up till almost in the morning. When I finally fell asleep I dreamed that Donna and me were in the secret spot under the cottonwoods by the river. There was good water full of trouts. And cotton was snowing out of the trees and it was in Donna's hair and on her clothes."

A mountain biker rode by, his tires churning up dust and shooting gravel into the sagebrush. I tilted back my head, stared up at bulging clouds. The sky held an iridescent sheen—the color of rotten meat, the color of a housefly's belly.

"Can I ask Donna under the cottonwoods?" Walter asked. "Can I take her to the secret spot and ask her to marry me?"

I leaned over, pushed him. "Just don't let her fish there."

Walter laughed and said, "When I told Mitch I was gonna ask Donna, he told me he wanted to marry Nancy. I said I didn't think that would work out too good. He told me there was a pretty cashier at Kmart and maybe he could ask her to marry him. He made a list of everyone he was gonna ask. It was a long list."

Across the glowing sky streaked lightning; I heard it sizzle the instant before thunder exploded, shuddering the earth. All the hair on my body stood up. The air crackled like radio static.

"I know what that lightning is," Walter said as we scrambled down a slope, away from the mountaintop, damp gusts laying the grass down, bending the trees.

I stopped hiking, turned to look at him.

"The world's a great big egg and we're inside it, and sometimes the egg gets cracks in it. Outside the egg there's lots of light. We get to see the light through the cracks before the egg heals."

I looked up at the sky. "How come the egg gets cracks in it?"

His good eye focusing on me, Walter said, "When somebody dies they don't leave the egg right away. They stay around like a ghost and watch the people they knew. If those people are so sad they can't do nothing right, then the ghost tries to help them. When they don't feel sad no more the ghost leaves. The egg cracks open for a second so the ghost can get out and go live where it's bright like lightning all the time."

We started hiking down. After a few minutes Walter said, "I'm ready to go back."

"To the deck?"

"To the place on the river where I fell down and broke my head. Where the old Walter ended and the new Walter started. I want you to go with me, Mike."

By the time we got to the base of the mountain, clouds had blackened the earth, and the sky was heavy with the dampness of a coming storm—the beginning of a wet spell that finally stopped the wildfires.

For the next few weeks, rain snuffed the flames, leaving soggy, smoldering coals, and watering piles of ash to a gray broth. When the storms stopped, the air lost its smoky stink, replaced by the clean fragrance that follows rain. Haze that had blued the mountains for most of the summer faded, and wet ash dried to a papery crust in the new sun.

25

The River

"You think you know how deep and fast it is," Walter said. "But you don't understand till you're in it." He nodded toward a white and curling wave guarding the entrance to a rapid. We were on a bluff overlooking the Green River in the desert of southern Utah. It was early autumn. We had returned to the stretch of river where Walter had fallen: the place, as he said, where he'd broken his head.

Walter pointed at the wave. "I rowed a raft through that rapid. It looks small from up here, but when you're down there on the river it's a great big wave. Water gets in your eyes, in your nose, in your mouth—it gets everywhere. The river's all around you and it goes on and on and you can't make it stop."

Walter glanced at me and kept talking: "If you fall into the river you shouldn't panic. If you fight it, it'll swallow you." He tilted his head. "Like a great big monster—it'll eat you up!"

Walter reached into his pocket, handed me something. "It's the elk's tooth I found by the wolf's den," he said. "I had it made into a ring. I was scared like shit when I asked Donna to marry me, but I wore it when I asked her and she said yes. It's my courage ring."

I took the ring. Squeezed it. Felt the cold metal, the smooth ivory. I tried to give it back.

Walter pushed my hand away. "You can use it. 'Cause you're my friend and I know you need it."

"You want me to keep it?"

"Someday I'll need it more than you do. Then you can give it back."

As I slipped the ring into my pocket, I stared at the desert: rock colored like rusted iron, shifting sand, blank blue sky. In the river below, water pooled as it flowed toward a gap; then it squeezed through in white and frothing bursts. And beneath that rapid was another pool, calm as a mountain lake. Waves wrinkled its surface and gently rubbed the shore.

Walter reached over, draped his left arm across my back. He clenched his hand and squeezed my shoulder. "Put the ring on, Mike. You're scared 'bout the baby you made with Nora. You need some courage."

I pulled the ring from my pocket, slipped it onto my finger.

Walter said, "You're gonna be a good dad. And if anything happens to you and Nora, I'll make sure everything's okay. Me and Donna—we'll take good care of your baby. You don't have to worry 'bout nothing." He stared at the desert a moment, then turned to me and said, "You and Nora are gonna be happy, right? You're not gonna fight no more? You're not gonna get divorced?"

"That's a hell of a story, Walt."

He tilted his head. "It's a good story, right?"

"One of the best you've told me." I laughed and stared into his eyes, one healthy and functional, the other an unseeing orb adrift in its socket, not in tune with the light.

⌒

That night, in the warm cocoon of my sleeping bag, with Walter snoring in a tent next to mine, I thought about what I had to do when I left the river and returned home. I had promised Nancy I'd help her find a roommate for Mitch. And I needed to make signs and charts for Walter to help him take good care of his dog: I was giving him Cap'n as a wedding gift. And I needed a job: the money from my parents' life insurance was running out. I was going back to school to become a social worker. Nancy had written me a letter of recommendation.

In the morning, through the window of my tent, I saw mayflies. They rode the river currents and then took flight, wings sparkling as they lifted off the water in the early light. I wiggled out of my sleeping bag and crawled from my tent into the crisp and shining dawn, then walked across a sandbar piled with the dead and fragmented mayfly bodies that were washing onto shore. I heard Walter rustling in his tent and turned to look. He pushed through the door, then stood up, stumbled, and walked next to me. I snatched a mayfly from the air and let it crawl across my palm, its threadlike tails wiggling, its wings trembling in a breeze. On my wrist I saw a scar. I ran a fingertip along the raised rib of flesh, the place where Walter's duct tape had sealed my wound.

After rigging the rafts, we floated down a flat stretch of river. Weeds fanned out in the current, feathering greenly beneath the surface. In the cliffs that edged the water, minerals sparkled like shards of glass. It was a peaceful place, but the thought of the whitewater ahead made it hard to relax. We stopped for lunch on a pebbly beach above the first rapid. I sat alone on a log and stared at a wave—churning, breaking into froth.

After lunch we climbed back into the raft and headed toward the rapid. Our guide, who called himself Sarge, was an ex–Army Ranger who told us he'd taught fighting tactics all over the world and shared nothing else about himself. Sarge rowed hard, pulling on the oars and pivoting the raft, making all the right moves. As we hit the first wave my stomach heaved. I grabbed a line on the side of the raft and squeezed it until the fibers burned my skin.

After the first rapid, as we drifted down a quiet bit of river, Sarge offered to let Walter guide. "Ever row before?" he asked Walter.

"I used to go rafting all the time. Right here on the Green River." He told Sarge his story: the accident, life before his fall.

"Then row away, bud," said Sarge as he shipped the oars and slid to the back of the raft. "We'll see if ya still got it."

Walter worked his way over the slippery rubber floor toward the oars, carefully gripped them, then gave a few pushes and pulls. The raft jerked; I grabbed the safety rope to keep from falling in the river. Walter had been working his left side, but his right was still stronger.

"You can't pull so hard with your right hand," I said. "You have to compensate."

"I can do it," he said. "Let me figure it out."

Walter's turns smoothed, and he began to pull one oar while pushing the other, spinning the raft. Then he spun it in the other direction and said, "Told you I'd figure it out. I can turn the boat just like I used to."

"Nice job," Sarge yelled from the back of the raft. "That deserves a golf clap." With bulking muscles and a booming laugh, Sarge brought his hands together softly, silently.

Walter laughed as he watched Sarge, a giant man gently clapping. Then Walter went back to rowing. "I still got it," he said as he pushed and pulled the oars, turning the raft as it moved down the river.

When we stopped spinning I saw a horizon line on the water ahead.

"Looks like the river drops off up there," I yelled back to Sarge. "Big rapid?"

"Not huge, but big enough. I should take over on the oars."

"I can do it," said Walter, his voice quiet but firm. "I remember how. I remember this rapid."

Sarge frowned. "Whatdaya think, Mike?"

"I trust him."

"Okay, Walter," Sarge said. "Guess our fate's in your hands, bud. Do good—I don't feel like swimming today."

A distant rumble was building to a roar. Froth from the rapid spewed into the air, and the wind blew sheets of mist toward us. I grabbed a safety rope, buried my feet in a crease at the edge of the floor, glanced at Walter. He pulled on the oars, ferrying us across the river; then he turned the nose of the raft into the rapid and pushed forward. I looked away from Walter, at the rocks and waves. I clasped the rope and clenched my teeth.

Walter maneuvered the raft, dodging churning holes, skirting boulders, slamming into small waves, avoiding big ones. Sarge shouted directions, his voice rising above the pounding water. Walter yelled; then the rapid silenced everything. A wave rose above us, crashed and fell. We went underwater, into the river, and for a moment all was quiet and cold.

Then I saw light and heard Walter's voice, and as the roar of the rapid faded behind us, I leaned over the side of the raft, coughing up water, spitting it back into the river.

"I'll be damned," Sarge shouted. "Never seen anyone take that line through the rapid. You went right through one of the biggest waves!"

"I've been through worse," Walter said with a crooked smile. He looked at me and tilted his head, laughing his gurgling laugh, the sound blending with the bubbly spill of the current.

After camp had been set up later that day, Walter and I hiked along a dry wash covered with cactus, their flowers cupped and red, like tiny goblets stained by wine. We found a thread of water and followed it to where it merged with a trickle, forming a pool in a deep draw—a sheltered place between walls of stone. I looked at the water and saw a reflection of the world above.

"I felt good today," Walter said. "I didn't have to think 'bout what I was doing. My broken head couldn't stop me. My body remembered how to row. I wasn't afraid of that wave. I knew we'd get through it."

In the mirrored surface of the water I watched the sky break apart, saw the sun burn through.

"Nervous about tomorrow?" I asked. "We're going to pass by where you had your accident."

Walter said nothing.

"We don't have to stop there. We can just float by."

"Maybe I should see it. Then it'll be done and I won't have to think 'bout it no more."

For a few minutes we were quiet. On the sandy bed beneath the pool, bubbles cast shadows—black disks ringed by light. Like little suns eclipsed by moons.

"I'm going for a walk," Walter said. "I need to think 'bout tomorrow."

I watched the bubble shadows for a few minutes, then lay down and stared up at sky. I squinted against the brightness, let my eyelids shut.

A shadow passed over my face. I opened my eyes and saw Walter standing above me. "I want to see where it happened," he said. "I want to go back."

The next day we camped near the place where Walter had fallen. We went there after dinner, walking a path around prickly pears, their flat and jointed stems armed with stiff spines.

"This is it," Walter said, pointing at a dome of red sandstone, glowing in the afternoon light. "I came with two friends. We ate lunch by the river and we split a can of beer between us, and then we hiked back here. My friends said there was some pictures on the rock. Pictures Indians made." He fell silent a moment, then said, "I remember seeing this mound of rock. Then nothing. My stupid head is blank. I don't know if I ever saw the pictures."

We stood and stared. The sun drifted lower, a molten ball in the blue and seamless sky. I began climbing the rockface, moving more carefully than I ever had. As I grabbed a knob and pulled myself up, a chunk of stone broke loose. It tumbled down, hit Walter on the shoulder. Walter said nothing. He was staring above me. I followed his gaze to a ledge, then worked my way toward it. I paused to wipe my sweating hands on my shirt as I inched along, trying not to loosen more stones. I climbed onto the ledge as the sun incinerated itself against a rim of desert in the west, and light drained from the ashen sky, turning the cliff the color of dried blood. Petroglyphs were carved in the stone: A snake, its body coiled into a spiral. A few animals that looked like deer or elk. A bighorn sheep. Something canine—dog or wolf. And in the center was what looked like a shaman, a person with a head huge and round. Wiggly lines streamed from it, as if the head reflected sunrays or leaked light from within.

As I downclimbed, pebbles rolled beneath my boots and rained from the ledges, tapping Walter's helmet like hailstones. When I reached the ground I told Walter what I'd found.

He looked past me in the dim light, staring at the pocked and fractured dome of rock, its darkening face holed with black sockets, fissured with shadows. "Who made the pictures?" he asked.

"The Anasazi, I think."

"Indians?"

I nodded.

"Do they still live here?"

"They're gone. Nobody really knows what happened to them."

Walter frowned. He opened his mouth to say something, then stopped. He gave a quiet chuckle, like a hiccup, then let loose with a gurgling stream of laughter. He said, "I broke my head to see those pictures. Old pictures—like graffiti from people who don't live here no more. And right in the middle of all the pictures is a man with a crazy head, just like me."

Walter's laughter spread through the cool silence as we walked back to camp, our feet crunching desert soil, a thin crust of life covering so much sandy waste. The first stars sparked in the gathering dark. We passed a dry streambed cobbled with pale stones. From its banks aspen grew, their leaves moving in a breeze. And in their peeling bark, as thin and crisp as parchment, were etched hearts and vows and the names of lovers—the symbols on the trees as strange to future worlds, I thought, as a shaman carved in stone to ours. I imagined people someday camping next to the river, seeking out the trees to study their messages, walking the desert soil and fingering the carvings, black welts hard as iron, wondering what stories they told, what world had passed.

Walter picked up a sharp pebble and left his mark, etched his love for Donna in the paperwhite bark. He asked me if I wanted to carve Nora's name. I told him I didn't want to hurt the tree; in truth, I wondered if Nora and I would be together in a week's time, and committing to each other for our entire lives seemed as unlikely a notion as a shaman soaring in and out of people's dreams. But still, I thought as I stared at Walter, it was a damn good story. I took the pebble from him, drew a heart, wrote my name and Nora's in the papery bark.

A raven rose into the sky, flapping its wings and cawing, its shrill voice filling the desert. The branch it had perched upon vibrated like a recoiling spring. I listened to the sound of shaking leaves. A soft rustling like the slosh and spill of running water. As if beneath its dry bed the stream still flowed.

"I know what those trees are," Walter said. "Those are laughing trees. They need laughter just like we need food. Crows land on their branches and tell them jokes. And when the branches bounce and the leaves are laughing, the crows get to eat the bugs that shake loose." He balled up his left hand, punched me in the shoulder. "You got a story 'bout those trees, Mike?"

I thought a moment, then nodded at the shaking leaves. "The leaves are baby hands waving." I pointed at an ancient branch, a gnarled curve of wood that forked into twigs long dead, bleached by the sun and weathered smooth. "And that dead branch is full of wizard's fingers," I said.

"Wizard's fingers and baby hands?" Walter said, shrugging his shoulders.

"There's a wizard in the tree that keeps the babies prisoner. When somebody walks by the tree, the babies wave."

Walter tilted his head and gave a half frown, as if trying to remember something. "Why does the wizard want to keep all those babies in the tree?"

"Bad things happened to him. He felt cheated and turned mean. Turned into a bitter, selfish wizard."

"Stupid old wizard," said Walter, walking toward the tree. He grabbed the dead limb and wrenched it free. Tossed it on the ground and trampled it. Beneath his bootsoles dry twigs popped like firecrackers.

We spent one more week on the river, a week of chilly nights and hot days filled with rapids. Rapids that hissed and growled like hungry beasts trying to devour our raft. Sarge let Walter guide, let him take charge of the trip. And while Walter pushed and pulled the oars, rowing through waves and whirlpools, my broken friend remembered who he once had been.

As the days drifted on, Walter stopped talking about the past, and what he had lost seemed to matter less than what lay ahead. He wore his Spam T-shirt under the noon sun, his duct tape sweatshirt under the night sky, crowded with stars. He spoke of Donna and his dad and the friends he'd made. A skillful guide, Walter led our raft down the river.

⌒END⌒

Epilogue

These fragments I have shored against my ruins
— T. S. Eliot, "The Waste Land"

About the Author

Stephen Grace has worked as a deckhand on Mississippi riverboats, a whitewater rafting guide, a laborer in national parks, a skiing and snowboarding instructor, a youth counselor, a social worker, and a volunteer firefighter and ambulance driver. He has backpacked throughout Africa and Asia. An amateur photographer and an avid mountain biker, he lives in Wyoming.